Invasi

Book 3 in the Sword of Cartimandua series

by
Griff Hosker

Published by Sword Books Ltd, 2013
Copyright © Griff Hosker
Second Edition

The author has asserted their moral right under the Copyright, Designs and Patents Act, 1988, to be identified as the author of this work.

All Rights reserved. No part of this publication may be reproduced, copied, stored in a retrieval system, or transmitted, in any form or by any means, without the prior written consent of the copyright holder, nor be otherwise circulated in any form of binding or cover other than that in which it is published and without a similar condition being imposed on the subsequent purchaser.

A CIP catalogue record for this title is available from the British Library.

Thanks

Thanks to Eileen, Vicky and David-without you there would be no books. Thanks to Rich for all his invaluable comments and support. To Ste and Julie for their kind words. And finally, thanks to the Parkwood Literary circle for keeping my feet firmly planted on the ground.

Contents

PART ONE- MONA

Prologue

West coast of Britannia 75 AD

Marcus Aurelius Maximunius, Decurion Princeps of the Pannonian auxiliary cavalry was finding their journey down the west coast much easier than he had expected. This was not the harsh landscape of the north with its hills, mountains and raging rivers. It was not the wild, undulating empty moorland of the east. This was good farmland with a people who largely ignored the Roman presence. Decius Flavius, his second in command voiced his views as they neared the legionary fortress of Deva, "It's like a different country. I haven't had to worry about ambushes or traps or treachery. I don't like it. Give me an enemy who hates me. That's what I like."

"Ever the pessimist. It is the land south of Deva where the enemy lies. Our general Julius Agricola needs to take the island of Mona back from the rebels and to do that we must fight the Deceangli who lived in the land before it. Happy now?"

Far to the south Decurion, Gaius Metellus Aurelius was happy. Even the scars from the unjust flogging he had received failed to hurt him. His turma was leading the two legions sent to punish the rebels and so far, like Marcus and Decius he had found it easy. The only person not happy was Sergeant Macro Curius Culleo, the weapons trainer for the ala. He loved action and he loved fighting. For him, the three-week journey from the far north had been torture. He rode next to the decurion, "Please tell me that we get to fight someone soon? This is killing me."

"When we do find the enemy then you will have more than enough fighting for the mountains through which we will be travelling are wilder and more rugged than those in the north and this time, Sergeant Macro, we will be seeking that witch Fainch so we will need to keep our wits about us. Try not to get killed before we find her eh?"

When the column finally halted at the new legionary fortress that was Deva there was an Imperial messenger awaiting Gnaeus Julius Agricola. After a short meeting in the Praetorium, the general sent for Marcus and the other senior auxiliary officers. The prefects of Second Adiutrix and Twentieth Valeria were already sat in conference.

"Gentlemen, it seems I have been appointed Governor of Gallia Aquitania. I believe I have time to recapture Mona before I take up my new position."

Marcus felt conflicting emotions; here was a leader he liked and respected and, most importantly one he could trust, a leader he did not want to lose. On the other hand, he realised that the promotion was a good one and a man would have to be a fool not to be excited. They all complimented the general who continued, "I am afraid I shall have to leave for Mona immediately. The two prefects, Pompeius Arvina of the Second Adiutrix and Sentius Musca of the Twentieth will have joint leadership here at Deva." He paused and looked directly at the auxiliary officers. "The Second Adiutrix will need to complete the construction of Deva if we are to have a sound base. The Ninth are even now finishing off Eboracum. It is the auxiliaries who will bear the brunt of this campaign and only when you have found the rebels and contained them will the Twentieth be able to destroy them. We, "he gestured to the legionary prefects," have decided that we will operate as a vexillation whose task it is to get to Mona and contain the rebels. We will take two cohorts of legionaries. Any questions?"

It had all happened so quickly that none of the three auxiliary commanders had had time to even draw breath let alone come up with questions. "No sir," chorused the three.

The general came and clasped the arm of each of the auxiliaries in turn. When he came to Marcus he said, "I would like to thank you again not only for your valour but for the way you and your men fought. I now believe that with enough auxiliaries this province could be captured by a single legion. We will try some new techniques during this campaign and we shall learn together. The task seems daunting but I have faith in you. We shall see if the auxiliaries can achieve in a few weeks what it took a couple of legions half a year to accomplish."

Chapter 1

As Gnaeus Julius Agricola dealt with the correspondence connected with his new position the prefects sat long into the night with the three auxiliary officers. As Decurion Princeps, Marcus was outranked by both of the auxiliary infantry prefects; however, his reputation was such that all of them treated him as an equal.

"The general was quite right. I need to complete this legionary fortress and that will take all of my legionaries."

Sentius Musca nodded, "My Twentieth will need to construct roads towards Mona. The reason the rebels captured it so easily is the lack of roads. I intend to start one following the coast west and one to the east towards Eboracum."

Cominius Sura, prefect of the First Batavians gasped, "That will take forever."

The two legionary prefects looked bemused. Sentius said, "On the land to the east my men can build a road one and a half miles in length each day, the sandy swampy road to the west a mile a day. Within two moons we shall be at Mona. Eboracum may take longer but when the fortress is finished then the second can aid us. Unless of course, you have summoned us when we shall down tools and finish off these priests and rebels."

Marcus looked at his friend Cominius and shook his head in silent amazement. The legions were impressive. The size of a job did not intimidate them and they would grind out the work until they were finished. They were the same when they fought, no matter how many enemies they faced their philosophy was '*kill them one at a time*'. Marcus had seen them do it with ruthless efficiency.

"The general has ordered the Classis Britannica to sail to us here so that we may use it to support us. As soon as it arrives it will make communication and supply easier."

The second prefect of auxiliaries, the Second Gallorum, pointed at the crude map. "How will we get across the straits here without the fleet?"

"Good question Cassius Bassus. The simple answer is that the fleet should be there by the time you have travelled that far but if not, you will have to improvise."

"I am a little worried prefect by the mountains which skirt the coast. We are on a narrow strip of land. We could be ambushed or they could attack us in the rear."

"Yes, Decurion Princeps and it is your cavalry who will have to prevent that. Your cavalry must be the vanguard, the rear guard and the flank guard."

Marcus let out a long sigh. "My men will be spread out thinly."

"We know. The general has requested two more alae of cavalry but until they actually materialise your single ala will have to perform the duties of three. You have three days to prepare. You will need supplies for fourteen days; by that time the fleet should be here but we will keep you informed."

When Marcus briefed his decurions Decius let out his normal expletive, "Bugger! It isn't bad enough that we have to protect the foot soldiers, we have to do it in land suitable only for a mountain goat and in a land where every barbarian wants to serve your bollocks up on a platter for their supper."

Gaius and the others smiled at the image but Gaius voiced their concerns. "We still haven't made up the numbers we lost in the last battle. We are at least two turmae down and we have few replacement mounts. Decius is right sir. There is a limit to what we can do."

When Marcus spoke, it was quietly and calmly. He had gone through all these problems with the general and he knew that they could protest all that they liked it would not make any difference. They had a job to do and Marcus would see that they did it if only to find the witch Fainch, the murderer of Queen Cartimandua and his wife and child. He looked at the young faces of his decurions; Decius apart they were all very young men, tested in battle and worthy of their promotions but young men nonetheless. "I know it looks daunting but it is not as bad as you are both making out. The Deceangli never really recovered from the last rebellion and they do not have large numbers. They certainly don't have the numbers the Brigante and Carvetii possessed. They succeed because the troops here were slack and lazy. They thought they had whipped their enemy and they were not ready for the ambushes and sneak attacks. We know better. We know that an ambush can come at any time and place." He paused, "As Drusus discovered and as Metellus nearly found to his cost." The memory of the dead decurion and the almost fatal ambush on the Dunum Fluvius made them all look at one another. Metellus almost unconsciously put his arm around the shoulders of Julius Demetrius, the youngest decurion. "If it had not been for the timely intervention of young Julius we would have been another turma down."

Agrippa leaned over and pointed at the map. "It looks to me as though there is much we don't know about the land away from the coast; just that there are some real mountains quite close to the coast."

"Good point Agrippa. We need to make our own maps. Each evening we will have a briefing to share information."

"At least we won't need to worry about our right flank. Not unless the Druids can walk on water."

Decius shook his head," Don't tempt the Fates Lentius. I for one am not looking forward to facing priests and witches."

As the others looked in surprise as the normally bluff and down to earth senior decurion Marcus realised that many of the men had had a fear of these people. Caesar himself had had to shame his legionaries to leave their boats when they first invaded and Aulus Paulinus had almost had a mutiny the first time they took Mona. The Roman soldier could face with complete ease any warrior but they feared the magic and superstition of the priests and their rituals. There were rumours racing around the camps at Deva of captives being place in huge wicker cages and burnt alive and they had all heard of captives being emasculated by the priestesses. "I for one am looking forward to finding one priestess but if you are that worried make sure they don't capture you, Decius!"

"Easier said than done when they use magic."

As they all looked uneasily at each other Marcus spoke sharply for the first time. "Enough of that. No matter what you think of the enemy do not let your troopers know that. They are young and impressionable. The Druids are not a problem. Is that clear?" They nodded. "Go and organise your men for the march tomorrow. Decius stay behind a moment."

As they all trooped out Decius stood with his head down. "Sorry about that Marcus. Me and my big mouth."

"Listen Decius we only have a couple of decurions with any experience. Most of the leaders have only been in the province for a few months. You, me, Agrippa and Lentius need to give a lead. If you want to express your doubts and fears do it in here with me over a beaker of wine."

Decius' face cracked into a smile. "That's the best offer I've had in a while. Decurion Princeps getting the wine in. Don't worry Marcus I will keep this big mouth shut!"

Fainch

Fainch and her sisters were already preparing their welcome for the Romans. The Deceangli might be few in numbers but the Ordovices lived in the remote mountains to the south of Mona and they had sent many warbands to defend the sacred groves of Mona.

Fainch looked at the King of the Ordovices, Gwynfor. He was a squat powerful warrior who hated the Romans even more than Fainch did for his whole family had been wiped out by the Roman legions thirty years earlier. He had spent his whole life warring with the Romans and inflicting both as many casualties and as much pain as he could. He had been more than willing to bring the ten thousand warriors north and he was even more willing when he found that he had the power of the Druids to call upon. The holy mountain of Wyddfa would become a terrible ally to the peoples of the mountains and the Romans would pay a heavy price. "Your warriors close to the holy mountain; they know what they are to do?"

Inside Gwynfor felt himself become angry, he was not used to being given instructions by a woman, even a priestess. It was, however, a necessary evil for they had tried to defeat the Romans the old ways and they had been beaten in the old ways, he knew that Fainch and the other priestesses had been responsible for the uprising which had thrown the Romans into such a panic. As he considered his answer he saw, for the first time that the priestess was ageing, almost before his eyes. The temptress, who used her sex as a weapon, was not as alluring as she had once been. Perhaps the strain of the magic and the spells was beginning to tell. "They know that the Romans must be allowed to get to Hen Waliau unmolested and then attack when they try to cross Afon Menai."

"Good."

Looking shrewdly at the priestess he added, "What if they do not come as far as Hen Waliau? They can cross much closer to their own lines."

"It does not make much difference for your men will still be able to fall upon them."

"But they will not Fainch, for you have given them instructions not to attack until the Romans reach Hen Waliau." He emphasised her name to leave all in the hut in no doubt where the blame for any failure should lie. He also noted the tic of annoyance that appeared on her face.

"Send a messenger then and tell them to watch the Romans. When they try to cross and they are committed then they will attack." Gwynfor nodded a smile of satisfaction creasing his weathered, gnarled face. "We will then fall upon them as they try to land on the beaches. "

"The Deceangli scouts say there are many Romans, at least one legion and many auxiliaries, some of them mounted."

"They all have the same problem. They have to cross to Mona and that is not easy."

"Unless they bring their ships."

Again, he noted with quiet satisfaction that she was not as confident as she had once been. "If they bring ships then we will fill coracles with brushwood and light them from the two ends of Afon Menai. They will burn and drown."

Gwynfor was not certain for the currents were notably irregular and the coracle so small it would probably burn out before it could do its job. However, he kept his counsel. The witch had the bones in her hand and she had thrown them. If they failed then Gwynfor would go back to the methods he knew best and harry them all the way back to Deva.

As the column turned its back on Deva Fluvium Macro nudged his horse so that it was next to Decius. It was Decius' turn to be the vanguard and they were heading away, briefly, from the security of the sea and river as the right flank. "I thought the mountains here were supposed to be enormous. Those hills don't look so big. We had much bigger ones than that in the north."

"It's a good job that you can handle a weapon because you haven't got the brains of a mule." He pointed forward to where the clouds were just rising to reveal the sharp, jagged white tipped peaks that were the mountains around Wyddfa. "Those are the mountains."

Macro looked at the mountains looming in the distance and his jaw dropped. "Oh! They are big. Do we have to go up them?"

"I hope not. No, we are just cutting across country because there is a valley up ahead we can travel down to the sea again. Gaelwyn reckoned it was the Clwyd or something but all their words sound like someone is coughing up phlegm." He looked anxiously around. "This is the part I don't like. We are spread thin enough as it is and now we have to be all around the column for protection. But who protects us." He turned to look at the plodding feet that were the infantry. He had plenty of time before they would catch him up. "Take two men and ride ahead. The sea is supposed to be about eight miles away. Ride until you can see it and then come back to us. And Macro be careful. No chasing warriors or investigating anything. Find the sea and then get back. Right?"

With the grin of a young child, the sergeant yelled, "Yes decurion" and galloped to find two other eager volunteers.

Over on the right flank, Marcus smiled to himself as he watched Macro and two other troopers gallop up over the skyline. He was smiling because he enjoyed Macro's enthusiasm and because it showed him that his old friend Decius was being as cautious as ever. Scanning his ala, he saw just how depleted they were. They had had over a thousand mounted men before the battle in the north-west now they could barely muster five hundred and twenty-three. He had had to reorganise the ala to enable them to operate. It also meant he had had to return temporary decurions like Macro back to their original roles.

Although it had not been an easy decision Marcus knew he had taken the correct one; he needed experienced heads in charge of his men for they would have to think without him looking over their shoulders. The fifteen turmae now had a formation of three in the vanguard, three with the rear guard, four to the south and five to the north. A sudden attack in this unfamiliar territory could easily result in many empty saddles. Decius was doing what Decius did best, he was being aggressively cautious.

Chapter 2

Inir was waiting with his warband close to the Afon Menai. He was a powerfully built young warrior and, unusually for an Ordovice quite tall. He stood out on a battlefield. It was said that he could shoot an arrow further than any man alive and no one had ever bested him in battle. Perhaps this was the reason King Gwynfor had detached him from the main army to ensure he did not outshine his king on the field of battle. Inir had ten thousand Ordovice with him and a few of the Deceangli who had not been either defeated or Romanised. His men were spread out in the gullies and sharply pointed valleys which littered this side of the mountains. The coastal plain was narrow; thirty men abreast could fill it in places. If the Romans could occupy that Inir knew they would be hard to shift, especially with their armour and testudo formation.

Idly chewing on a piece of wild garlic he pondered his latest instructions. He was not to attack until the Romans turned their back upon him. Those instructions made no sense; he was a puissant warrior and he had a military mind as sharp as any. He would know the best time to attack not some witch, no matter how strong in magic on an island forty miles from the enemy. He did not like the idea of taking orders from a woman anyway. A woman had two places where she was useful, in the bed and at the fire to prepare food. He preferred the company of men, men whose conversations were about war and heroic deeds not the problems of mewling children or the cleanliness of the home. He was proud of his warband. The men who had followed him had chosen to follow him because of his deeds. One day he would rule the Ordovice and then he would make all the decisions.

Agricola stood with Marcus and the Batavian prefects as they gazed across the small bay to the promontory which stuck out into the sea. To their left the land drifted in low hills towards Mona, a faint smudge on the horizon. Rising behind the hills were the high mountains. The scouts had returned despondent for they reported that the only things which could move on those hills were goats or sheep. They had however reported a river that would halt their progress. There was a crossing place but it was a couple of miles inland.

“Gentlemen we are deep inside enemy territory. So far, we have seen no sign of the enemy. Decurion what is the latest intelligence?”

“My scouts report that the plain narrows considerably towards Mona with the mountains almost blocking the path.”

Agricola nodded, “And still no sign of the fleet. The plain looks too narrow for the legion.”

Cominius could not hold in his reaction. “But we need legionaries if we are to take Mona!”

Agricola smiled, much as a father smiles indulgently at a child’s outburst. “Calm yourself prefect. I will leave one cohort at that place. What did your scout call it?”

“Caerhun.”

“How these people communicate with words like that I do not know! We will build a fort at Caerhun and the remainder of the men will come with us to Mona. Still no sign of the fleet eh?” This was a rhetorical question for they all knew that the fleet had not arrived and that meant they were not as well supplied as they might have been. Marcus also realised that it gave them a headache. How would they cross the straits? “Let us push on. I would like to camp at this Caerhun tonight.”

Decius and his turma were eating well. Macro had gone hunting and returned with a mixed bag of game, rabbits, gulls and even a fox. “They must have no sense at all these foxes; it was still daylight when I saw him.”

“So, young Macro I know the Allfather forgot to give you brains but at least he gave you a keen eye and arm.”

Marcus wandered over. “Any problems today decurion?”

“I might have known! We start cooking and the senior officers just happen to come over.”

Marcus grinned. “Decurion, you know I always do my rounds at this time. Just because I happen to come when you are cooking what I hope is a magnificent stew is happenstance.”

“And I know that you wouldn’t want your old friends to miss out.”

“Gaius! Can’t your men hunt?”

“Not as well as young Vindonnus over there.”

Later as they all mopped up their game gravy with the last remnants of the hard bread they carried they discussed the campaign so far. The three of them had served together for long enough to speak their minds. "We lost no more horses today?"

"No but this land is leg breaking country. I would hate to have to gallop. You only get twenty strides and you find a chasm opening up in front of you."

"I know what you mean Decius. We are travelling barely faster than the infantry."

"That suits our leader," commented Marcus. "They will have good, close protection. What about the men?"

Decius gave an almighty belch. "It just shows that if you cut out the right pieces of bad flesh you can end up with a healed arm." Gaius looked at him in confusion. "Get rid of the bad men and even though you have fewer men you are stronger."

"Ah, you mean Modius?"

"Not just Modius although he was the worst but Flavius Demetrius and his turma. They were all a bad lot."

Flavius Demetrius had been the son of the former prefect. Over promoted at a young age he had been a corrupt and demoralising influence in the ala. He had had Gaius unjustly flogged and promoted his own cronies to positions of power. Fortunately, when his turma was massacred in the northern forests the canker had been cut out. Modius had escaped to join the rebel Brigante.

"Julius has turned out to be a fine officer."

"Yes, young Gaius and that just shows that if you train 'em right they turn out all right."

Again, Gaius looked confused and then he grinned with understanding. "Oh yes I forgot you trained him."

Decius nodded, "And you, remember that I trained you."

Gaius looked over at Marcus who had remained silent throughout. "But remember who trained all of us."

It was an embarrassed Marcus who changed the subject. "Let young Julius take the van tomorrow." They both looked in surprise at him. "I know but we have used all the experienced decurions and they all have to know what it is like. That is how we learned."

"I know Marcus but we don't know these people. They aren't going to fight like the Brigante. Look at this country. They can't use horses and I have heard they fight with witches at their side."

Marcus' face hardened. "Camp gossip. The women might fight but we had that at Stagh-herts didn't we? And they died just as easily. As for the witches, we have met a witch before, and their power seems to be in poison; men's minds and food! Julius will be fine and I have a feeling that we will be in action sooner rather than later. They have allowed us to get far closer to Mona than I thought they would." He gestured at the plain. "This would have been a perfect place to hold us up and ambush us. I can't think why they didn't."

High in the foothills overlooking the camp Inir was thinking the same thoughts. The Roman invasion force was like a flea on a dog. His scouts had reported they were building a fort. Perhaps this was the total sum of their invasion! He would wait until the following day to decide what to do but he had made his mind up, witch or no witch, he was going to attack the Romans before they got to Mona and if the king did not like that, then there could be a new king ruling the west of Britannia before the turn of the year.

Julius Agricola rode his mount next to that of Marcus as they headed North West towards the coast. Marcus turned to view the vexillation which followed them. The four hundred and fifty legionaries seemed a pitifully small force. The Batavians and the Gallorum auxiliaries added fifteen hundred and Marcus could only muster five hundred and twenty-three troopers.

"You are thinking Decurion that, perhaps, we have too few men?"

"I was thinking sir that we could have done with a few more legionaries."

"I disagree. On a battlefield that is unencumbered by rocks, rivers defiles and trees then yes, the legion is invincible. However, look around you. Do you see such a battlefield?"

"No sir but the terrain suits neither my horses nor my men."

"Your horses, I agree but your men no. They can fight on foot." There was a silence as Marcus pondered this. "Do you see a problem Decurion?"

"No. it is just that Prefect Demetrius wouldn't have dreamed of taking his men from their horses. Had I known I would have had the men training for that different style of warfare. Luckily Sergeant Macro has had the men sparring on foot."

"The advantage we have over the tribes is that not only do we have the superior weapons and armour but we have the discipline. We don't need to fight as the legions do, in fact, that would be too difficult."

They were interrupted by a trooper from Julius' turma. "Yes trooper."

"Decurion Demetrius' compliments and we have arrived at the straits."

"And?"

"And, that is all sir." The trooper looked confused.

Marcus smiled and said, "It is his first duty as vanguard and I think he is trying to make sure he does not make mistakes."

"Return to the Decurion and ask him to wait for us at the coast." The trooper galloped off glad to be away from the senior officers. "We will make camp there and then we can launch our attack in the next few days."

"Will the fleet be there?"

"It doesn't matter. I have a few ideas." Enigmatically he ended the conversation leaving Marcus to wonder what he had in mind. The idea of fighting on foot was an intriguing one but it would necessitate training, how Decius would love that!

As the column snaked its way down the foothills towards the coast Inir mustered his men. "The Romans have divided their forces. We outnumber them five to one. We will attack." His men were gathered in their warbands and they began to filter down the hillside using all the cover that was available.

Agricola and Marcus were met by an eager Julius. "You can see sir, there is Mona." He pointed across the short stretch of water to the island lurking in the afternoon mist. Although the day was bright and warm the island had attracted a veil of fog which shrouded the shoreline and all that they could see was a low rise of hills emerging from the mist. The troopers looked with trepidation at the sinister sacred isle of Mona. As soon as the weary foot soldiers slogged up they were instructed to begin to erect their camp.

Marcus ordered Quintus and Levius to throw out a picket line to the north. "Gaelwyn!" The grumpy Brigante scout reluctantly arrived at Marcus' side knowing that, unlike the others he would still have work to do."

"Yes sir."

"Head down the coast and see if we have any surprises." The wiry warrior trotted his horse along the beach and Marcus noted with some admiration how he used every morsel of cover he could find.

Inir's men were less than half a mile from the picket line when they were halted by Inir. He signalled for them to squat down. The sun was lowering in the sky and the mountains behind them cast a shadow. Although a young leader Inir was a wise one and he wanted every advantage he could have. Unlike the tribes to the north the Ordovices used dull colours which camouflaged them well against the rocks and sparse vegetation. Inir gestured for the men on the extreme right and left to outflank the picket line which was struggling to keep formation on the rocky hillside. The troopers could smell the food which was being prepared and, whilst they were pleased they did not have to erect the camp, they also resented the fact that they would eat later than their comrades. It was slowly falling to night and they would have a two-mile ride to reach the camp. Quintus and Levius were also a little unhappy. Levius had only just been promoted and had taken over the turma of Modius. They were already a truculent troop and Levius had found it hard to garner any trust. Quintus' troop was much more experienced but they too were eager to return to camp.

The first they knew of the presence of an enemy was when a flurry of arrows descended from the dark. Levius just did not react as his men were plucked from their saddles; Quintus' experience stood him in good stead and he yelled at the nearest trooper," Get to the camp, tell them we are under attack. Troopers form ranks!" Levius' men obeyed the commanding voice as a war axe flew through the air and hit the unfortunate decurion in the chest. It was a chaotic scene as thousands of tribesmen poured down from the hillsides intent on slaughtering as many Romans as possible. Quintus saw the impossibility of their situation. They could not manoeuvre, they were well outnumbered and the enemy had the dark and surprise on their side. He had no other recourse than to shout, "Retreat!"

As they made their way down the hazardous slope the arrows and missiles continued to thin their ranks. The tribesmen were moving as fast as the cavalry and Quintus could see that the retreat had merely delayed the inevitable. They would die. He determined to die as a warrior and he kept turning his horse to face the enemy behind, slashing down with his spatha and killing many tribesmen. As soon as he had despatched one he continued down the hill. The rest of his turma, those that lived, attempted to do the same. Those in Levius' turma just fled making them easy targets for the spears, stones and arrows hurled at them. Quintus' men's retreat made their pursuers wary. He wondered whether to make a stand and was debating whether or not to order his men to turn when he heard the welcome call of the buccina. The Decurion Princeps was on his way to help. Almost as the last note faded away a solid line of cavalry appeared. Those in the centre had bows and they launched a volley at Quintus' pursuers. The unprotected tribesmen fell like leaves and the last few troopers were able to disengage and find shelter behind their comrades.

Marcus had no time for pleasantries. "One more volley and then fall back." As Quintus, bleeding heavily from his arm and legs, emerged through the cavalry he saw a solid hedgehog of auxilia and legionaries.

When the cavalry filtered through Cominius Sura dropped his arm and a hail of arrows stopped the attack in its tracks. The tribesmen were spread out and the arrows did not kill as many men as the Batavian would have liked but it was enough for Inir who signalled a retreat and his men disappeared into the murk. He had done what he had intended. He had defeated the vaunted Romans and killed many of their men. As his warriors climbed back up the hill Inir could see over seventy slain Romans. Tomorrow they would attack again and this time they would slaughter the rest.

"Thank you, sir."

"Don't talk Quintus. The surgeon is on his way."

"They surprised us, sir. How many ....?"

"How many survived?" Quintus nodded. "There are seven of you."

"I am sorry sir."

"Don't be a fool. There were thousands of them. Even the general knows our horses are useless in this country. Rest now and we'll talk in the morning."

As Quintus was led away the general arrived. "So, Decurion Princeps we have our war eh?"

"Bit of a disaster sir."

"How many men did you lose?"

"Seventy-one so far and a couple of the survivors don't look as though they will last the night."

"I don't think they will attack again tonight but I will keep the Batavians out there until the camps are built."

Marcus watched as the general rode off. He was amazed by how calm he was. Perhaps the high casualties were acceptable but this was the biggest single loss that Marcus had experienced and he was angry. Decius came up along with Gaius. "A whole turma gone eh? That hasn't happened, well not since Drusus."

"It is my fault, Decius. I should have trained the decurions better. Levius was too inexperienced and his turma was not the best one we had, Modius saw to that."

"We haven't had enough time to train them, sir. We didn't have the time."

"We will have to train on the job; Gaius get Macro, will you? And Agrippa."

Gaius trotted off and Decius looked curiously at Marcus. "What is going on in that head of yours?"

"Something that the general said to me. About adapting to our enemies and our terrain and I think these two might be able to help." Agrippa and Macro arrived together both wondering why and macro wondering what he had done wrong. "You have heard about the loss of our men?" They both nodded. The general almost anticipated this. It looks like we will have to change our style of fighting. We need to fight on foot." The look of shock on Decius' face could have been comical were the situation not so serious. "As Quintus and Levius discovered the horses get in the way. Cavalry works best in open country; the prefect for all his faults, knew that. This is not open country.

When we go into battle tomorrow we will fight on foot. I want the two of you to get around the men tonight and show them how to do it." He held up his hand to silence the protests forming. "When we had the tournament, I saw that they could fight with a sword. You two are the best weapon trainers I have ever seen. You can do it. We will fight in the same formation as on horse, javelins at the front with a row of the best archers behind. Oh, and tell the decurions, they fight on foot as well."

The two men walked away bemused and a little apprehensive. Decius was almost boiling over. "Us fight on foot? But it's never been done!"

Just then Cominius who had been nearby walked over. "Actually, Decius it has. We have some units which are mixed cavalry and infantry. It works quite well although they are trained specifically for that task. I have seen your men fight. They have the skills in arms. In fact, it might be easier. They won't have to control a horse."

"Yes sir but some of them will struggle to walk and wield a sword!" He walked off shaking his head as Marcus and the prefect laughed.

"He will do it. He might complain but he wants this ala to be the best one ever. My only worry is that we fight tomorrow and looking at the numbers we will be seriously outnumbered."

"I am not worried Marcus. Our general is a calm man and a thinker. We will beat them, of that I am sure. I am just not certain if that will be tomorrow or another day."

Just then Gaelwyn arrived in the camp. He looked around at the wounded being tended and sniffed. "I see you missed my nose again."

Slightly irritated by the insensitive comment Marcus snapped. "What did you find?"

Ignoring the rebuke, the Brigante warrior idly picked his nose and, examining the result said, "There are a few thousand tribesmen waiting all along the beaches of Mona. And before you ask there was no sign of the fleet. I found a stream a mile up the coast with a path going into the hills." When Marcus looked him at expectantly he carried on, "I only mention it because when I went up it I found the Ordovice camp." Their faces showed their surprise.

"Thank you, Gaelwyn, now go and have your food."

Turning to leave he added more seriously. "And there are thousands of them, a legion and half in your numbers."

"I think we had better find the general."

Chapter 3

The general was up well before dawn. The cold night had left more mist around the beach and the camp. As Marcus and the two prefects made their way to Agricola's tent he wondered about the magic of the island. The mist did not seem natural for it also hung around the tops of the hills and mountains as though the gods were protecting this sacred and holy land.

"Thank you, gentlemen. Thanks to Marcus' scout, a most interesting man by the way Decurion, we know where the enemy camp is. I propose to attack at first light."

Cassius Bassus looked incredulous, "But they outnumber us by at least five to one and we will be attacking uphill!"

"Do you doubt your men prefect?"

"No sir but uphill and outnumbered!"

"You forget our advantages. Arms, training and discipline with those we will win. Our plan of battle is quite simple. The legionaries will be in three lines in the centre, The Batavians on the right and your men Cassius Bassus on the left. We have no artillery but I will require one cohort of your men Prefect Bassus to guard the wounded and the supplies. Decurion Princeps Maximunius will take his men on foot," the gasp from Bassus was so loud they all looked at him, "will take his men on foot." He repeated, "That is right prefect on foot. Have you a problem with that Decurion?"

"No sir the men are all prepared."

"Good. Your scout can take you behind their camp and when they engage my front-line fall upon their rear. Should be simple. Any questions?"

Any questions they might have had died on their lips. As they left Bassus turned to Marcus. "I'll say this for him, he has balls of iron that one. Your lads manage the fighting on foot?"

"It is not as if we have to make a frontal attack, ours is the easy part."

"Only if we win, if we don't then this could be the end of the Pannonian cavalry."

Inir and his men were in position as the sun lit up the island of Mona gleaming like a jewel glinting in the west. The

Ordovices took this to be a sign that the gods smiled upon them and they eagerly took up their battle line. The Ordovice warrior was small and squat and whilst in many places this could be a disadvantage here on a steep slope it was an advantage. They could run quickly down the hill and be less likely to fall over. The speed down the hill would increase their momentum and Inir was certain that a pathetic three deep line could not stand against them.

As his men marched down the hill he was shocked to find the Romans advancing towards him. He had expected them to wait until he attacked but they were going to win the battle for him. If they were moving then it would be harder for them to stand their ground. With a roar, his men crashed down the hill like rocks from an angry Wyddfa. If he thought this would intimidate his enemies and make them flee he was wrong. They continued their steady and remorseless march towards the screaming barbarians. He could see the centurions in their distinctive helmets and the standard-bearers looking along the lines to make sure they were straight and he wondered at this war machine he was about to take on. They appeared to be calm as though on a parade not being charged by the Ordovice. He had not time for further thoughts as they approached within forty paces. Suddenly, and without a command being spoken the whole line hurled their javelins, spearing warriors and throwing them back into their comrades following on. The front line disintegrated as warriors fell and others, coming on behind tripped and fell over the dead and dying or trampled them where they lay. Still the Romans did not falter. The front lines passed their javelins to the men behind, locked their shields and went to work with their gladii.

Inir found that he was unable to land a blow which did any damage. He was the tallest man in the Ordovice line and able to smash his sword down on the legionaries in front of him but there always seemed to be a shield in the way. Next to him he felt men fall as the deadly blades slid under, through and over the shields to find the vital organs of the unarmoured men. The javelins continued to be hurled by those in the second and third ranks whilst the archers amongst the auxiliaries sent flight after flight into the rear ranks. The centurions were calmness itself, killing efficiently and warning those legionaries who were in danger of dropping their guard to '*pick up that bloody shield*'. Seeing the general himself in the front line Inir determined to end this in the way of the tribes by killing their leader in single combat. Once their leader was dead his men would surely flee. He and his bodyguard left the front rank and made their way through the sea of enraged warriors until they were facing Agricola. One of the legionaries to the left of the general stumbled and Inir took the opportunity of smashing his sword down on the shield of the Roman leader. In all his previous combats such a blow would have ended the contest for he would have broken the shield. Agricola merely turned the shield slightly so that the blade slid harmlessly down. So surprised was Inir that he failed to counter with his own shield and the general's blade sliced through his unprotected side. Although not a fatal blow it was a disabling blow and Inir's bodyguards closed around him to protect him.

The momentum of the charge had now left the tribesmen who had many ranks deep but their front ranks were being butchered in a clinical fashion by legionaries and auxiliaries alike. Although the legionaries fought in a tighter formation the auxiliaries kept a tight line and were well disciplined.

High up on the hill, behind the extreme left flank of the Ordovice line, Decius was heaving to catch his breath. "Sod this for a game of dice. I just want a horse."

Macro was barely breathing, "I will tell you what, sir, after this is over I think I will have to give you some extra training. You are not fit."

"You two shut it!" Marcus' whispered command sounded like a crack of thunder. "Decurions form line!" The whole ala formed an oblique line with Marcus in the middle, Decius on the extreme right and Agrippa on the extreme left. "Sound the buccina!" The strident call of the buccina seemed to echo around the mountain tops and the ala moved down the hill, not at a charge but a fast walk. Marcus was determined to maintain cohesion. The first warriors they encountered were fleeing towards them and were so surprised to find Romans in their rear that they were easily despatched. Soon they could see the rear ranks of the Ordovice who were looking nervously over their shoulders having heard the screams of their slain comrades.

When they saw the approaching Romans many of them panicked and they ran towards the Romans advancing down the hill. Others bravely charged the Roman line led by Agricola but in both cases, they met the solid line of Romans piecemeal and were slaughtered. In the centre Marcus wielded the sword of Cartimandua effortlessly and it seemed to sing a song of death in the early morning breeze. Its razor-sharp blade sliced limbs from the warriors regardless of any armour.

Soon the lines of warriors thinned out as they tried to escape but they were encircled. There were Romans all around them. The net tightened inexorably and more and more barbarians fell to legionary and auxiliary alike. Finally, there was a knot of men gathered forlornly around their wounded leader and Marcus wondered if the general was in a mood for prisoners. He could see however that Agricola's face hardened and the legionaries continued to chop their way through the ever-decreasing circle of bondsmen until the general himself decapitated the erstwhile king of the Ordovice and held it aloft waving it to a cheering and rampant Roman army.

As they began clearing the dead from the battlefield Marcus could not believe how few Romans had died and how many barbarians had perished. He looked over at Agricola who was wandering the field talking to his men. The next time Agricola made a decision which appeared to go against logic Marcus would trust his judgement. Watching his own men, he was proud. They had fought in a way which was unnatural to them but coped as though they had been doing it their whole life. None of his decurions had died or even sustained an injury. The only worry though was that not only Decius but some of the others had shown they were not as fit as they might be. Marcus decided that Macro was right and they should become fitter warriors. When they had the time, he would initiate a training programme to build up muscles not used when on horseback.

Fainch

Fainch was beside herself with anger. Watching from the shoreline she had seen her Ordovice allies disobey her orders and the result was the slaughter of more than half the warriors available to her. She watched as the Romans built and burnt pyres of warriors whose lives had been thrown away needlessly.

She turned to the king, "King Gwynfor you obviously picked the wrong warrior for the task."

"I cannot understand it; Inir was a brave and cunning warrior. Perhaps he thought there were too few Romans."

Fainch considered this. "Perhaps. Certainly, there were fewer than I expected." She hated it when her planning was thwarted. The warriors had every advantage, terrain, numbers, time of day; how could they have lost? What if this general had already sent his fleet to the other side of the island? She knew he had another legion perhaps they were already moving to the northern coast? "You may have been right when you said they would use ships. We will await the fleet for I cannot believe that they will launch an attack with the pitiful numbers we saw."

In a quiet voice a chastened Gwynfor added, "Those pitiful few destroyed my warriors."

Glaring at the downcast king she snapped," We will await them inland make sure your watchers send the signal when the fleet is sighted."

The next day was spent preparing for the invasion. Cassius and Cominius shared with Marcus their worries about the actual invasion. "Without the Classis Britannica, I cannot see how we will affect landing on the beach."

Cominius gestured at Marcus. "His scout Gaelwyn said that there are many trees close to the shore just down the coast. Perhaps we will build rafts."

"That would take too much time. No, I think he will wait for the fleet."

"I do not think so."

"Why Marcus what do you know?"

"I know that he does not always take the easy approach and he does things which his enemies and even his friends do not expect. I will wait. When he is ready to tell us, he will do so. I think it will be an interesting experience, whatever it is."

The general called them together for a briefing late in the afternoon. "I have set the legionaries to felling some trees." Cominius looked at Marcus and tapped the side of his nose. Marcus merely shrugged. "We begin the crossing at first light. We will cross there." He gestured to the narrowest point between the mainland and the island. Marcus estimated it about fifteen hundred paces. Not far to punt a raft."

Cassius spoke up. "What opposition can we expect?"

"The barbarians appear to have moved from the shore but we estimate their numbers to be the same as we fought yesterday. The difference will be, Prefect, that we will attack without the legionaries." The shock in the meeting was visible in all the faces except for Marcus. The legionaries were the elite, the cutting edge of any attack it was madness to leave your best troops cooling their heels.

"But sir."

"Trust me prefect. Trust me." He glanced over to Marcus. "The Decurion does not appear to be perturbed, why are you?"

"Well… it is not normal to attack with just auxiliaries when there are legionaries available."

"As it is not normal to fight with dismounted cavalry or uphill or any of the things we have done. Do you not see Prefect Sura that it is by doing the unexpected that we will win? They have learned over the years how we fight and they count on us fighting the same way. Make sure your men are well rested for the success of the invasion lies with them."

As they left Marcus turned with a wry smile, "I wish I had put some denari on the general's decision."

"You have the gift Marcus, you can foretell the future."

"No Cassius but I am coming to know our general. I think we will succeed tomorrow."

Decius and Agrippa were not too certain when Marcus briefed them. "I don't know sir. I mean he has been lucky so far but I hate boats and a raft is not even a boat it is just a log that floats."

Julius and some of the younger decurions were quite excited. "I think they will get a surprise when we suddenly arrive on the beach."

"It might be fine for us but what about the horses. Some of them are jittery at the best of times and a raft is fairly unstable."

"Stop speculating." They all looked at Marcus. "We don't even know it is a raft. It may be something else entirely."

Decius smiled, "A bridge! It could be a bridge. Now a bridge I don't mind."

Just then Cominius came hurrying past after a meeting with Agricola. He was grinning. He gestured for Marcus to join him. "I have been sworn to secrecy but I can tell you Marcus it isn't a bridge and it isn't a raft. I have to go and choose a couple of likely lads I have a job for them." Marcus deemed it unnecessary to frighten Decius any more than he was already.

The next morning as dawn broke over the snowy tops of Wyddfa, Marcus led his men down to the beach. Marcus apart, they were all expecting to see rafts constructed by the legionaries. It was a shock to see that the straits were empty apart from two ropes about half a mile apart which went from the mainland to the Mona shore. Peering into the gloom, Decius expressed the views of most of the troopers. "Does he think we can do a tightrope walk over that?"

Laughing Marcus pointed across the straits to where eight armed Batavians stood guard at each end of the two ropes. "Look. The Batavians have secured them I think we are going to get wet. Dismounting Marcus led his horse to the water's edge to where the general awaited.

"Ah Decurion. From your expression, I think you have deduced what we intend to do?"

"Yes sir but I think it has come as a bit of a shock to my lads. Should I tell them or do you want that pleasure?"

"Your command Marcus, you tell them but be quick about it. I want the men in the water as soon as they are informed. The infantry auxiliaries will be going on either side of you. You and your horses will go in the middle."

"Right sir."

Turning to his men who stood with expressions ranging from horror on Decius' face, to a bemused look on Julius' childlike visage. "The general has decided that we smell a bit and has asked us to take a bath. While we do it, we will cross the straits so that when we meet the Ordovices we will smell a little sweeter." He allowed a moment for that to sink in. "Dismount. On my command, we will lead the horses into the water. Hang on to their manes and they will swim us across. For those of you who have never done this you will find it easier if you kick your legs in the water."

A lone voice piped up, "But I can't swim!"

Decius had regained his composure. "It seems to me that now is the time to learn. Besides all you have to do is hang on to the bloody horse. Be thankful you aren't the infantry; the non-swimmers have to hang on to a log."

Glancing at the general who nodded, Marcus shouted, "Decurions lead off your turma and keep it steady." The first one in the water was Marcus who hoped that he could hang on, if not his armour would drag him to a watery death.

He found it remarkably easy, all of the horse's movements were below the water and the powerful beasts made little of the current. The trooper behind hazarded a question many had been thinking. "Why the two ropes sir?"

"Simple. Any man who falls off will be swept along to one or the other. He just hangs on and then pulls himself across."

Gaius shouted over, "What about the barbarians?" He gestured with his arm to where a few hundred had gathered to watch in amazement. Marcus saw someone point inland and a warrior ran off as fast as he could.

"If these are the only ones then I don't think we have a problem." He raised his voice above the splashing. "Decurions form up as soon as we land. Pass it on." The message rippled across the water as the message was taken up. To his surprise Marcus found that Argentium was touching bottom. They were almost there. He slid the Sword of Cartimandua and raised it above his head. As soon as all four feet of his mount were on the dry sand he yelled, "Mount!" He looked around and was pleased to see that there were over a hundred of them already on their mounts. Some of the stronger Batavian swimmers were also standing in defensive stance. The tribesmen had fled.

Looking over at a dripping Decius who was shaking water from his helmet and ears he shouted, "There you are, that was fun wasn't it?"

"I don't know who is madder, you or the general."

By the time the men had formed up the general had swum ashore. "By Neptune that was exhilarating. I may never build another bridge again."

"Just out of interest sir where did you get the idea from?"

"Britannia of course!" He saw the quizzical look on the decurion's face. "When we first invaded the general ordered the

Batavians to swim across the Tamesis and outflank the enemy while the legions built a bridge. Batavians are good swimmers. Between you and me, I think they are part fish. Still, it worked. Now the legionaries can swim across and we can tow their arms on small rafts. Simple eh?"

"Yes sir."

"Now then take your men in a long sweep. Find the enemy. We will build a camp here, just in case they attack." He paused, "I don't think they will but remember what happened when the garrison of Rome failed to make a camp and that slave Spartacus slaughtered them. Wouldn't do, would it? Not when things are going so well. I should be able to leave for Aquitania by the end of the week."

When Marcus and his troopers returned to the beach they were dry although their legs and those of their mounts were covered in dried salt. "Can we find some clean water soon sir and wash them off?"

Marcus looked down at Sergeant Cato who was responsible for the horses. It would not bother the man to be covered in salt himself but he would hate the idea of his horses suffering.

"Yes sergeant, as soon as we have made camp take your old turma and scout out a good spot."

All the troops were ashore and the camp in place. The general had his headquarters tent set up and the prefects were all there. "Ah Decurion. Find anything?"

"No sir. The tribesmen we did see were all on the skyline moving away from us. I don't think they were ready for such an… interesting invasion."

Agricola beamed. "No, we seem to have caught them napping. What about the terrain? Any problems?"

"No sir in fact it is flatter than anything we have seen so far, including the north. It is just low rolling land with a few woods but no forests. Nothing my lads couldn't get through."

"Excellent. In that case we will move off tomorrow and head for," he pointed at the map, "this little island where the centre of the Druidic religion appears to be. Caer Gybi. What a name!"

When Marcus told the decurions the only comment came from Decius. "I bet a month's denari we will be swimming again!" This time there were no takers.

Caer Gybi

Fainch looked around the small island at the disconsolate warriors who sat dejectedly in little clumps. She had to admit that the Romans had outwitted her and yet, irritatingly, her Ordovician army still outnumbered them. Unfortunately, their morale was so low that any attack by the Romans would result in disaster. She had to come up with something which would inspire and terrify at the same time, inspire her warriors and terrify the Romans.

She called over King Gwynfor who had both aged and shrunk over the past days. She spoke quietly so that none could hear but the king. "Have you thirty or forty warriors you can trust?"

Bridling at the comment he spluttered, "I can trust all my men!"

"As you trusted Inir?" His silence was eloquent. "Have you a small band of warriors who have the courage to go behind the Roman lines without hope of glory to bring back one prisoner?"

Intrigued the king replied, "Yes but what…?"

"I want your men to capture, alive, one of their officers. They are easily marked out by their helmets. Or even a standard-bearer but it must be someone of importance."

"Why?"

"A cold hard look spread across her face and her eyes narrowed. "Do you question me? It was not I who led half the army to its death disobeying orders it was one of you trusted warriors." She sighed as though having to explain something to a truculent child. "Their officers, all their officers, are leaders. Without their leaders, any leader, they are weaker. The ordinary soldiers believe in the strength of their officers. I want them to bring one such here and we will display him in the wicker effigy so that when the Romans arrive here they will see one of their own leaders helpless and bound and we will burn him before their eyes. It will embolden our warriors and please both the god Taransis and the Mother. It will put fear into the Romans for they fear our priests more than they fear our warriors. When they attack us, they will do it reluctantly and our warriors will destroy them."

The king had to admit that it was a good plan and he could see its merits. "I will send my son Gryffydd. He is clever and he will not let us down."

"Good."

Chapter 4

The crossing of the island of Mona was conducted at a steady pace. The general was confident that he could defeat anything the barbarians threw at him but he was ever mindful of the ambush of the cavalry and so he was more cautious than usual. The loss of a turma was a serious one. Gaelwyn and the other scouts reported that the barbarians were gathered on the most sacred and holy part of Mona, Caer Gybi.

After crossing the Cefni, where the cavalry took the opportunity to wash all the salt from their mounts and themselves, the column headed for the coast and made their last camp before the assault at a small bay about ten miles from the island. Marcus and his decurions took the opportunity to discuss the new tactics employed by Agricola.

"We can fight on foot but what is the point? We are cavalry!"

"No Vettius we are only cavalry when we can operate as cavalry." The decurion looked puzzled. "Here is a problem for you then, for all of you. Tomorrow we arrive at this little rocky island. What do we do?"

"We make sure we aren't ambushed."

"You dozy lump! All the barbarians are on the island."

"Thank you, Decius, but Domitius has a point. That is what we should do but all of the enemy are on the island, a rocky island. Do we let the auxiliaries and legionaries just attack on their own?"

"You can't do that sir."

"I know Agrippa and the only way we can help is by fighting on foot. By wading across the stretch of water while they are hurling missiles at us, climbing up the rocky cliffs and then fighting them on foot." They nodded finally seeing his point. "However, when we can, we will be cavalry again although it looks like this part of the world does not suit us as horsemen which probably pleases Sergeant Cato." They all laughed for the blushing sergeant was known to care more for horses than humans. "When we get the chance ask Macro and Agrippa to help train your turma in foot tactics. It can't hurt."

Leaving the decurions to drink and talk Marcus retired to his tent. He cleaned his armour and then spent half an hour cleaning and sharpening the sword of Cartimandua which he reverently placed in his chest. As usual he went to his small altar and said a prayer for Macha, his dead wife and Ulpius Maximunius, his dead son. Perhaps tomorrow he would have the chance to avenge them and his friend Ulpius Felix; perhaps tomorrow would be his day for this was where the Druid's power was concentrated and it was where Fainch awaited him.

Gryffydd and his men had coated their flesh with mud making them as invisible as it was possible to be. They had watched the gates of the camp close with a dark and sinister finality. The warriors with Gryffydd looked at him. How would they get in and how would they escape? Gryffydd was young but cunning. When asked to carry out this mission he had planned his escape route first; he had a small fishing boat moored less than two hundred paces from the camp. The Romans had no ships nearby and if he could snare his quarry he would be away before they knew that they had kidnapped one of their own. Watching from the rocks he had identified the places where the leaders were. As much as he would have liked to snatch the general himself Gryffydd had seen the sentries posted around his tent and he knew that there would have been no chance of silencing the guards and escaping. He was flexible; the witch had said an officer, any officer. He had seen where the prefects and centurions were gathered and the tent with the cavalry officers. They were all noisily drinking and laughing that meant they could not be taken but their noise would mask and disguise the kidnap. That left the tall cavalry officer who had retired to his tent early.

The palisade was meant as a barrier to those who would attack at night but Gryffydd and his men were not attacking, they were sneaking in and there would be neither roars nor war cries to accompany him while the other ten kept the guards under close observation their arrows notched, their slings at the ready. Gryffydd found the place he was looking for between the two gates where the guards would not tend to look. It also happened to be a dozen paces from the tent of the victim, the Decurion

Princeps. Two men boosted Gryffydd and two others over the palisade and then one man boosted his colleague. The four of them peered around in the unfamiliar dark. That was the weak point in the attack for the Romans knew every uncia of the camp having erected hundreds of them in their time. They froze as a sentry walked by and Gryffydd had to restrain one of his warriors who attempted to raise his knife. Shaking his head, the leader pointed at Marcus' tent. While one kept watch the other three slipped under the back wall of the leather tent. Inside it was pitch black but they could hear the heavy breathing and snuffling of the man who lay in the comfortable sleep of a man who believes himself to be safe. The decurion was soundly asleep. Gryffydd's eyes gave the signal and the two men grabbed Marcus' arms and covered his mouth while Gryffydd swung the club at the side of the Roman's head. Unconsciousness arrived quickly. They bundled him under the tent and then, each man taking a leg or an arm they hurried to the wall. Although they were quiet they could have made as much noise as they wished for the drinking parties amongst the officers were in full swing and masked all other noises. They also distracted the sentries who kept looking at the tent and laughing, speculating about their officer's behaviour. When they arrived at the palisade they checked that the guard's attention was elsewhere and they unceremoniously threw the unconscious decurion over and into the ditch.

A few moments later, with extra arms to help them they had scurried over the small rocky mound, onto the beach and the waiting boat. While Gryffydd and four others began to row back to Porthdafarch, the rest made their way back silently along the beach. There was no alarm, there was no chase. Decurion Princeps Marcus Aurelius Maximunius was captured and would soon be in the clutches of the woman he hated most in the entire world. He would be in the hands of the Druidic priesthood and few Romans had ever survived such an encounter.

When Marcus came to he found that not only did his head hurt as though a wall had fallen on it but his hands and legs were tightly bound and he was incapable of movement. He thought he must be in some sort of hut for he could see wicker branches before him but how he had come to be there he had no idea. He remembered going to sleep and then… nothing. He woke up to this. As his ears became attuned to the ambient sounds he could hear an argument. He could not tell the direction for the sounds were not clear it was as though they were in a different room. The voices appeared muffled but as his head hurt it was difficult to tell.

"Why did you not bring this soldier's weapons? Do you not know that he is one who possesses the Sword of Cartimandua? If we had that sword then all the northern tribes would rise with us. You knew who it was you brought did you not?"

"Yes!" The man's voice was young and threatening. "I was told to bring a prisoner not his weapons. Do you know how difficult it was to capture him alive and with no alarm given? No. And why not? Because you are a woman who just gives orders! You are the witch who commands. You are the witch who stays behind the safety of this isle while others do your bidding. You are Fainch! And unlike others around here I am not afraid of you." The young angry warrior squared up to the diminutive witch who refused to back down.

Although his mind took in that a door of some sort had been slammed it was immaterial. He had heard her name. His enemy, Fainch was here. The one who had murdered the Queen of the Brigante, tried to murder Ulpius Felix and had murdered his sister in law, wife and son. She was here and he was tied like a helpless sacrifice. Suddenly a chill spread through his bones. Sacrifice! A wicker room! He saw now that was what he was in, a wicker coffin. And that meant he was to be burned alive. He had heard Decius talk of it but he had ignored it as a superstitious fantasy. But it was true and that was the cruellest irony, he would burn to death within touching distance of the being in the entire world he most wanted to kill. He vowed to stay alive as long as possible in the hope that he might be revenged and prayed to the Allfather to help him.

It was as the camp came to life before dawn that Marcus' disappearance came to light. Decius and the other senior decurions had gone to wake him when he did not come for his food. This was not the Marcus they knew for he was always the first up, organising and chivvying. At first, they thought he had gone to an early meeting with the general but when the general sent for him they knew that something was amiss.

When Decius entered the tent, he could see the covers on the floor and footprints in the dirt. "Get Gaelwyn. That old dog will sniff what went on here or I'm a Greek bum boy." When Gaelwyn arrived, unusually, he did not make a disparaging comment or give one of his usual sniffs instead he began to feel around the edge of the tent and then under the bed. He quickly leapt to his feet and set off like a greyhound around the outside of the tent. The auxiliaries followed as quickly as they could. When he came to the palisade he amazed them by lithely leaping over the barrier as though it was not there. By the time they had exited the gate and caught up with him he was down by the beach. "Well?"

"Four men came into the camp and captured the decurion. They climbed the wall and met others. Half went in a boat and the rest went along the coast. Probably to the isle." He gestured to Caer Gybi.

Showing more affection than he normally did Decius put his arm around the scout's shoulders. "You have earned your pay today old lad. Tell me is he still alive?"

He looked straight at Decius, "I did not see any blood. He could be." Closing his eyes for a moment he said, "And I do not feel his death. He lives."

Decius went straight to the general as the other decurions roused their turmae. "General!" His guards tried to stop the intrusion but Decius was in no mood to be halted and he pushed aside their spears.

Agricola looked up more bemused than angry at the interruption. "Yes, Decurion?"

"The Ordovice. They have captured Decurion Princeps Maximunius."

Had he slapped the general in the face he could not have a greater impact. For the first time since he had seen him Decius saw a man who was not in command of himself. "Are you sure? Of course, you are. Tell me."

"Looks like four came in last night, hit him and then took him to their island."

"So still alive, "he put his hands together and half closed his eyes. "They want him for something which means he may be kept alive for a little longer. Oh tribune, have all the guards from last night flogged, this should not have happened. Now where was I, ah yes, what do they want him for? The sword. That damned sword. Is the sword still there?"

Confused Decius looked around as though the sword was behind him. "I er, I don't know. I'll find out." Forgetting to salute he raced out.

"I think gentlemen that; until we have a better picture of what they have taken him for we will put off the assault until tomorrow. It isn't as though they are going anywhere and it will give us time to reflect on this disturbing turn of events. Oh, and send for that barbarian they like to keep with them, the scout."

Gaelwyn arrived with Decius and the sword. "At least that answers one question. They didn't get the sword. Decurion, you are to take charge of that thing until we get the Decurion Princeps back. Now," his clerk whispered in his ear, "er Gaelwyn. You probably know these people better than we do. I know you are not of this tribe but you know their ways."

Gaelwyn nodded, "I know the Ordovice. They are rats, for they live in holes."

Smiling the general continued, "Quite. I would like you to find out what has happened to the Decurion Princeps. Can you do that?"

"Yes."

"Good. Decurion have an escort get him as close to that isle as possible without showing yourselves and make sure he gets back, here right?"

"Yes sir."

"Oh, and decurion do not go yourself. I don't want to lose all my senior officers." The disappointment showed like cracks on the bluff trooper's face. "You will have your revenge but this is a task for a younger man."

"Sir!" Once he left the tent he said, more to himself than anyone else, "All this because I got out of breath climbing that bloody hill." He turned to Gaelwyn. "Right then. What is the plan?"

"We will go along the beach as they did. When we get to the isle I will swim around to the far side where there is a cliff. I will climb and be able to see into their camp. I will return to your men." He looked at Decius. "I do not need to be guarded."

Decius' voice softened. "I understand and I know what you think of the Decurion Princeps but look at it this way. If you have four or five men with you then it might be possible to rescue him. Difficult on your own eh?"

For the first time he could remember, Decius saw the scout smile. "You are not as addled in the head as you make out are you decurion?"

"Gerroff with you!"

The choice of two of the rescue party was obvious, Macro and Gaius it was the other two who were not as easy to find for they had to be tough, quick and fearless. It was Macro who gave them the answer. "Those two troopers who Modius and Flavius sent back to us. Cilo and Galeo, they are as good a pair of fighters as I have trained and they would give their lives for the decurion. Oh, and one more thing."

"Yes?"

"They are Atrebate, from the south. They might know about the customs of the tribe. We need all the help we can get."

That settled the question. "Right. No horses, they will make too much noise. Take your slingshot and just swords, don't bother with shields." He looked over his shoulder. "And there will be a turma within a mile of the isle. I want your ugly faces back. May the Allfather protect you."

Caer Gybi

There was a sudden movement and Marcus found himself lying on his back although still contained within the wicker structure. He was roughly bounced around and then flickering daylight began to flood in through the gaps in the wicker and he involuntarily tried to shield his eyes with his tethered arms; the pain was excruciating. After a few moments, he found himself upright. Again, there was some movement and a piece of the wicker from directly in front of his face was removed. He found himself seemingly hovering above the sea like a gull, for it stretched before him blue and grey in the early light. He turned his head to the left and saw, with some relief, the land that, he assumed was Mona. He still wasn't certain whether he had died or not but the pain in his head and his arms seemed to suggest that he was still in Britannia.

"Roman!" He looked around for the owner of the voice. When he looked down, an action which increased the pain in his head he saw that his wicker coffin, for so he thought it was, was on a wooden platform at the edge of the cliff and there before him was his nemesis, his enemy, Fainch the witch. He did not know what he had expected but he was disturbed to find that he was oddly attracted to her and, despite the pain he was in, felt his loins stirring. She was older than he had expected and there were flecks of grey dotted in her hair but, as she stared at him, had had to admit that she had a power. Her violet eyes, or were they blue, seemed to exude a power that bored into his brain. "Do you know where you are Roman?"

He tried to speak but he was dry and he had to cough. The witch stared at him, a grim grin like a savage slit in her face, enjoying his discomfort and pain. "I assume this is a sacrifice to the god Tanasis and I am to be burned alive."

She seemed surprised and annoyed for she had hoped to shock and frighten this Roman who had thwarted so many of her plans. "You know our ways Roman but I forget you had a bitch whelp you a pup did you not?"

If she was hoping to anger him she failed for his anger was a cold vengeful anger which was stored up inside him, powerful and patient. Ignoring her comment, he continued, "If you hope to hear me beg for my life you will be disappointed for in my death I will join my wife and child. You will be making me happy. And when I am dead my men will come and kill you. You will be crucified."

Her face showed more than a hint of irritation but she had expected nothing less of this man. That was a good thing for her warriors would see it as an even more powerful sacrifice, a warrior who was fearless. "How you die is immaterial but I shall enjoy the anguish it causes your men when they arrive to see you burn!" Suddenly she was gone.

That was their idea. They were trying to demoralise his men and the rest of the Romans. Marcus smiled grimly. They would be thwarted for his troopers would fight even harder to revenge themselves on those who had killed him. He idly wondered as he closed his eyes for a moment, what would happen to his sword. He was glad that they had not taken it and he wondered which of his men would claim the honour of wielding it. Perhaps Macro as the ala champion would want it but Marcus knew who he wanted to be the new owner, Gaius. Gaius had become the son who had died. He had replaced the young Ulpius and become Marcus' hope for the future. He still regretted having to watch the innocent Gaius being flogged on the whim of an arrogant young patrician and he had sworn then to make it up to the fine young decurion that Gaius had grown into. Yes, Gaius would do the sword justice and give it honour.

Even as Marcus contemplated death and his reunion with Macha and Ulpius his men were already moving noiselessly along the shoreline. They were not moving swiftly for there were many rocks and inlets but those obstacles ensured that they arrived unseen behind a rock outcrop. Gaelwyn was in command, regardless of Gaius' rank, and he signed for them to wait as he slipped into the water and, like an eel, disappeared beneath the waves.

"He scares me he does. Look at that you can't see him. How does he do that?"

"The same way, Macro that you are able to hurl a slingshot so accurately and I am not. It is one of Gaelwyn's skills; be glad for today they may save Marcus' life." Gaius had been particularly troubled by the kidnap for he blamed himself. He had the tent next to Marcus and, had he not been drinking and carousing he might have heard the kidnappers and prevented this tragedy. He vowed he would never allow drink to interfere with his duties again.

It seemed an age that Gaelwyn was away but Gaius could tell from the sun's movement in the sky that it was a short time. When he returned dripping and breathing heavily he led them away from their rocky outcrop to a place where they could talk. Gaius could tell from the expression on the scout's face that his news was not good and he braced himself for the worst.

"He is on the cliff across the water," he paused, "in a wicker cage. He is to be burned alive."

Macro had not been expecting that, in reality this was beyond Macro's comprehension but the thought of Marcus being burned alive evoked a gasp of shock. "The bastards let's…"

Gaius grabbed his young friend's arm. "Let us hear what our friend has to say." Turning to Gaelwyn he said, "What can we do? Can he be rescued?" None of the party was privy to the plans of Fainch and they had no idea that she would wait until the whole army appeared before igniting the unfortunate prisoner, as far as they were concerned speed was of the essence and delay would mean death for the decurion.

"We could approach under the water, climb the cliffs, for they are not steep, and release him."

"Right, let's go then."

Gaelwyn restrained Macro this time with a paternal smile on his grizzled old face. "Be patient. We will have to wait until dark."

Gaius asked the question which was on everyone's minds. "When do they normally burn these… things?"

After a pause Gaelwyn said, ominously, "After dark."

The looks on each of the faces of the four troopers was the same, dismay, despondency and dejection. They were ready to rescue but they might be too late. "There's nought we can do until dusk. Let us rest." Gaius looked at them all. "We will rescue Marcus, or die trying."

Back at the camp, Agricola had finished his briefing with Decius and the prefects. "We will arrive before dawn. I want every man in position before the first hint of the sun appears." Decius knew that every man in the camp would go without sleep all night if necessary for the barbarians had violated their camp. Even the sentries who had been flogged felt the same. They wanted to avenge their shame. "Our scout has not reported back yet. That means that either they are dead or they are trying to affect a rescue," he looked pointedly at Decius, "against orders. Perhaps they are using that turma of cavalry which left for a patrol this morning. However, we cannot let that change our decision. The Decurion Princeps will either survive or he will not, it is no longer in our hands. However, the fate of the island and Wales is. We will ensure that every person on that island is destroyed and obliterated from history. When we have finished with this pestilential hole then we will return to the heartland of these Ordovices and kill every single man woman and child. Every animal will be killed and every dwelling burned. Nothing of the Ordovice will remain. The people of these lands will find out what happens when you kidnap and kill Roman soldiers. They will pay with their land and their lives."

Fainch was becoming increasingly concerned when the Roman army did not appear. She had expected a swift reaction as there had been when Inir had destroyed their cavalry. She had counted on a swift response to this challenge. She had thought they would come charging across the island and attack. That was why the wicker effigy had been placed on the eastern side of the island ready to be burned. The only positive side to their delay was that the Roman prisoner was in agony with bound arms and legs and a day and a half without water. By the time the Roman army came and they burned him he would be begging for death. There was satisfaction in that.

Chapter 5

Gaelwyn gathered the auxiliaries around him in a small circle. "We could walk through the water, for it is shallow, but I do not wish us to be seen by scouts and sentries. We will slide through the water as fish, making no sound. The sound of the surf should hide any sounds you might make. Once on the other side we will need to move as animals on all fours. There is some soil at the foot of the cliffs; when we get there rub it on your faces and arms to darken your skin. The moon will soon rise and white skin will stand out." He had already told them to discard their armour leaving them only with a sword, knife and, in Macro's case, a slingshot. "I will go around the back and release the ropes which hold the decurion in place. You and you," he pointed at Gaius and Macro will make sure no-one is near, kill any sentries silently. You two, "he pointed at Salvius and Numerius," will help me to carry him down to the water."

"Good plan. Remember we have one chance and once only. Macro and I will wait at the top of the cliff until we see you in the water. Our lives are not important but we must rescue the Decurion Princeps." Macro nodded his agreement but in his head, he knew that they could kill any warrior who even came close.

The water seemed icy as they slipped into it although it was relatively warm. The five men spread out like an arrowhead with Gaelwyn as the point. Keeping their heads beneath the waves they occasionally lifted their mouths out for air, when they did so they glanced up at the cliffs where they could see the sentries peering across the water to the island of Mona. They were not looking down. For the first time Gaius thought that their plan might have a chance.

Gaelwyn's raised hand halted them as they lay in the shallows barely breathing. On his signal, they scampered to the gorse lined patch beyond the beach. Above them they could see the platform built over the cliff and Gaius realised that it hid them from prying eyes. Of course, once they left its security then they would be vulnerable but it gave them an edge. They each grabbed handfuls of soil and spread them over the bare, wet patches of flesh which helped spread the mud like paint. Soon they were darkened shadows, wraiths. Gaelwyn gestured for them to do the same to their blades to prevent them gleaming in the light which was just beginning to glint from a rising moon.

Taking a breath, they all stepped out from the gorse bush and began to ascend the slope. They took their time, securing foot and handholds before moving on. Gaelwyn caught Macro's attention and signalled the sentries talking to their right. There were none to the left. Macro nodded and, taking Gaius' arm led him in that direction. As Gaelwyn and the other two slipped around the back of the wicker cage Macro and Gaius edged slowly towards the two sentries. As long as they stayed together the would-be rescuers had a problem. They needed them apart for then Macro could take one with a slingshot whilst Gaius could slit the other's throat. After what seemed an age one of them lowered his breeks, telling the two Romans he was about to urinate. His companion wandered a few yards away more to avoid being splashed than any thoughts of discretion. They both had their backs to the troopers and rather than risk a falling body they both rushed and each grabbed a sentry, their hands clasped over their victim's mouth. The other handheld a razor-sharp knife which sliced effortlessly through the throats of the doomed sentries. As their warm, dark lifeblood oozed from their bodies the Romans laid them gently on the ground. They dared not roll them down the bank in case there was a splash. Immediately on guard they scanned the encampment. The tribesmen seemed remarkably close but the Romans were hidden, as they squatted by a row of thick gorse which disguised them.

Gaelwyn saw the sentries fall and he rose up to sever the rope which held the wicker effigy together. Within moments he had cut a hole big enough to get the decurion out. The two troopers joined him and they all cut through the bonds. Gaelwyn held his hand over Marcus' mouth as he felt the soldier stir, "Friends," he whispered and Marcus gave a faint nod. Gaelwyn supported the man's body as the two troopers made short work of the bonds. The weight of the body suddenly increased as the support was removed and the extra weight almost made Gaelwyn drop him and it was only the lightning reactions of Salvius that prevented a disaster for Marcus, who had taken neither water nor food for a day and a half had no strength of his own. The three men manhandled the unresponsive body towards the slope down the side furthest away from the dead sentries. Gaelwyn kept his eyes on Macro and Gaius; when he saw that they had seen him the three men moved more quickly. Gaius and Macro moved swiftly down the slope listening for any alarm. At the water's edge, they turned Marcus on his back and Gaius was delighted when he saw his mentor open his eyes and smile. Macro squatted in the shallows, slingshot at the ready while the other four half dragged, half towed the decurion back to safety. When they were halfway across the narrow straits Macro started across slithering backwards through the salty surf. He was halfway across when he heard the shout of alarm as the bodies were found at the base of the tower. The man who found them made the mistake of running to the edge of the platform to attempt to see where the killers were where he was silhouetted and Macro's slingshot ended his life. Although it only delayed the pursuit any delay might give them time to escape and time was not on their side.

Macro emerged from the water to see his four companions pulling Marcus along the rocky covered beach. He ran up to them, grabbed the decurion and unceremoniously slung him across his shoulders like a sack of grain. "We are in the shit now lads so let's run! They know where we are." They ran along the beach for there was a gentle path about six hundred paces down, it would be easier to ascend and it would prevent them being lit on the skyline. They could hear the noise of their pursuers as they splashed through the water.

"I hope Decius sent that turma!" gasped Gaius.

"We had better shout so they know where we are!" Numerius began to roar, "Romans! Romans ho!"

They had just reached the top of the slope when the first of the Ordovice caught them. Leaving Gaelwyn and Macro to race on the three troopers turned at the top of the slope and faced their enemies. The first four who climbed the slope had not even looked up for they were struggling up the sandy, rock, littered bank and the three blades chopped them down before they even knew the Romans had turned to face them. The ones below saw them and began hurling spears. Unarmoured the three troopers were vulnerable and when Numerius was hit in the shoulder

Gaius shouted, "Run!" As Salvius supported his friend Gaius sliced his sword down on one attacker's shoulder and, throwing his knife at a second took off after his companions. Glancing over his shoulder Gaius could see a horde of enemies; he was just contemplating turning to delay the inevitable by a few minutes and perhaps give his companions the chance to reach safety when he heard the sound of the buccina and the thunder of hooves. Even as he turned he heard Agrippa's voice yell, "Down!" and he dropped just as the volley of javelins thudded into his pursuers who were barely paces from the lone Roman. He felt the horses jump over him and he raised himself to follow his companions. He found them already mounted on the spare horses brought by Agrippa. He was no sooner mounted than Agrippa returned, "Much as I would like to finish off these barbarians I think we need to get these two to the surgeon."

"Thank you, Agrippa."

"Let us just call it a favour for Drusus." Nodding Gaius thought back to the moment they discovered the slain and butchered bodies of Drusus and his men, Agrippa had been the only survivor. Marcus was right they were a band of brothers.

As Marcus was brought into the camp Agricola could not believe the cheers and roars from the troops, legionaries, infantry and cavalry alike. He looked at the Decurion Princeps weakly waving his arm at his fellow warriors and thought that this was the acclaim given to a gladiator or a general. Shaking his head, he thought he could only dream of such feelings from fellow warriors. He had known that the camp was angry at the kidnap but he thought it was their professionalism that their walls had been breached; now he saw that it was more it had been anger that someone they respected, possibly loved had been stolen from them. He made an instant decision. He walked over to the drooping man barely sitting in the saddle and grasped his arm. As he did a silence fell upon the whole conclave. Agricola looked around then said, "Welcome back to your men Prefect Maximunius." It took a few moments for the words to sink in but when they did Agricola realised he had made the correct decision. The whole camp raised their cheers and roars to a new level. "Rest and your men will exercise their revenge on these savages and then we will talk." He turned to the camp,

"Tomorrow we wipe this pestilence from the land!" He was gratified that the cheer was as loud for him as for Marcus. He had made the correct decision. When the island was taken he could leave for Gallia Aquitania.

The next day the whole force arrayed in battle order on the shoreline facing the holy and sacred isle. Every man was eager for combat. They knew they were outnumbered. They knew they would have to wade across the sea. They knew they would have to attack uphill but most importantly they knew they would win. The rescue of Marcus, the attack on the Ordovices near Wyddfa had all convinced them they would win. As they stared across the tiny gap from the isle their enemies gathered to repel them and they saw fear on the faces of their foes. The rescue of the decurion and the destruction of the wicker man had made them doubt that they could win. The grim faces of the Romans and the memory of Inir's slaughter told them that they would lose.

On the isle Fainch and Gwynfor were doing their best to talk up their chances of winning but even Gryffydd was beginning to doubt that they could win. Had the gods deserted them? What had they done to upset the gods who had long protected this sacred land? "We can throw these dogs into the water! Look my warriors they are only a few in number! My bodyguard alone could destroy term!"

As Gwynfor extolled their chances his men began to doubt him even more. True they were only auxiliaries but it had been auxiliaries who had beaten them near Wyddfa and had affected the dramatic rescue. Gwynfor lied. They looked to the witch for magic. Fainch for the first time looked despondent; she looked as though for the first time in her life she contemplated defeat. Could the Roman army be stronger than her magic? She had tried everything she knew, every spell, every chant, every potion, and every prayer. Had the Mother forgotten her? She tried one last invocation. "Caer Gybi send your powers to throw back these invaders, these unbelievers destroy them and let your servant Gwynfor triumph again!"

It was a desperate throw but it was enough to steel men's hearts and they stood their ground as the two thousand warriors of Rome rolled over the water, rolled up the hill and rolled over the Ordovices who died where they stood, slaughtered as they faced an enemy who was intent on their destruction and they had no avenue of retreat available. Some took the only option they had; they hurled themselves into the sea; the water at least held a chance of life. The land was a butcher's shop. It took half a morning but finally the warriors of the Ordovice, Gwynfor, and Gryffydd, all died on the spare, sparse and sacred isle of Caer Gybi.

In the aftermath of the slaughter, as the Romans scoured the battlefield despatching any wounded foes, the decurions all searched for one thing, the body of the witch. The Batavians and legionaries busily salvaged weapons, coins and jewellery but, unless it was a woman then Marcus' closest friends moved on. By the time they had combed the entire isle they had not found any women.

"Well she can't just have disappeared."

"She is a witch Decius."

"Lentius she is a woman, she might be an evil bitch but she is still a woman. She is either hiding or she has escaped."

Just then they heard the recall and they headed despondently back to camp. They all looked at Decius for they knew he would have to be the one to give the bad news to Marcus. The new prefect was still under the care of the surgeon for he had been in a much-weakened state when he had been rescued. He had, however, made it clear to his decurions that the witch should be found and they scoured the isle searching every nook and cranny to no avail. It was as though she had disappeared into the bowels of the earth. Many of the troopers were especially grateful that they did not find her for they feared her more than any barbarian warrior. They feared her power and her magic.

The witch herself was hiding with the other five survivors of the massacre whilst some of her sisters had chosen a watery death from the steep cliffs to the north west of the island; Fainch had led the others by way of a twisting and precipitous path to a cave. It was their last refuge and had been the hiding place for the Druids when the Romans first took the isle almost forty years earlier. "We will be safe for a while sisters and, when the Romans leave we will go back to the mainland and continue our work." She could see downcast faces for the survivors were all younger than she. “This is a setback. We have obviously offended the Mother and we need to sacrifice to her. Had the Roman been sacrificed then we would have won and I blame myself for that. I should have sacrificed him sooner rather than waiting for the Romans to arrive. Be patient for we will triumph.”

“Where will we go?”

“I will go north for there are still rebels in the land of the lakes.” As she named each tribe she pointed at each of the priestesses in turn. “You should go to the Silures. You to the Dumnoni. You the Belgae. You the Dobunii and you the Dematae.” All of the tribes she had named were to the west and were still fighting the Romans; they were her best, although faint, hope of fermenting unrest to loosen the ever-tightening grip of the Roman hydra. She knew that the Canti, Regni, Iceni and Atrebates had all surrendered and would pose no threat. Even her journey, dangerous though it was, would probably end in failure for the Brigante were not strong enough to defeat the Romans. She would have to travel further north. She had met some of the leaders of the Caledonii and Pictii. They were still powerful enough to thwart the Romans and their land was like that around Wyddfa, it did not suit the Romans. She had noted how few legionaries this general had brought with him. The legions were difficult to defeat but these others, they were like the tribes themselves, one step away from being barbarians. They could be defeated. “Come sisters let us offer to the Mother and pray that she protects us as we work to rid the land of these Romans.”

The day after the isle had been cleared the general summoned his prefects. “We have completed the first part of the subjugation of this land. I will not be able to continue this part of the journey with you as I have to take up my post as Governor of Gallia Aquitania. I have sent my reports and recommendations to Governor Cerialis and, until you hear from him then you will continue to follow these orders. Prefect Bassus and Sura you are to eradicate the Ordovices. That is your priority. From what we have seen they will not offer much opposition however as their homeland is on the far side of that mountain it may be difficult to find their rat holes."

He gestured through the leather tent wall to the distant peak of Wyddfa. "You will leave one cohort here Prefect Bassus to build a fort and make sure that the Druids never return. The legionary cohort will return to Deva. Prefect Sura you will leave a cohort at the new fort of Canovium to enable the legionaries there to return to Deva. Prefect Maximunius your cavalry has performed wonders, not least in their rescue of you. It seems that we should rename the Pannonians the Rescuers eh? First a Queen, then Batavians and now their Prefect. However, they are ill suited to the terrain and I am mindful that it is difficult to replace horses. You will return with me to Deva, "he smiled, "a fitting escort. While we were travelling south I noticed that the land north of Deva was perfect cavalry country and close enough to the land of the lakes. I would like you to return to Glanibanta and rebuild the fort as a permanent fort. Find those Brigante rebels who fled there and destroy them." He sat back in his chair and put his hands together in a thoughtful way and half closed his eyes. "I can see a time when we will have to move north and complete the subjugation of Britannia. I have already written to the Emperor with my ideas on how this could be completed. If you three can complete the tasks I have set then when the time comes we can use our bases here to launch an invasion of Caledonia." The general was gratified to note that they not only nodded their agreement but from the grins across their faces they wholeheartedly endorsed the venture. "Right I am sure we all have things to do but one last thing. Thank you." As they nodded their gratitude and began to leave Agricola grabbed Marcus' arm. "And you prefect, are you ready to ride?"

"Yes sir. I am recovered."

"It is a shame the witch escaped, "he paused, "or drowned. Perhaps you ought to forget her now eh?"

"I can never forget her and she did not drown. I know not how I know I just feel it; she lives, for the moment; but do not worry sir my quest for revenge will not interfere with my duties."

"I know prefect which is why you are now a prefect. Good. You know the thing I should have done was build a bridge to this damned island. We will either have to build rafts or risk a swim."

Marcus laughed, "I think my lads are getting quite used to swimming."

"Swimming it is then."

Part Two
The Land of the Lakes

Chapter 6

North West of Eboracum

The war was long over and there were no Brigante warbands roving the country. The merchants had new markets as the Roman influence spread from the pottery in Petuaria, Isurium Brigantium and Derventio to the iron mines at Danum and lime workings at Morbium. There were the new forts springing up to defend the hard-won province. The same merchants were aping the Romans they had met. They were building villas and baths bought with the new-found wealth as Britannia emerged from the Iron Age into the Roman age.

The very prosperity brought with it the attendant dangers of prosperity, bandits, thieves and robbers. They were, in essence the same warbands which had fought the Romans but as the finest and noblest of these had died the ones who remained were, by their very nature, those who had survived and not fought to the end. They were the ones with the skills in warfare but not the aptitude. They were the ones who did not want to go back to their farms to eke out a living but they wanted to prey on those who did work hard and tried to better themselves. While the south of the province still had some order with many natives embracing Roman values and mores, a good road system and tax collections the north of the province had fewer influences, fewer roads and more opportunity for banditry.

Aed still called himself a rebel; he still felt himself to be a legitimate heir to Brigantia but in reality, he was a bandit, a powerful one, but a bandit nonetheless. His lieutenant, the former auxiliary Modius ruled the circle that was the land of the lakes with an iron fist. The mountains which surrounded the fine farmland meant that it was easy to defend against anything other than a legion or an ala. There was neither. The nearest force was a cohort of infantry at Brocavum and another at Morbium. The legionary fortress at Eboracum might as well have been in Rome for all the influence it could exert. Aed had quickly discovered that he could raid with impunity during the summer and spring months when the merchants were talking advantage of the fine weather to move their goods to the new markets. Lime, iron, pottery and tiles were in demand in the south and would fetch a higher price as there was so much building going on. It was worth the risk and the roads from north to south made easy pickings for Aed who used a small force of mounted men under Modius to rob and kill the merchants bringing the contraband to a safe place. Aed could then transport the goods under heavy guard, to the very markets that had been their destination. He was becoming quite rich and quite powerful as other disenchanted bandits flocked to his banner. If a vexillation appeared from Eboracum he could quickly retire to his stronghold knowing that they did not have the resources to follow him. The legionaries would then go back to building the roads which in time would bring both security and order but as the spring grew into summer Aed's empire was still growing.

Prefect Maximunius and his ala had spent the end of the winter at the newly built fort of Mamucium. There they had replaced broken equipment, trained new horses, practised the new skills needed for fighting on foot and reorganised the ala. Macro had taken over Marcus' turma as a reward for his increasing maturity and his bravery during the rescue. He still kept his role as weapons trainer. As Decius had said, "He'll burst into tears if you take it off him. He's still the volunteer." Decius himself had been made Decurion Princeps. A role he seemed to have been born into; he was a different Decurion Princeps to Marcus but as Marcus himself commented, that was no bad thing.

As the spring grew into summer they began to get increasing reports of banditry and brigandage. The Governor broke off from an inspection of Mona and the west to brief Marcus on his new role.

"Well prefect you have done well for yourself. Governor Agricola praises you and your men highly and you have earned your promotion." He lowered his voice and spoke conspiratorially, "Tell me prefect did he order you all to swim across the sea?"

"Yes sir, although it wasn't wide four or five hundred paces only."

"Four or five hundred paces! Gods man, I wouldn't swim ten yards in armour. Well, well so it is true. If you can do that then I suppose nothing is beyond you. I am more confident now that you can cope with the task I am going to give you. It seems there is a large band of bandits operating from the area west of Glanibanta, where you built the fort. They are preventing trade. Complete your mission from the general and rebuild the fort but then I want this band destroyed. Utterly! Do I make myself clear? I want no survivors. They have to realise that if they disrupt the life of the province they will pay with their lives." Once more he leaned in, "Next year we will be moving north to repay those warriors from Caledonia who sided with the Brigante. We need this part of the province secure. Anything I can do for you?"

"More men and horses sir? Those Atrebates you sent last year worked out well. We don't need to have replacements from the homeland, those from Britannia appear as committed."

"I'll see to it. Good luck prefect."

With that the busy Governor left a bemused Marcus. It seemed that life came in full circle and always came back to the same people. Cresens, Fainch and now Aed, for he was in no doubt that it was Aed who was running the bandits. He and Julius Agricola had discussed what happened to the survivors of the battle of the Taus. There had been too many of them to forget and Marcus had begged his general for the chance to destroy the man who killed his wife. Agricola had been adamant, Mona came first. Upon reflection Marcus realised that the general had done his best to aid him in his quest by sending him back to Glanibanta.

As Marcus waited for his decurions and senior sergeants to arrive he began to appreciate the pleasures a brick building and hypocaust could bring. He would have to forego these pleasures when he rebuilt the primitive fort up by the edge of the icy cold lake. Decius would undoubtedly roll his eyes and utter some unintelligible curse. Marcus made a mental bet with himself. When they arrived and saluted Marcus felt a real pride. He believed himself to be unique; all of his decurions were the best he could hope for. He had sergeants and chosen men just waiting to be promoted. The number of rogue troopers, normally quite a high proportion, was almost negligible. Indeed, most of them had either died with their decurion Flavius Demetrius or deserted following their decurion Modius.

"You have all become far too comfortable. We are going for a little ride." The younger decurions looked delighted, being bored with fortress life. The older ones and especially Decius looked wary. "We are going north."

"Morbium sir!" Decius glared at Macro who sheepishly sat down.

"No Decurion Macro oh and congratulations on your promotion. I am pleased that it has not changed your impulsive nature," the blushing decurion had to endure hoots and laughs from his peers. "No we are going back to the land of the lakes." All laughs, smiles and snickers stopped in an instant for they all knew they were returning to face the Brigante again. If he had demanded close attention Marcus could not have achieved it more effectively. "We are going back to Glanibanta."

"Shit! That means building a frigging fort again!"

Even Marcus joined in the laughter. "Eloquently put Decius. The Senate missed a fine speaker when you chose the auxilia over politics." Marcus waited until the laughter had died down before he continued. "We will have to rebuild the fort first and then our task is to destroy the warband which is rampaging through the north." He paused to allow the words to sink in. "Yes, we will destroy them. As with the Ordovices there will be no prisoners taken. Rebels now will pay the full price of their crimes." He was pleased that they all nodded in agreement. "Sergeant Cato please let me know of any deficiencies in mounts. Quartermaster Verres we will need to get as many supplies as possible. We may not be re-supplied for some time." Again, he paused for effect and he said with great emphasis on every word, "Scour the fortress for anything you think we might need. Understood?"

The huge man grinned, tapped the side of his nose and said, "Understood, sir."

"Well if there is nothing else we leave in the morning." There were gasps as the gathering realised the short time scale. The room emptied much quicker than it had filled.

The first part of their journey was over the familiar territory they had traversed heading south with Agricola the last year. They were even able to use one of the camps they had made which made that day, at least slightly easier. They were encumbered this time by pack mules and a couple of wagons for Porcius Verres had outdone himself with his scavenging. Decius had been delighted to see many amphorae of wine disappearing into the wagons and from the look of the one carrying their armour it suggested that the quartermaster had taken Marcus at his word and obtained spares of everything. As it was spring the weather was unpredictable but for the first few days they were lucky to find either sunny or cloudy skies beneath which they could plod their way north.

They reached the first major river since leaving Mamucium and they were in unfamiliar territory for the first time. The prefect ordered the camp built south of the river close to the point they had turned south the previous year. North east they knew for the next thirty or so miles, according to the basic map Marcus was reading, and after that they would be in unfamiliar land. The furthest they had patrolled, all those years ago, was the southern edge of the lake upon which Glanibanta stood. Once they reached that point Marcus would be content for then he would know the land. The next thirty miles were potentially the most dangerous for he knew nothing of the land or the brigands who waited there.

As the camp was being set up he sent for Gaelwyn and Decius. Gaelwyn had not mentioned the rescue of Marcus despite the profuse thanks offered by Marcus and the offer of any reward. It was not in the Brigante warrior's nature to expect reward. He had rescued Marcus because he liked him, he owed him loyalty and in a barbarian way he was his chief. When he married into the Brigante royal family then Gaelwyn owed him more than loyalty he owed him fealty. When a Brigante, a true Brigante, gave you his oath it was for life and death. "Do you know the land north of here Gaelwyn?"

He nodded and looked at the map not understanding its writing. Instead he pointed due north, "There are hills with forests and woods." He pointed north west, "There it is flat with woods, some farms." He then pointed further west, "There lies the sea with dangerous beaches which eat both men and horses."

Decius looked at the Brigante sceptically, "Eats them?"

Marcus shook his head, "Ever hear of sinking sands and quick sands. They would eat us quickly enough." Gaelwyn gave a quick sly knowing look in Decius' direction as the Decurion Princeps coloured brightly. "Well we have wagons which rules out the sands and the hills so it looks as though we will be taking the middle road. Decius, I want a turma with Gaelwyn five miles ahead of us as we travel. Change the turma at noon I want them all to get the lie of the land as we travel. Keep another turma one mile behind the column. We could be in ambush country and although I think our rebellious friends will be further east I am taking no chances. When you have detailed tomorrow's, duties send Sergeant Cato to me."

The prefect was studying the map when the sergeant came in to his tent. "You sent for me sir?"

"Yes, sit down." As he sat down Marcus leaned back in his seat. Riding was a little more uncomfortable now that he had reached more than forty summers. He remembered how Ulpius had complained of the horse's back, now he understood why. "What is the state of the herd?"

"We only have ten remounts and a couple of the horses are coming to the end of their useful life. If we had to campaign we would struggle." He paused thoughtfully. "If we are just patrolling then we might manage until autumn." Cato knew the prefect well enough not to ask irrelevant questions. He would get to the point in his own time.

The sergeant had recognised both a problem and a solution at the same time. If they were patrolling they would only need eighty mounts at any one time, injured horses could be rested, older horses kept out of action. A campaign meant attrition, injuries and losses. "Very astute of you sergeant. At first, we will be patrolling but within a couple of weeks we will need to mount a serious campaign. When we get to Glanibanta I want you to take your," he searched for the word because it was an unofficial unit, "horsemen and travel to Derventio and the stud. There should be remounts there and if not, you could buy them. You know the farmers." Marcus and Decius had always kept back part of any loot discovered by or freed by the turmae. It was used to buy horses, extra rations and occasionally, if a trooper was wounded and could not continue, provide a sort of unofficial stipend. It was one of the reasons that the ala pooled their loot, everyone benefited. Cato would have plenty of money to buy horses.

Cato nodded. They had been around the farms in the horse country around Derventio and made many contacts. They had set up a stud and, whilst there would not have been enough time to produce numbers of horses, there would be a number of new mounts they could bring. "Ask our farmer friends if they could supply us with horses until the stud begins to produce numbers. We will need many horses in the next two years. Do you understand?"

Cato was an old soldier and recognised what Marcus was saying without using words. They would be heavily campaigning. "I'll do that sir and money?"

"I will supply you with enough denari but ask the farmers if there is something they would like to barter rather than using money." Cato looked at him curiously. "If we catch these brigands there may be things we capture which are more valuable to farmers than money."

"Right sir."

Pontius Brutus had been a centurion in the Ninth; upon his discharge, he had been granted some land. He had found farming not to his liking and he had decided to become a merchant. His contacts at Eboracum enabled him to get some slaves at a ridiculous price and he soon found a lucrative trade route transporting limestone and lime from Morbium down to the forts being built at Eboracum Deva, and Mamucium. He had finished his contract with Eboracum and now had the longer journey to the south west of Brigante land. This suited the ex-centurion for he could charge a higher price and it gave him the opportunity to buy items not available in Eboracum. He found he had a penchant for trade. His slaves did most of the work and the guards he hired were both loyal and tough. The grey haired florid

Roman had a good life and he intended to build a huge villa with the proceeds of his latest investment.

The Brigante bandits watched as the slow column made its way down the slope towards the river. They counted only ten guards which could easily be taken by their fifty warriors. It was Calgus' first raid as a leader and he was keen for success. Aed might reward him if he was successful. The way the wagons moved suggested they were packed with trade goods. It would be a rich haul. He also noted the weapons and helmets worn by the guards, they too would be a bonus. His only concern was the merchant who led the column. From his bearing, he looked to be an ex-soldier and Calgus, veteran of battles against Romans, was always wary of Roman soldiers, retired or not. He waited until they halted at the ford to allow their animals to drink. His men watched for his signal. As soon as the drivers began to walk upstream to drink he gave it.

The warriors ran swiftly and silently down the slope; the first the guards knew was when one of their number fell screaming from his horse with a spear impaling him. They quickly turned to face the threat and Pontius roared his defiance. Drawing his gladius, he charged his horse at the line approaching him. His mount trampled the first two and then he hacked down with his sword. His victim had no helm and the blade split his head. Calgus could see that his men were wavering and he hurled his spear at the horse, and although it was not a lethal strike it caused the horse to drop its front legs just as Pontius was leaning forward to strike at a second bandit. He tumbled from the horse and as he lay winded, on his back the last thing he saw was the tattooed Brigante warrior bringing the axe down on to his head. The remaining three guards saw their paymaster die and they galloped south to safety. The wagon drivers just ran for their lives. Calgus stopped his men from pursuing. He had already lost four men; he did not want to risk more. "Check the wagons; let us see what treasure we have found." As his warriors clambered aboard the wagons Calgus quickly relieved the dead Roman of his gold, armour and sword.

As he strode towards the wagons he was feeling very pleased with himself until one of his men shouted, "Stone! Wagon loads of stone."

Another one commented, "Why would anyone want stone?"
The disappointment was immense. They had only six horses and ten mules to show for their endeavours and losses. They could not even use the wagons for they would have had to empty the stone which in their mind was useless. Aed would not be happy when they returned empty handed.

Gaelwyn saw the fleeing riders as they crested the rise. He turned to Metellus, "Riders and they are riding as though pursued."
Metellus could now see them. If they were Brigante they would turn and go in the opposite direction in which case he would pursue. He was about to order his men into extended line when he saw them turn and come towards him. When they arrived, he could see they were not native warriors although they were armed.
"Who are you?"
"We are the guards of Pontius Brutus the merchant. We were attacked by Brigante and they have killed our master."
Metellus had had his orders made quite clear. Their job was to protect the merchants. "Gaelwyn ride back to the column and report to the prefect. You men take me back to where you were attacked." The guards looked at each other fearfully; they had just escaped the danger why should they go back? Metellus could see the indecision. "Just show us from a distance then you can piss off wherever you like." Reluctantly they led him over the slope. In the distance Metellus could see movement. "Is that them?"
"Yes sir."
"Right wait here and point the way for the rest of the column." To his turma he shouted, "Draw your swords!"
Galloping down the hill they caught the bandits completely unaware. They were busy extracting the mules from their traces and, being mules, the animals were not cooperating. Just as Calgus had found his prey helpless and vulnerable now he became the prey. The forty Romans quickly killed most of the bandits and Metellus barely had time to halt the slaughter before his men killed them all. "That's enough we need prisoners."

By the time the prefect arrived with two turmae Metellus had bound the prisoners and tended to the wounded guards who had remained close to their charge. Metellus noted, with some surprise that the three guards who had been reluctant to return to the ambush were with the prefect.

"Well done decurion. Any casualties?"

Inwardly Metellus smiled, the prefect always thought of his men first. "No sir. Five prisoners for interrogation."

Marcus nodded and beckoned over the three guards who had fled. "Your master," he pointed to the bloodied corpse, "did he have family?"

"No sir."

"Land?"

"Yes sir, up near Morbium."

"Mmm. That gives us a problem. What were you carrying?"

"Quick lime and limestone for Deva."

Marcus turned to Metellus. "Our quartermaster could be a very happy man tonight. We will take your wagons and guards into our safe keeping. You three return to you master's home and guard it until we can decide what to do about his land." He saw them exchange quick furtive glances. "Oh, and before you think of running, my cavalry is based here and in Morbium. When I visit Morbium I will expect to find you three there. If you are not then I would have to think that you were rebels and have you crucified. Do I make myself clear?"

"Yes sir." Metellus smiled their faces showed quite clearly that they would be there.

"Take whatever food you need from your wagons. If you leave now you should make Stanwyck before dark." Marcus emphasised Stanwyck to let them know he knew the area well. With slumped shoulders, the three riders rode off rueing the fact that their freedom had been short lived.

"I'm surprised they didn't show a clean pair of heels before you arrived sir."

Marcus grinned, "Oh they tried but they were so dozy they ran straight into us. This is a true stroke of fortune."

"Why sir?"

"Lime and limestone. We can make concrete, pazzolana and have stone buildings at the new fort. Should make Decius happy. Now let us interview the prisoners."

The fear on the prisoner's faces was clear. They had recognised the uniforms and remembered the Pannonians from the battle. "Where is your base?" They all sullenly looked at the ground. Marcus nodded. "So, it is to be that way. Trooper!" He gestured to the nearest trooper who stood stiffly at attention.

"Sir!"

"Choose one of the prisoners, any one. Your choice. "

The trooper grinned, reached down and dragged one to his feet by his braided hair. "This one'll do sir."

"Stick your spear in the ground," he paused and looked at the quaking prisoner, "point uppermost."

The grinning trooper roared, "Yes sir." The other troopers began to grin in anticipation as they saw the wet patch forming at the prisoner's feet. The trooper had succeeded in driving his spear into the ground so that the blade and the length of a man's leg protruded from the soft soil of the riverbank.

"So, I will ask you again where is your base? And before you look at the ground again if I receive silence then my men will sit you on that little seat." The prefect pointed at the spear. Marcus then looked at the other men. "When you have died I will repeat the questions to the others."

The man could not get his words out quickly enough. "Over there, the land of the lakes."

"Where in the land of the lakes? On the big lake where the Roman fort is?"

"No nearer the sea, further away!" He gestured northwards.

Marcus turned to Gaelwyn who was chewing on a piece of liquorice root and cleaning his teeth. "Do you know where he is talking about?"

"There is another big lake not as big as the one you know but big. Yes, I know where the dogs are hiding."

"Good." He looked at the man. "Then you live. You can retrieve your spear trooper." The trooper looked disappointed as he pulled it from the ground. "Keep them bound and we'll decide what to do with them later. For the moment tether, them to the wagons. "

When his raiding party failed to return Aed was not concerned for he had had desertions before. Chiefs who took their raiding party to other pickings. He had enough warriors still flocking in from every direction. They were the displaced warriors who sought a paymaster and Aed could still furnish arms and shelter. So far, the Romans had not bothered him and he felt he had Fainch to thank for that. Mona was still a thorn in Rome's side. He knew that sometime they would come which was why he had small groups of watchers on all the major routes in and out of the land of the lakes. When they came he would destroy them. His only fear was the presence of the legions; if they arrived he would find it hard to motivate his men to fight. Too many of them had seen the relentless way they had slaughtered waves of their fellow warriors. The auxiliaries he could destroy, he had done so before and he would do so again. He had over two and a half thousand warriors and the goods he had stolen had made each one of them richer than they had been in their lives. Although he was still hopeful of recapturing the whole of Brigantia he was happy enough to rule this part.

He looked up as Modius entered the roundhouse. "Still no sign of Calgus then?"

"I told you he was too weak and too inexperienced to lead a warband."

"I agree Modius, but we need to blood the young leaders; you know that it is the Roman way."

He nodded, "Yes but the Roman way trains them. I will lead my men and see if can find where he went."

"Good. Check that our watchers are still doing their duty."

The column made much better time as it travelled along the low coastal plain. They could see the sea in the distance but Marcus made sure they did not get close enough to lose either man or beast in the treacherous sands. Soon they saw the peaks rising in the distance and they knew they were getting close. Gaelwyn and Gaius with his turma left one morning on an extended patrol to see how far it was to the fort. They returned in mid-afternoon. "We will be there tomorrow."

"How does it look?" asked Decius who had made it quite clear to anyone who would listen what he felt about rebuilding the fort again.

"You can still see the ditches. It looks much the way it was when it was dismantled."

"Yeah and we haven't got the legionaries to help us build it this time."

"Stop moaning Decius. We will be much more comfortable this time. It won't be wooden and we won't have to share it with foot soldiers." Marcus pointed at the slaves driving the wagons. "And this time we have slaves to do some of the jobs that you and the lads hate."

Decius sniffed, "Well I suppose if you put it like that."

It was quite nostalgic for the older veterans who remembered the last time they had seen the lake, then they had been heading for the battle with Venutius under the command of Ulpius Felix for the last time. They pointed out features to the recruits as they passed them. "That was where we had stables."

"We had a landing stage there."

"That was a guard post."

Marcus smiled for the recruits could only see lumps of discarded rotting wood but for the veterans they could see the building and hear their comrades now with the Allfather. When they arrived at the head of the lake Marcus was pleased that the outline of the fort was still visible. Laying the lines out again was not complicated but this simplified things and made it easier for them. "Build the camp here inside the old fort. Tomorrow we start to build. Gaius, you and Decurion Demetrius can take out your turmae tomorrow."

"Are we to find the bandits?"

"No not yet. Let's get this built. Just take a sweep from west to east. You know the paths and lakes. Show young Demetrius the lay of the land. We need to make everyone as familiar with this land as you and Decius."

The next day Julius Demetrius was quite excited as he left the camp. Even in the early dawn Decius had the men mixing concrete and others chopping down trees. Gaius leaned over, "Confidentially we have got the best of the deal. I would rather be riding than building. Ride next to me and I will explain the land to you."

They headed north and Gaius halted them a mile and a half from the camp. He pointed out a knoll and a field filled with bleached bones. "That was where we halted the Brigante. That knoll had a tower and the young decurion on duty died along with half his turma. This is a dangerous land. We won't see it today but there is a trail through those woods which goes along that escarpment. The Brigante used it to ambush us. You will see it better from the rise over there."

With that he headed west and crossed a roaring river which fortunately barely covered the lower legs of the horses. They climbed steadily behind a hill until they emerged at the top and Julius could see the lake with the fort as well as two lakes to the north. "I see why they call it the land of the lakes."

"There are many more lakes close to us hidden in little dells and coves. You are never far from water here. Remember that. Look yonder you can see the trail I told you of."

"And yet we could not see it when we were next to it."

"This is why the prefect wanted you to see the land. It cost us many men's lives to discover that."

The rest of the morning was spent gradually heading up the twisting trail to the north west. Julius could see that by using the trail you could see huge distances in every direction. When he mentioned this to Gaius who nodded. "I know but the drawback is you can be seen by hidden watchers. Today we tell any watchers that the Romans are back."

The watchers he mentioned were watching from the very trail Gaius had shown Julius. One of them was running back to Aed even as Gaius and Julius turned east to drop down to the narrow neck of land between two lakes. They rested their horses in a flat area between the two still pieces of water. As they chewed on their stale bread Gaius pointed out where their Brigante allies had fought with the rebels. "We nearly managed to destroy the whole warband but instead we lost some fine warriors that day. Just there."

The afternoon saw them climbing along the high escarpment to the east. "We will not go to the top but on the other side there is a dark valley and a long deep lake. We travelled up that way when we went to Brocavum and now we head back to see what Decius has managed in the way of building." It was a pleasant ride back along the escarpment and then dropping down to the lakeside with the sun slowly setting over the incredibly still waters. When they crested the rise, which overlooked the fort Julius was surprised to see the progress. "That's because Decius hates building. The sooner it is built the sooner he can do what he likes doing best, killing Brigante."

Aed was not surprised when the news reached him of the Roman incursion into his land. It had only been a question of time. Knowing that it was just the Pannonians made it sweeter for he wanted revenge and he knew that they must have many recruits in their ranks. Modius too was pleased. "I'll finally get to gut that jumped up decurion Decius."

"Patience. Patience. We will choose the time we will choose the place. To reach us…"

"He doesn't know where we are."

"I suspect either Calgus or one of his rabble will have talked, it is no matter. To reach us they will need to cross the high pass. We can easily stop them there if we have to but I want them observed. You served with them what will they do next?"

"Build a camp or a fort so that they have protection then send out patrols."

"How many men?"

"One turma would be about forty but sometimes they send two."

"I remember." Aed had almost massacred a single turma and would have but for the intervention of a second. "Good when we find their routine we will ambush and slaughter one of the turma. Our man did not know how many men there were but it cannot be more than a thousand."

"Not even close to that with the men and horses they lost in the last battle."

"Good then we will whittle them down. We will maim their horses for they have no replacements. We will ambush their foraging parties and, when they are weakest we will take their fort from them."

Modius was not certain that they could achieve all that Aed hoped but his personal goal was the deaths of Decius and Marcus; anything else was a bonus. He would repay every scathing comment and rebuke with a wound and when they were begging for death he would emasculate them and then, only then would he end their miserable lives.

The following day Marcus sent out Lentius with Vettius, this time following a different route. As he explained to his decurions, "All of you need to be familiar with the land here. It is only a small area but it is full of high mountains, valleys and lakes. We cannot travel in straight lines and the paths are few. That is where the enemy has the advantage. He can travel on foot where we cannot on horse. He can take short cuts and we cannot. I want every man in this ala to be able to get back here, on foot if needs be for before this campaign is over we will need every trooper we have."

As Lentius trotted away in the early morning half-light Marcus and Decius walked around the partly rebuilt fort. "How long Decius?"

"We have broken the back of the work. It was lucky for us that we found that stone. Pontius Brutus had quarried it well and the lime was perfect for the concrete."

"He was a centurion, he knew it could get a higher price if they were well prepared and presented. It is sad that we were not able to save him."

"Aye, but when you finish soldiering life must seem a little boring. Flavinius Bellatoris seemed to shrink when he stopped being a prefect and started farming. Perhaps Pontius went out as he would have wanted, fighting not sitting in some villa remembering the old times."

"I think we will send those Brigante prisoners back to Eboracum when Sergeant Cato returns. We will all make a little money from the slave market and it will save us guards. Besides we will need more supplies soon. Once it gets to winter nothing can get over those mountains. I want us well stocked. I'll go and make sure Quartermaster Verres knows what we need."

"I think you made a wise choice there. He is the best Quartermaster I have ever seen."

Laughing he said, “Yes I noticed your uniform was a little tighter.”

“I washed it and it shrank!”

“I am tempted to keep the slaves. We can use them for cooking, cleaning and growing our own food. It will free up every trooper for duties. All we need to do is feed them and they will be growing their own food anyway.”

“Good idea sir, if they can cook.”

“There you are then Decurion Princeps when you have started the building off go and find out.”

By the time Sergeant Cato returned there was a substantial wall and ditch built. The Porta Praetoria was rising already with solid stone at its base. The Praetorium was taking shape and the sergeant could see that by the end of the month most of the men would be housed in buildings rather than leather tents. For his part, the prefect was delighted when his sergeant trotted through the gate with a string of thirty horses.

“You have done well sergeant!”

Smiling modestly the sergeant said, “Luckily they remembered us clearing out that nest of bandits and they had a surplus so I got them at a bargain price.”

“How is the stud coming along?”

“Twenty mares with foals and I left some more brood mares with the lads there.” He pulled a pack mule towards the prefect. Untying two amphorae he said, “Prefect Strabo wondered if you and the decurion princeps might like a drop of this. It is, apparently from Capri.”

“I think all the decurions will enjoy this. When you have rested you might put your thoughts to a place to stable and graze the horses. As I remember the meadow where we fought our battle against the Brigante is a fine meadow for horses but not secure.”

“That’s not a problem sir. We can take them down each day to graze and build a secure stockyard here.”

That was what Marcus liked about Sergeant Cato, he was supremely confident about all things equine. “Good see to it and well-done sergeant.”

Marcus walked to the main gate and climbed the partly built tower. As he gazed around he felt some satisfaction. His men had worked wonders and soon he would be able to take his men on their first offensive action. They would take the battle to the Brigante. North west, that was where the rebels hid. That was where he would go, he would take his men to the very heartland of his enemy.

Chapter 7

Summer was past its best by the time the fort was secure enough for the ala to go on the offensive. The quartermaster and Sergeant Cato had ensured they were well stocked and well mounted. A few replacements had trickled in with the supplies and they were almost ready to field another turma.

Leaving two turmae to guard the now defensible fort Marcus led his men north. When they reached the knoll and the scene of the battle Gaius and Julius were sent with their troopers along the escarpment path through the woods. "Your task is to make sure we are not ambushed. Wait for us at the second lake."

Metellus and Agrippa were sent with their turmae to climb the high ridge and do the same from the left flank. Marcus, Decius and the other six turmae trudged up the valley.

Modius and his warband had been watching the fort from the thick woods which encircled the fort. Moving swiftly through the woods they could travel faster than the horses. Modius did not have enough men to attack the ala but he could certainly cause casualties amongst a turma or two. When he saw Gaius lead off the two turmae he grinned wolfishly and turned to his lieutenant. "Those we can have."

Leaving the path, they raced, like mountain goats, up the steep path to the hump back lump of rock which rose like a giant Roman nose. The trail they took was a goat and sheep trail, impossible to follow on horse but easily traversed on foot. Once they reached the top the hard climb was done and they began to catch up with the red crested Romans below them. Modius knew exactly where he was headed. There was a sheer cliff and a recent landslide had decimated the trees which littered the hillside. The result was an unstable mass of rocks and broken trees; an ideal spot for an ambush. They reached the spot before the Romans and Modius set his men to the task of gathering the largest rocks they could. He had ten of his men armed with bows and their instructions were clear, they were to target those at the front and the rear of the column to jam up the narrow bridleway. The spot he had chosen was perfect for the path took a steep twist and the horses would be forced to slow down dramatically.

He almost held his breath as he saw the red crests of the two decurions appear. They were riding side by side; his archers could take out the leaders which would cause even more confusion. His smile turned to a snarl when he saw that he would not be able to target the front and the rear of the column at the same time for the column was strung out too far on the narrow path. He nodded and his archers began to rain arrows down on the turmae. The rest of his men let out a roar and hurled the boulders and rocks they had gathered.

On the path, the troopers had no idea what was happening. Even Gaius was taken by surprise. He felt the arrow shave his face and slam into his horse's shoulder. As it reared he saw that Julius had taken an arrow in his shoulder. Turning to shout an order he was horrified to see boulders and trees cascading, crushing and crashing into his men and their mounts. There were screams and cries from men and beast. Gaius saw that he was trapped. His only recourse was retreat. "Retreat! Retreat! Go back!" The order was given more easily than it was followed for his men had to turn on a narrow path. Their discipline held them in good stead and, whilst still taking casualties, they managed to turn. This helped as their shields could now protect them from the arrows. Fortunately, many of the trees which had started rolling down the steep slope became jammed together so that the main danger to his men was the arrows.

"How are you Julius?" Gaius could see that his companion was pale but still conscious.

"I am alright." His tone belied his comment.

"Get on my right your shield arm is injured."

High on the escarpment Modius' delight had turned to frustration as he saw the dam of logs which stopped the avalanche. It also prevented him from seeing the result of his attack for the Romans were now hidden. He turned to his archers, "Keep firing! The rest of you throw rocks high in the air, over the barrier."

Down on the trail Gaius could assess the disaster. There were at least eight dead horses and he could see many men lying on the ground some were dead but others were obviously wounded. "Julius can you command?"

"Of course."

"Good then take the men who still survive back to the open ground away from this sheer cliff and wait there. You six troopers here." As soon as he had the six troopers and Julius had led off the rest Gaius dismounted. "Cassius hold the horses. You two protect us with your shields. The rest check for the wounded. We can do nought for the dead but we can help the wounded put them on any horses which are not dead." The arrows continued to thud into the trees and the shields but fired blind the chances of a direct strike was low. They managed to put eight of their wounded comrades on horses, the rest lay dead. "Right back along the path to Decurion Demetrius."

By the time he reached his companion Julius had organised a defensive ring and had one of his troopers tending to the wounded. "I have sent a trooper to the prefect sir to tell him what has happened."

"Well done Julius." Mentally Gaius was chiding himself for not having thought of that himself. He looked around. Out of the eighty troopers who had ridden into the pathway of death there were only fifty not wounded. Another ten, including Julius were wounded but the catastrophe was in the damage to horses. Many were injured, some were lame and there were more dead horses than dead troopers. All Sergeant Cato's work had been undone. "Julius, you wait here. I'll take ten men and see if we find the rebels who did this."

Julius looked up at the steep hillside. "Up there?"

"If they can do it we can. Keep a good watch here and get your shoulder looked at." Selecting ten men from his own turma Gaius set off at a trot up the narrow pathway which twisted and turned around the escarpment.

Modius felt satisfaction. He did not know how many men he had killed but he had killed many for he had seen both horses and men fall. He had lost not a man. He laughed aloud and his men looked at him in surprise. "They are mounted we are as safe here as anywhere for they did not bring infantry. Come we will return to Aed with news of our great success." His men set off in a long line at a gentle walk believing that they had nothing to fear from the Romans.

Gaius and his men were breathing heavily when they reached the top of the hill and looked along the ridge. Unlike the barbarians they wore armour and carried shields but even so Gaius was pleased that none had dropped out. He was also pleased to see the path undulating gently away. They soon found the spot where the ambush had been sprung. He could see from the crushed vegetation where the raiders had waited and also the path leading away. For a moment, he thought about returning to Julius but then he caught a glimpse down the slope of a dead trooper and his mount. His face hardened. No, he would pursue until he found them.

Inevitably the laggards at the back of Modius' band began to lose contact with those in front. The best and fittest warriors were at the front following Modius who was keen to return and report his success. As they lost touch they slowed down even more.

"Well he said they couldn't catch us so what is the hurry." The fifteen of them sat down and began to drink from water skins. They had chosen a small dell which sheltered them from the wind.

One of them pointed up the ridge; in the distance, they could see the other forty warriors in a line. "What's the hurry?"

His answer came swiftly. Gaius and his men were almost as surprised as the resting raiders when they came upon them. Gaius had seen the other, larger band of men in the distance and was just contemplating returning as the odds were not in his favour when he almost tripped over the fifteen who were in the dell. The Romans reacted first. They were angry with their enemies for the cowardly ambush and they were tired and knew that the sooner they disposed of them the sooner they could rest their aching legs. They set about the raiders with a rage which shocked even Gaius. They were killing for their friends lying slaughtered on the path and for their mounts, those animals who were cherished and loved by their riders. It was over as quickly as it started. Each trooper took a head and with a roar waved them at the mass of men in the distance whose white faces showed that they had turned when they heard the noise of the melee.

Modius was white with anger. His success was negated by the lazy laggards who had not followed orders. He turned on his warriors. "That is what you get when you don't follow orders. These are Romans we fight, not a bunch of farmers and merchants. You cannot take risks with them. Now this time keep together and when I say move, you move!"

By the time Marcus received the report from Decurion Demetrius he had met up with the other patrol and was resting men and horses in the shady spot between the two lakes. "Sneaky bastards eh sir?"

"We should have anticipated that Decius. Those hills are perfect for infantry ambushes; our horses can't climb as well as men and they are immune from our attacks."

"So, what do we do? Fight on foot, again!"

"No, it just means we bring Aed to battle sooner rather than later." He gazed up at the hillside to their right as though trying to see Gaius and Julius through the trees. "I just hope that Gaius and Julius are safe."

"It was Julius who had the wound wasn't it?"

"It was but you know Gaius. It would be just like him to try to capture those who attacked him. We need to let our young decurions know that saving our lives is more important than taking their lives. They can afford to lose two to each of our one and they will win."

"To be honest sir when you were a young decurion didn't you want to take it the enemy all the time?"

"You are right Decius but who reined us in? Ulpius; and we have to do the same for our boys. I can't see the point in carrying on with this patrol. They have shown their hand. We will need a different strategy."

It was a chastened atmosphere back at the fort when all the turmae returned. The surgeon tut-tutted his way through the wounded and Sergeant Cato sadly shook his head as he saw the savagely wounded beasts being led in by, sometimes, tearful troopers. "Briefing in headquarters when you have sorted out your turmae."

Marcus called over the quartermaster and, after a hurried conversation the portly man trotted off to his store.

"How is the shoulder Julius? Shouldn't you be resting?"

"No sir. There is no pain and the surgeon managed to remove the arrow." He looked around apologetically. "I just didn't want to miss the meeting." They all laughed and Decius ruffled the likeable young man's hair in a paternal way.

"We learned a valuable lesson today. I am just sorry it cost so many troopers from turmae ten and two." He looked around at the downcast faces. His leaders were demoralised. They had come from a successful campaign in Mona and they had lost more men in one day than in some battles on the island. He gestured at Porcius who brought out some amphora of wine.

"I was going to save this for a special occasion but the prefect felt tonight was the time to drink it. It looks like I will have to take another trip to Eboracum." The men laughed as they were each poured a beaker of wine.

"Tomorrow we push on to the rebel camp." There was an audible gasp from the gathering. "We go straight up the valley. I sent Gaelwyn scouting whilst we were resting. He has told me there is only one place we could be slowed up, just a mile or two from the second lake where the valley narrows. Once we are through there it is a clear route to the rebel's camp. Gaius showed yesterday that, even on foot, our men are superior to the rebels. Ten troopers killed fifteen rebels and did not suffer a scratch. We only lose if we are too cautious, let us be bold. Julius, you will remain here with the Quartermaster, Sergeant Cato half your turma and the wounded." He could see the disappointment on the decurion's face. "Someone has to stay here and would you take the place of an able bodied decurion?" Julius blushed and shook his head. Gaius will command the two turmae. And now gentlemen let us enjoy the wine the good Porcius has provided."

The troopers heard the cheer and wondered what was going on in the Praetorium.

Fainch unerringly found Aed even in his secret location. He found himself aroused as soon as he saw her despite the fact that the journey had taken much out of her. "It is good to see you."

"And you my love." She stroked his head and kissed him full on the lips. Soon they were wrapped passionately in each other's arms; Aed had taken slaves but Fainch was a woman full of passion and surprises; it seemed as she aged, like good wine she improved and she introduced Aed to new experiences which took him to the edge of ecstasy and back. Their lovemaking was exciting and each time they managed something different. When they had finished and they lay breathing heavily the same thought fleetingly passed through both their minds. '*Why could they not do this every day*?' The answer of course was obvious to them both and dismissed by both just as quickly. They both had important work to do and they needed to do it apart. Aed could fight the physical battles but Fainch needed to fight the diplomatic battle.

"When do you leave?"

"Tomorrow. We can only delay them here it is the Caledonii and the Pictii who must defeat them for they have the numbers of men. My plan for the tribes of Britannia to throw off the yoke failed because the southern tribes were too Roman. There is nothing wilder than our northern brothers. They are my last hope." Aed nodded. "And you, my love what of your plans?"

"We managed to ambush a patrol today but we did not kill enough troopers. Our men are not disciplined enough. I hope to ambush more tomorrow when they send out a patrol. We are getting warriors all the time and the Romans do not have enough men."

"Be wary. The Ordovices also had many men and they were slaughtered."

"That is true but the Romans were led by a fine general that time. These are just auxiliaries."

She put her fingers on his lips. "Be careful. This Roman leader has luck with him. I had him in my grasp and he was spirited away. If you get the chance then kill him and kill him quickly. I made a mistake, I delayed and we paid the price."

Julius felt at a loss as he watched the nine turmae ride away. He glanced around at the fort and it seemed empty, almost deserted. He knew that the prefect was right and he would have endangered his men had he travelled but he was gratified by their calls as they had left.

"Don't worry sir; we'll bring a few heads back for you."

"We'll teach these bastards a lesson."

"We'll pay them back."

He was surprised that he was held in such affection; when he looked at leaders like Macro, Gaius and Agrippa he could see real heroes, leaders that men would look up to and admire. When he thought of himself he felt unworthy. He did not know that his men held him in the same regard as the best decurions in the ala. To them he was the best leader they could have.

Gaelwyn, as usual was riding ahead with the Decurion Princeps and his turma. They were riding swiftly as they were in more open country. Decius pointed at the narrow saddle they would have to cross. "That is where I would ambush." Gaelwyn nodded. Decius pointed to the slope to their right. "If you could get up there you could see over the saddle and see if there is an ambush."

"I will go. "He held up his spear horizontally above his head. "This means an ambush. "He then held it vertically, "This means it is safe."

Decius halted his men about a mile from the saddle. If he had taken them forward and it had been ambush the first they would have known would have been when they crested the rise and were assaulted. This way was safer. He watched the scout become a faint dot on the hillside. Had he not watched him constantly he would have been invisible. He went so far that he worried he might lose him. Without turning he shouted, "Arrius, you've got young eyes watch Gaelwyn and tell me what he is doing with his spear."

"Yes sir."

"He's stopped and… he's holding his spear."

He growled, "I know he's holding his spear, you useless excuse for a dog's dick! Which way?"

"What do you mean?"

Rolling his eyes Decius held his spear first horizontally and then vertically. "Which way?" When the blushing trooper held it horizontally Decius said," Ambush then. Right, Arrius because you did so well there you can ride back to the prefect and tell him there is an ambush and the Decurion Princeps is going to sort it. Got it?"

"Got it sir."

"Right we are going to close with the saddle and then dismount. I want the archers to split into two groups. We are going to belly up to the top of the saddle. The archers will take out anyone who looks like they might have a missile weapon of any type. The rest of us run in one line, shields together like Caerhun and rush the bastards."

Grinning the turmae all shouted, "Yes sir!"

"Good, four horse holders. Whose turn is it?" In Decius' turmae they had a rota for holding the horses; it saved argument and was generally fair. "Three men held up their hands and one said, "And Arrius sir but you sent him…"

"Then whose turn is it next?" The trooper reluctantly put up his hand. "Good. Let's go."

Decius hated the technique known as bellying up but it was the only way to get close. He also hated it because he had to remove either his helmet or his red horsehair plume. He chose the former as he could never remount the crest quite as well. As he peered over the top he could see fifty warriors all armed with a variety of weapons but they had no horses. He idly wondered where Gaelwyn had got to and then realised with grim satisfaction that there would probably be some Brigante having his throat sliced right at that moment. He turned and was gratified to see thirty-five faces trained upon him. This was the moment. He raised and dropped his spear. As one man, his turma stood. As soon as they did they had a clear view of the enemy who had been surprised having expected the thunder of hooves as a precursor to an attack. As the archers wreaked havoc with their opponents Decius led a wedge of troopers fielding a solid wall of shields and spears. Macro's training had paid off as had watching the legionaries train. Ten paces from their enemies his men hurled their spears and, without a pause, hit the shocked second line with the weight of shields, armour and bodies muscled by good food. The action was over so quickly that Decius was almost embarrassed. He cursed as he saw a seemingly dead body rise from the ground and race off up the hill. Before he could order an archer to bring him down he saw

Gaelwyn rise like a wraith and sliced off the warrior's head. As he wiped his sword against the dead man's breeks he nodded to Decius. It was the closest to a compliment Gaelwyn had ever come and Decius was quite touched. His men began searching the bodies for treasure and Decius signalled the horse holders. The prefect had been right, these men were no opposition.

He heard the column before he saw it. The thunder of the hooves vibrated and travelled through the ground. He would have to tell Marcus about that. The ala was telling its enemies when it was coming. On a battlefield that was a good thing for it inspired fear. In this land where there were many places to hide it was not.

Fainch kissed Aed goodbye. Modius stood in the corner like a sulky boy who has had his nose put of out of joint by a pretty sister. He turned in disgust. The sooner the priestess left the better. "Be careful my love. These Romans are dangerous. Delay them but do not put your life at risk."

Aed looked down at the diminutive love of his life. He was touched that she would think so much of him. "Do not worry. My men will delay them at the pass and then we will withdraw through the hills to the north and slip over the Taus to the land of the Novontae, I have friends there. Already my treasure is heading north. "

"We will meet at the court of King Calgathus." With a long, passionate kiss they parted and Fainch the witch slipped north to continue her war against the Romans

"You have done well, Decurion Princeps. These were obviously the advance guards intended to slow us down and then warn their lord. We will push on. "Gaius take Gaelwyn and find their stronghold."

Gaius galloped off with his strong turma. He was confident he could deal with any enemies he met. Gaelwyn inspired confidence. He would find their enemies and then the Pannonians would strike.

Decius explained to Marcus the problem with the cavalry and how he had defeated the guards. "So, Decurion Princeps, your views have changed since you questioned the general at the foot of Wyddfa?"

"No, I am just saying that here, in this desolate land perhaps we might want to change the way we work. Gaius managed to kill plenty on foot and I did, you might be right sir here. But mark my words when they need the cavalry we will do what we do best, ride and charge!"

"You are right Decius. You are right. If Agricola has taught me one thing it is this, learn to adapt or die."

Gaelwyn stayed close to Gaius as they cautiously trotted up the steep sided wooded valley. They had avoided one ambush and neither scout nor Decurion wanted to stumble into another one. As they approached a narrow neck of land between steep outcrops Gaius halted the turma and gestured Gaelwyn forward. The turma sensed they were nearing their objective and the veterans began checking that their swords slid easily from their scabbards and that the horse furniture was tight. The newer troopers aped their more experienced comrades. Gaelwyn approached a moment later then signalled them on. Once they crested the rise the land began to flatten out and they could see smoke in the distance.

"Gaelwyn go up the rise and tell me what you can see." The scout trotted his horse as far up the slope as he could safely manage and then dismounted tying the beast to a lone hawthorn tree standing defiantly against the relentless winds which whipped over these northern hills. Gaius watched him scurry up the hillside, occasionally turning to find an easier route. Some way from the top he slid on to his stomach and began to slither along. After a few moments he turned and, pointing to Gaius beckoned him up.

"Right lads I won't be long. Fabius take charge." Tying his horse to the hawthorn tree and resting his spear and scutum on the ground Gaius followed the same route as Gaelwyn. Having seen him he found it easier but he was still breathing heavily. Gaelwyn tapped the top of his own head and Gaius suddenly remembered his helmet which he removed before the horsehair crest could give them away.

When he arrived next to the scout he beheld a huge lake with an untidy camp of warriors spread out along its northern and western edges. There was a small settlement a short way from the lake which appeared to be unfortified. The position and size of the camp had been determined by the terrain for there was a steep hill to the south. The ridge they were lying on was even steeper with a dizzying drop down to the water side. Gaelwyn pointed out all the important features and Gaius soon ascertained that the only approach to the camp was from the east. Had his men turned west then they would have been seen for there were sentries posted across the plain before the town. The decurion was just grateful that they had not posted sentries at the top of the ridge he occupied. Had they done so then there would have been no chance for surprise.

"It will have to be an early morning attack sir or a night attack. They could hear us and see us long before we reached their camp and they could escape easily. Gaelwyn hasn't been there but when we descended from the ridge we could see many valleys heading south and west. They would be like rats leaving their hole; they could take twenty or thirty different escape routes."

"Thank you, Gaius." The prefect stroked his chin thoughtfully. He had much to mull over. He shaded his eyes with his hand and looked up at the sun. They would have another two hours of daylight. If they were going to attack tonight he would have to give the order quickly. He suddenly had the image of Agricola charging up the hill at the head of his legion. The general would not hesitate. If they waited until the morning his quarry might flee. They would either reinforce the ambush site they had destroyed or wonder why they had not returned at dark. "Right we attack tonight. Gaius, you take the lead, you know the way. Take out the sentries, silently. As soon as they are eliminated we will charge. Are they spread all around the lake?"

Gaius drew the crude shape of the lake in the soil and marked the position of the barbarians. "The land next to the lake looks to be marshy. They are camped about forty paces from it. If we keep the lake fifty paces to our left then we should sweep them away."

"Good. Decurion Princeps, you take the left. Agrippa take the right. I will be in the centre. These bandits are the last remnants of the Brigante rebels when these are destroyed then we may have peace. Let us ensure therefore that we destroy them, completely."

Chapter 8

Aed and Modius had just finished their inspection of the camp. With men arriving each day and others deserting it was important for the two leaders to know who was in their camp. Every new arrival was inspected and interrogated to make sure he was not a Roman spy. Modius had a nose for Roman deserters. Although they had not discovered spies he had found Roman soldiers who had fled their units because of some disciplinary indiscretion. The cruel Modius always got the truth and it inspired just a little more honesty from all. Their inspection also enabled them to see if any of their warriors was hording treasure. Aed made sure they were well rewarded for their banditry but as leader he took the bulk of their loot. They were in the middle of the camp when they heard the alarm. At first, they assumed it was some squabble between clans, a fairly common occurrence but then Modius heard the distinctive call of the buccina. "Romans! To arms! Romans!"

The two leaders had been leading their mounts but now they sprang on to their backs. Modius cursed. The auxiliary troops were attacking from the east and his men were silhouetted against the setting sun whilst the Romans were all but invisible. The men in the camp were panicking and Aed had to slap them with the flat of his sword to make them stand. "Turn and fight. These are cavalry. If you flee you will not escape you will be hunted down. Stand!" Aed turned to Modius, "You take the right and I will take the left. We outnumber them still." Aed's voice betrayed his uncertainty.

"Yes, but they have the surprise."

The camp was a chaotic scene but the sheer numbers in the camp had slowed up the attack. The horses had lost impetus as they ground to a halt on the dead bodies of those killed in the first charge. Pockets of warriors gathered around their chiefs and heeded Aed's words. They formed shield walls and threw their javelins at the Romans who circled them like starving wolves. The sudden appearance of Modius on their right flank heartened them and the shield walls coalesced into a slightly more solid line. Decius could see the organisation and he shouted his voice strident above the din of war. "Turma five reform."

His men were trained so well that they performed the manoeuvre as though in the gyrus. Once they were in a line Decius just pointed his sword at the enemy. The mailed and armoured auxiliaries swept through the warriors who still fought isolated combats with great courage but no support from other warriors. The auxiliaries were relentless and in the rhythm of killing striking down almost in unison. The barbarians had no answer and they fell to sword, spear and horse's hooves.

Suddenly Decius caught a glimpse of Modius trying to rally his fleeing troops. Decius' face was a mask of hatred and anger. Spurring his mount, he charged at the traitorous auxiliary. As he screamed, "Modius you bastard!" the rebel turned, shocked at the use of his name. He tried to wheel his horse around to face the Decurion but the press of bodies around him was too great and he only managed to half turn around. Decius' horse struck him as he was turning and he tumbled to the ground. Decius' mount cleared the jumble of arms and legs enabling the Decurion Princeps to hurl his javelin at the writhing body of Modius. Although it failed to hit him the deserter had to turn away from the blow making him disorientated. Decius swung his horse around and leaned down to strike his long sword at Modius' body. The edge nicked Modius' arm and opened a slit the length of a man's hand. Blood began to pour from the wound and he had no option but to drop his shield from his now useless arm. Roaring in anger Modius swung his sword in a backslash which luckily for the rebel caught Decius' horse. As the horse's head reared up Decius felt himself slipping off and he went with the action landing nimbly on his feet. Modius was a bigger, heavier man and he rushed at Decius with his sword held as high as he could manage. The blade crashed down and had he not had quick reactions it would have split his helmet and his skull. The Decurion Princeps fended the blow off with his scutum and stabbed upwards the edge ripping through the edge of the body armour. They both stepped back breathing heavily. The warriors and troopers surrounding them were all engaged in their own private battles and it was as though the two were in a world of their own. Modius looked down at the blood seeping from his arm and he felt with his fingers to see what damage had been done to his armour; the blade had weakened it and Modius knew he would have to finish the fight quickly. He quickly twisted and turned his blade as he struck Decius repeatedly on his left and his right. The blows were well delivered and were coming too frequently for Decius to do anything other than defend with his shield. Modius was becoming weaker and Decius waited his moment. One double handed slash went too high; Decius ducked beneath the blow and thrust his spatha into the unprotected neck of the ex-decurion. As the life left his eyes he looked down in surprise to see the blade protruding from his throat. Decius withdrew it swiftly in one fluid movement. He was covered in the flood of arterial blood as Modius' life gushed from his throat.

His men had already been weakening but the sudden defeat of a warrior they feared took the heart out of them and they began to drop their weapons. Despite the prefect's instructions about prisoners, the beleaguered troopers were almost too exhausted to carry on with the slaughter. Many of the barbarians fled across the boggy and marshy ground close by the lake. When the Romans failed to pursue others joined in and soon there were forty or fifty men splashing across the darkened lake.

Over on the far side of the battlefield, there was almost as much confusion. The only way Marcus and his decurions knew who enemies were and who were friends was by the fact that their friends were mounted. Aed and his bandits had not fought a serious enemy since the battle of the Taus but the Pannonians were a finely honed and well-trained machine. The end was inevitable but Aed continued to fight. His bodyguards were whittled down as sheaves of corn at harvest time. Realising that all was lost he stabbed at a trooper with his spear and, as the trooper defended with a shield he turned his horse and ruthlessly rode down those of his men who stood in his way. He heard a voice cry, "After him!" He did not make the mistake of turning and showing a white face in the dark night instead he put his face as close the mane as he could and galloped over the dead and dying remnants of his erstwhile rebel army. All was lost here and Aed would ride to the Taus and join Fainch. The battle had been lost but not the war.

Macro heard the shout and saw the figure streaking away. He dug his heels in and his mount responded instantly. The grain fed horse began to outstrip the rebel horse which had not been well looked after. Aed could hear the thunder of the hooves but he knew he dared not look around for fear of missing his footing on the treacherous, rock filled plain. Macro had no such fear and he was already sliding his spear in his hand to extend it beyond the tip of his horse's nose. He used his knees to guide his horse and he reacted to the movement of the horse in front of him. The end, when it came, was a sudden shock to both men. A deer had been drinking at the lake and when it had heard the thunder of hooves it had panicked. It suddenly leapt in front of Aed's horse causing him to swerve in front of Macro. Macro had the lightning reactions of the young and in one fluid movement he had thrust his spear through the gap in the breast and back plate of Aed's magnificent armour. As he felt the life blood ooze from the fatal wound he wondered if Fainch knew of his death and how she would take it. The puzzled expression on his face made Macro wonder about the last thoughts of this, the last Brigante rebel. Had his last thoughts been of the power he had so nearly had or perhaps it was of his victories? Macro spent the long ride back to the battlefield with the dead rebel and the dead dear slung over the horse's back pondering on such thoughts.

"Sound the recall!" The prefect did not know for certain if he had won. From the lack of enemies around him he assumed he had but he could not see far on this cloudless night. Night had fallen heavily as the battle had progressed. Any further pursuit was fruitless and he did not want to lose any men unnecessarily. He could hear the moans and cries of the dead and the dying and the last few combats played out in darkness. He turned to the men around him and shouted. "Form up in your turmae. Decurions report to me when you have ascertained casualties Gaelwyn!"

He almost jumped when the wily warrior's voice came from behind him. All through the battle the scout had protected the prefect's back, having saved his life once it was now his duty to protect his life for ever. "Yes, prefect?"

"You gave me a start. Find us a good place to camp." Without acknowledgement, the man melted into the dark. His decurions started to arrive with their reports. He smiled as he realised that they were all there and then he counted again. Macro was missing! He hoped the impulsive but likable young man had survived. From the casualty figures supplied by the decurions he discovered that they had lost barely a handful of men so swift had been their attack and the shock it had created.

Decius was the last to report and he held the grisly remains of Modius' head. "Found one deserter sir."

They all turned, their hands going to weapons as they heard the thunder of two horses. "Friends! Friends! It is Decurion Macro." As he reined in his horse Decius shook his head. "Killed their leader sir and I got us dinner, tonight we have venison."

"You know son if you fell in a pile of shit you'd end up with gold in your hands."

The next day as they surveyed the battlefield the prefect saw what a complete victory it had been. True, rebels had escaped and in that had disobeyed his orders but the number of rebels who had escaped was so small that a couple of turmae could have defeated them. At long last Brigantia was safe and the northern rebellion was over.

Gallia Aquitania 77 A.D.

Julius Agricola almost jumped for joy when he received his new posting. "Britannia!" He yelled at his wife. "Britannia. I am to be governor of Britannia."

His wife looked decidedly unhappy, "But it is such a damp little province and they have no baths nor theatres…"

"I know my love which is why Emperor Titus wants me to finish the task of conquering it so that we can release the legions and make the natives lot in life better. You do not need to leave here. I chose this villa rather than the governor's residence so that we could have a long-term home. And one day we will return to Gallia Narbonensis and Forum Julii." It made his heart glow when he saw the pleasure that brought. He would build a villa in his home town so that when he retired he could live in that idyllic land by the sea of blue and warm his southern born bones after the vicissitudes of his service in the cold harsh northern lands.

Glanibanta

The Prefect and the Decurion Princeps were enjoying the pleasant autumn morning. They were travelling the pleasant ride which encompassed the two small lakes closest to the fort. It had become daily exercise for the two warriors who had spent the autumn and winter tracking down and destroying the small bands of bandits who had escaped their clutches. The summer had been a time to consolidate, build roads, train recruits and manage the new trade routes.

"Do you know this is the first time since we came to this province that I have felt safe, almost peaceful. It is a strange feeling. I keep looking over rises and behind bushes for Brigante and they are all gone."

"You are right Decius. It has been a long journey since we rescued the Queen Cartimandua and began to fight these Brigante."

"They were a tough bunch, not very bright but tough." He gestured around with his hand at the steep hills and valleys. "This is a natural fortress. They should have held us here for years."

"Yes Decius but they are not builders. You have seen Stanwyck; it is not as strong as this little fort and yet it is much bigger. Had they been builders we would still be fighting."

"Well I won't be sorry to get some fighting in and stop this road building. I hate it."

"It is necessary and look how peaceful the land is now. Time to head back I think."

"At least we have had the chance to get all our replacements trained and kitted out. These southern volunteers are quite good you know."

"That's grudging praise from you, Decius. There was a time you thought they were one step away from pigs."

"I admit it I didn't like them but once they take to Roman ways they change somehow. Perhaps they just needed civilising." Decius glanced up at the prefect who seemed to smile a lot more these days. "Speaking of civilisation and such matters have you finally reconciled yourself about the witch?"

"What you mean do I think as you and the others do that she is dead? No. She lives." Decius shook his head. "It is not just a feeling Decius there have been rumours of a woman being seen in the camps of the Pictii and Caledonii; I am sure it is she. She was ever the mischief maker using Venutius, Aed, Brigante, Carvetii, and Ordovice. She seems to have a power over all men." He looked down at the back of Argentium's head. "Did I tell you of our meeting? When she spoke to me?"

Decius looked at the prefect and was taken aback. The prefect never revealed himself. Perhaps it was a sign that they were becoming closer as leaders, much as Ulpius and Flavius before them. "No, you didn't. I mean I knew she must have spoken to you when they captured you but you never said about a conversation."

Marcus sighed. "The woman I hated. That woman had destroyed all that was dear to me and yet when she spoke I found that I became aroused." He shook and hung his head. "I was excited and it shamed and angered me. I only glimpsed her but her eyes have the ability to see into your soul but it is her voice, Decius, it has a power. A frightening power. If you ever see her do not let her speak. Kill her. Kill her as quickly as you would kill a snake in your bed."

Decius had never heard his friend speak so powerfully and with so much hate. "Don't worry prefect. She will die. Of that you can be sure."

The land of the Venicones

Fainch was tired. She was no longer the young woman who had bedded kings and chiefs, who could move around quickly and silently like a ghost. She had travelled through the lands of the Novontae, Selgovae and Votadini seeking support for opposition to the Romans. She was tired because she had to repeat the same arguments and she received the same responses. The kings and chiefs would fight the Romans to the death when they crossed into their lands. She had tried to tell them that the peoples in the south had tried the same tactic and been swallowed piecemeal as morsels at a Roman feast. Finally, she had heard of one King Calgacus, who lived in the far north, who hated the Romans as much as she did. He seemed to be her last, if not her only hope to spark a fire which would engulf and destroy the Romans. Her guides were passing her from kingdom to kingdom to enable her to meet this mighty king. That they did so swiftly showed just how much they wanted her out of their kingdom. They did not want to offend a witch but they feared her nonetheless.

"Messenger coming in and he looks like he's in a hurry."

"Who trained you to give a report you lump of duck shit?"

"Sorry Decurion Princeps."

Julius smiled and turned to Gaius. "I just love his turn of phrase. He is so eloquent. Reminds me of Socrates or Aristotle."

"Yes, but he is effective."

The Imperial messenger was taken straight to the Praetorium. Imperial messengers were rare and the decurions all found excuses to gather near to the Praetorium to find out quickly what was going on. They did not even bother with idle desultory chatter they just lounged. When the clerk came out to give his instructions to the guard he looked around with his mouth open. "The prefect would like to see all the decurions as soon as they can be found." He paused. "Very efficient gentlemen, very efficient. The Prefect will be pleased with such a prompt response."

"Sit down." From the look on his face they knew that it was good news. "We have a new governor. Gnaeus Julius Agricola." The sentries heard the cheer from the office and wondered what it meant. "He is at Deva and will spend the next few months tidying up the area south. Next year he marches north and we are to conquer the rest of this province. We are heading for Caledonia."

"When do we start sir?"

"Macro don't be so keen. We have to wait for the troops who will be guarding Glanibanta. They are a local auxilia force from Eboracum. Once they arrive we head north to the Taus and wait there for the general. We have at least six months before we start."

The portly quartermaster groaned, "That means living in a tent and sleeping on the floor."

They all laughed and Decius snorted, "What do you mean? You sleep in a bed in one of your wagons."

"I know I was talking about you not me!"

Part Three
Caledonia

Chapter 9

When Marcus arrived in Deva he immediately noticed the vast changes which had taken place. The building was strongly built in stone and his journey to the impressive building had been on Roman roads. Travelling down the west coast he had seen the peace which the Roman influence had wrought. In the lands of the Carvetii and Brigante through which he has first journeyed also displayed this prosperity now that the warriors had been defeated. He had felt so secure he had travelled alone, enjoying the peace and solitude it brought. It was the first time since he had arrived in the province that he had had any time to himself.

The fortress itself was a hive of activity and the Prefect of Cavalry was surprised to see so many different units represented. When he presented himself to the sentry he was directed to the Praetorium where he was greeted by Agricola himself. The general warmly grasped Marcus' arm and greeted him as an old friend.

"Marcus, it is good to see you. Thank you for doing such a fine job for me up near Glanibanta." He looked thoughtfully at him. "You are fully recovered from your ordeal?"

"Yes sir. "

"Good for I shall need both you and your cavalry if we are to subdue the north. You now complete my leaders. Return here after the noon break and I can brief all of you at the same time." He smiled. "I think you will find some old friends here."

Marcus did indeed and he was greeted loudly by Furius and Cominius as soon as he entered his quarters. As Marcus looked around Cominius said, "We are no longer the only auxiliaries Marcus. As he glanced around the room he saw that his friend was right; the room was filled with auxiliary prefects some cavalry and some infantry.

"It seems, "said prefect Strabo chewing on the bone of some deceased animal, "that this invasion will not be the work of the legions but of the auxilia."

"I see that the general has carried out his idea."

"What?"

"Oh nothing, it is just something he said while we were travelling to Mona how he could conquer this land with just the auxiliary units. He said that he did not need the legions to conquer the province."

The meeting was the biggest one Marcus had attended and the room was crowded. One wall was dominated by a crude map of Britannia; it was detailed up to the land of the Caledonii but just drifted into nothing north of that. It was a sobering thought for Marcus and the others. They knew not where they were ultimately going and what awaited them there. The superstitious Roman soldier still believed that the edge of the world and the abyss beyond lay somewhere close to this barbaric land.

The only legionary presence was the prefect of the Ninth although Marcus noticed an officer from the Classis Britannica stood in the corner. The rest of the room was filled with an eclectic mix of auxiliary officers. Some of them had the pale skin of northerners, some the olive complexion of the Mare Nostrum but some had the dark skin of Africa. General Agricola had certainly gathered a varied force drawn from all four corners of the Empire.

"Gentlemen. Welcome. I know some of you," he nodded towards the trio of Marcus, Furius and Cominius who were sat together, "from our wars against the Brigante and the Ordovice. Others are new to me. You will all have noticed we only have one legion with us. That is because I am leaving the legions to consolidate our success in the west and maintain order in the north. The Emperor Titus may well need those legions for the wars in Dacia and it is our task," he emphasised the word *our*, "to conquer this province as quickly as possible. I have faith in your ability to defeat the barbarians without the need of our legionary brothers. It is you the auxiliaries who will fight the battles and enable us to win this war. When we win the war, we will have conquered the province. There will be more lands to the west for us to conquer!"

There was a buzz around the room as the prefects commented on and discussed the idea. The general smiled and studied his maps briefly. "You may have noticed a sailor amongst us, Marcus Maenius Agrippa. Some of you may know him from his time in the auxiliary. He knows Britannia and I, for one, am pleased that he is to control the fleet in the east for I also intend to supply us using the fleet as an aggressive arm. Our ships will sail up the east and west coast. They will not only act as supply ships but as scouts for the barbarians have neither ships nor the ability to build them. Our fleet can act with impunity. They can sail into bays and inlets before we arrive and support our attacks with their artillery. First, we will gather at the Taus and conquer the tribes north of Danum Fluvius. Thanks to the Pannonian cavalry and the Batavian infantry this will be easier than it was. I intend to raise local cohorts to build forts and guard the key routes across this mountainous land. That will not be the role of you and your men. You are the cutting edge of my blade not the spade. Others can build, you must fight."

He paused again to allow his comments to sink in. "Another change will be that we will take prisoners if only to provide slaves to help build the buildings in the southern half of this province. I will also try to negotiate where I can. Any questions up to now?" His briefing had been so detailed that all the questions had been answered and the prefects sat, some of them bemused at the radical ideas he had put forward. The only man who looked unhappy was the prefect of the Ninth, Tulius Broccus for he had been relegated to a supporting role, a reversal of the normal way the legions worked. Marcus suspected that Agricola must have spoken to him prior to the meeting for he kept his mouth shut and offered no comment. "We will meet," he pointed at a spot on the map north of Glanibanta at Luguvalium where the Ninth will build a fort. It should control the area and means we have a large base of operations. Those prefects whose units are in that area will sail with me and a cohort of the Ninth to begin the construction. The remainder can rejoin their units and make their way there as soon as possible."

Walking back to their quarters the three prefects who had shared such trials in the north and Wales each caught up on the exploits and events of the others. The two Batavians were most interested to hear of the demise of Aed. "That decurion of yours, he is a handy bugger in a fight. I certainly wouldn't want to face him."

"Me neither Furius and yet he has such a gentle looking face."

Marcus laughed, "His fellow decurions call him the baby-faced killer. It does annoy him but then a few moments later and he is smiling again."

"Well I for one am pleased to be travelling on a ship. It is more comfortable than the roads, or what passes for roads."

"Aye and we will get to see what the land looks like from the sea that has always interested me."

"I didn't see Prefect Bassus. Any idea what happened to him."

"Oh he's here but he is with the surgeon he fell over and broke his arm."

"Fell over Cominius?"

"Fell over drunk. It was Strabo's fault he gave him unwatered wine."

"These Gauls can't handle decent wine. They are too used to drinking gnat's piss. It was a waste of good wine."

"Thank the Allfather you never change prefect."

Furius stopped and looked offended, "Me change? Why should I? I am perfect as I am. I am the perfect prefect."

As the bireme sailed on the sluggish wind northwards Marcus found himself looking south to the towering peak of Wyddfa and the other terrifying mountains which towered over Mona. Despite his assertion to Agricola that he was unchanged by the incident with the wicker effigy it had affected him. It was as close to death as he had come. What had frightened him was that he was not afraid of death in fact part of him wanted to die. That was worrying. Would he feel the same when leading his men for he had their lives in his hands? Would his death wish result in the deaths of friends? His hand went, as it did in times of worry, to the hilt of his sword, the sword of Cartimandua and he found it reassured him. It was the physical link to his closest companions, Ulpius, Macha and the Queen Cartimandua. He could only hope that the Allfather still protected him from himself through the power of the sword.

"Reflecting on the past Marcus?"

He almost jumped when the quiet voice of Agricola spoke. "A little. That campaign changed the way we fought and the way we thought about fighting. Yet we are travelling to the very edge of the known world."

"Yes, but the enemies we face are the same. They all fight the same way. It is only numbers that cause us problems. Our men are worth five of theirs. If we continue to be flexible, to use good defensive positions, to use missiles, men on horse, men on foot then we will beat them." He leaned in confidentially. "Have we ever found a leader who could beat us? Have we ever been in danger of losing a battle?"

Remembering Prefect Demetrius, Marcus found the courage to say. "It was close up near the Taus."

"You are right Marcus and that taught me a valuable lesson. It is the prefects and leaders that I need. If they trust me as I trust them and follow my orders exactly then we shall win." He looked around conspiratorially. "That is why you and the other prefects I have fought alongside before are invaluable. Some of the others may turn out to be like Prefect Demetrius, I hope not but," he looked directly at Marcus, "I would hope that you and the others would tell me next time before a disaster occurs. I need loyalty."

Marcus was shocked, "Are you asking me to spy on the other prefects?"

"No. I am expecting you and Strabo, Sura and Bassus to make sure that all the prefects follow my orders and tell me if you think they are not." His voice had become hard and Marcus could tell that he was being given an order.

"You know you never need to doubt my loyalty sir."

The smile returned, "I know Marcus. I know."

Marcus and his fellow prefects were astounded by the variety of landscapes they viewed. Once they left the estuary and turned north they saw vast beaches backed by huge sand dunes and pine forests. There appeared to be no humans at all, no sign of settlement, house, hut, shack, tumble of twigs, there was nothing to show man's mark on the land. Even as Cominius saw land to the northwest the other two saw the peaks of the land of the lakes slowly rise like a smudge of smoke on the horizon, "That must be an island, look it is steep and has a mountain top but it does not spread like those mountains to the north east."

"There is much more to this province than meets the eye."

"And we are about to see much more of it I believe."

They reached their destination soon after dark and Agricola decided that they would stay on the moored ships rather than risk a camp close to the enemy for although Marcus had cleared south of the estuary the lands to the north were most definitely hostile. The arrangement suited the prefects who enjoyed the fine food and wine of a generous general. "The fleet will be invaluable. I am assigning a marine to each auxiliary unit so that he can translate the signals from the fleet and transmit your requests. As you have experienced they can travel far faster than we on horses or foot. Today we were lucky to be able to use sail but they can row against the wind and still travel faster."

"They do have powerful storms here general."

"The commander knows that but there are many inlets and estuaries such as this one. I have ships from the fleet on the west coast. Even now they are sailing up to Morbium with reinforcements for the east coast invasion."

"Do you think the tribes will fight or negotiate sir?"

"Good question Marcus. I am prepared to fight but I hope to negotiate. The Carvetii proved amenable to diplomacy after the last battle."

Furius let out an enormous belch, "Was that the negotiations which followed the slaughter of thousands of their warriors?"

A slight tic was the only sign that Agricola did not like the comment from the outspoken Batavian. "A good point well-made prefect. But if you remember there were Pictii and Caledonii there that day so they may negotiate having had a lesson paid for by their Carvetii brethren."

As the prefects left the next day to bring their commands to the new camp Agricola said to Marcus, "We will not be needing the fort for a while but we will need it. Do you think the locals would be likely to invest it?"

"I do not think so. We will be leaving the servants and slaves there to maintain the land so it will not be unoccupied. All the men who could fight fled or died. The land is empty. We need to encourage settlers for it is good land."

"I know. Perhaps we will offer those soldiers who have served their time the opportunity to use the land."

Marcus rode back to his fort excited for the first time in many years. He felt that they were on the edge of a major event. It had taken various Roman commanders thirty-five years to defeat the southern half of the province; Agricola had taken less than four to finish the task. However big the land was they were about to invade Marcus had no doubt that this charismatic leader would accomplish that sooner rather than later. He was also filled with anticipation for he would be at the forefront. He would not be on the periphery as he was when Cerialis was governor, relying on the legions, he would be used decisively as in the campaigns in Wales and Mona.

Riding over the saddle near the two lakes he felt almost sad, like coming home for the last time. This fort had been his home for longer than any other place since he had left his home in Spain. He had built it and rebuilt it. He had started a family within it. He had lost comrades around. He knew he should not be sentimental but he could not help it.

"Call out the guard Prefect returning." The bellowing voice of Decius welcomed him back to his command. "Good to have you back sir. When do we leave?"

If Decius had been expecting some time to pack he was mistaken. "Today. The general needs us. We are going to war."

"Today! But…"

"Decius, it is Marcus you are talking to. You and I know that you have everything ready to move and had I said within an hour you would have been ready."

The grin in his face told the prefect he had been right. "Right sir. We taking everything? Knocking it down again?"

"No, we are leaving the servants and the slaves they can continue to maintain it. Send them to me."

While Decius raced around shouting orders to the whole ala, Marcus sat in his office to explain to the slaves and servants what would happen.

"You can't leave us sir. We will work for you in the campaign."

"Thank you Attius, thank you all." He was quite touched that they seemed to hold the command in such high esteem. "We do not know where we will be campaigning but when we return we will be coming home and you need to make sure that we still have a home to come to. Sergeant Cato has arranged that the remounts will be sent from Derventio to here. They will need care. The vegetable gardens you have planted will need to be tended. The animals we have bred will need to be cared for. We are going to do what soldiers do. You who remain here must do what you do. Keep our home safe."

Each one promised and swore the most sacred oaths that they would do so and Marcus felt slightly guilty for he did not know if they would ever return. However, he felt he had done all he could for these people who had served his men so well.

Chapter 10

By the time the Ninth had reached Luguvalium all of the auxiliary forces had arrived. The fleet had sailed up and down the coast ferrying the legionaries to their new fortress. The First Cohort had laid out the site and Marcus was amazed at how quickly it rose from the ground. The fact that it was half built told Marcus that the legion would not be participating in the first part of this campaign. Agricola's engineers had built a bridge close to the fortress and the auxiliary camps were all on the northern bank.

Marcus saw a different side to the general when he was summoned to the headquarters. Agricola was dictating to a clerk and Marcus offered to withdraw but Agricola beckoned him in. "And I would urge you to encourage the chiefs and nobles to adopt Roman habits and customs. To that end I authorise you to build baths, schools and public buildings for the people around Eboracum." He turned to another clerk. "Have copies sent to Lindum, Deva and Luguvalium, just change the names. I will sign them later. Sit down Marcus." He noticed Marcus' look. "We can never win the war simply by winning all the battles. If we can make their leaders Roman then the tribesman will all become Roman. Baths and schools are not expensive and they are certainly cheaper than men's lives. Now then this is what I require of your ala…"

As Marcus walked back to his tent his mind was partly on the instructions he had just been given and secondly the master class in diplomacy he had just received. He thought back to the first governor he had encountered, Marcus Bolanus; it was hard to picture a bigger contrast. Bolanus had despised everything about the natives and went out of his way to disparage and degrade them. Had he not done so perhaps his soldiers would not have approached mutiny and the Brigante might not have rebelled.

"Right Decius, mount the ala, full marching kit and rations for four days. The general has sent a bolt thrower stick it on a pack mule."

"Yes sir." If he was surprised then Decius did not show it. Within the hour the column was moving northwards across the newly finished bridge heading for Novontae territory. Ahead of them Gaelwyn had galloped off and was now a distant speck on the horizon. They appeared to be heading northeast and Decius ventured the question which was on all their minds. "Sir, where are we going?"

"Actually, I don't know." The answer stunned the normally voluble Decurion Princeps into silence. "That is why Gaelwyn is scouting. Do you remember a couple of years ago when Flavinius Bellatoris was wounded, when we defeated the Novontae?" Decius nodded. "Well this is their land but they don't appear to have one place which is a large town. Our job is to find them."

"Find them and fight them?"

"Find them and neutralise them."

"Neutralise them? Is that another way of saying slaughtering them?"

"Not necessarily. If they are small bands then we might be able to frighten them with our numbers or perhaps persuade them that we want nothing from this land, just peace."

"That is, well, that is different."

"You have seen the general. Does he ever do things the way other generals do?"

"Well no," he suddenly started as though stung by a bee, "that's why we were chosen, because we beat them and let them leave with honour."

"Well done, Decius, got it in one."

Puffing up like a child praised for reciting Homer well Decius beamed. "Well now I understand it I can explain it."

"Not yet Decius, let us see how the Novontae take to our invasion of their heartland."

Gaelwyn returned in the mid-afternoon. Marcus was contemplating a camp when the scout galloped in. "There are three settlements close by. One is a hill fort, a Roman day's ride away."

Ignoring the sarcasm Marcus said, "And the other two are they closer?"

"One is in the next valley and the other at the head of the valley."

"Good we will visit the first one. Decius warn the decurions we are going to be in potentially dangerous territory. Be alert but I want hands off weapons. Take your turma to the rear where you can cover us with your archers if there is a problem. Send Gaius and his turma to take your place." Now that he understood the strategy Decius rode cheerfully back with his turma. "Gaelwyn ride next to me. You may need to translate.

"Then perhaps you had better get a duck for these people speak their own language which sounds like ducks mating."

"Just translate, leave the insults to Decius, he has had more practice." When Gaius joined him, Marcus ordered them forward. "Gaius, we are going to try to persuade these people that we are their friends. We may have to fight but I hope not. I have chosen you and your turma because your troopers are like their decurion, calm and measured. That is what we need today Not sparks to ignite fires."

Blushing at the compliment Gaius murmured, "Yes sir. Thank you, sir."

As they crested the rise Marcus saw the tiny stockade of round huts. Their appearance sent the tribesmen into a panic and he saw them racing around like ants when a rock is moved. Keeping his hands from his weapons Marcus and Gaelwyn led the silent column down. He could feel himself sweating; when he had heard the idea put forward by Agricola it had seemed reasonable but what if they unleashed a volley of arrows? He, Gaelwyn and Gaius would be the first to die and then what? The whole thing would be a catastrophe. He saw some armed men rush to bar the gate whilst the others lined the palisade. In itself it was not a barrier; his horses could leap it and his men outnumbered the warriors he could see. He halted the column a hundred paces from the settlement and rode forward with the scout.

Speaking Latin, he said, "I would like to speak to the chief."

There was no reply and Marcus nodded to Gaelwyn who spoke, "The Roman wishes to speak with the chief."

The gate opened a little and a large, squat warrior with an enormous war axe in his hand stepped out. He spoke in halting Latin. "I am Ferdia and I am headman of these people. What do you want we have done nothing wrong?" His tone was that of an injured party who has been accused of some crime.

"I come in peace Ferdia."

"You come in peace with a warband bigger than my whole village. That to me does not look like peace."

"It is not long since the Novontae made war on Romans. I remember a warband raiding close to the hills to the south."

The man nodded. "I was in that warband. We fought your cavalry." He peered at Marcus. "Was it this cavalry force?"

"Yes, it was this cavalry."

"We have been peaceful since then, as we promised."

"You have and yet some of the Novontae joined the Brigante king in rebellion."

"Not from my people."

"Perhaps but how would we know? We need to find who are our friends and who are our enemies which is why we travel as a warband but a warband which brings peace to those who would be our friends."

"Peace?"

"Indeed, my general is moving north to make this land part of Rome and bring the benefits of Rome."

"Wait here Roman."

"What do you think Gaelwyn?"

"This man does not fight."

"I agree."

The warrior returned, without his weapon and he opened the gate. "It is not right that men discuss such things in a field. If your men make camp then we can talk in my home."

"It is good." He turned to the Brigante scout, "Ride back to Decius and ask him to set up camp, but out of sight of the village. I don't want to offend them for our camps look a little too much like forts."

Gaelwyn nodded his approval. "You have learned much from me prefect, including wisdom."

Ignoring the comment, he continued, "Then return to me for I may need your translation skills." He lowered his voice. "I will need you to listen to them speak amongst themselves."

As he ducked into the hut he was hit by a fug of heat from the fire roaring away in the middle. The hut belied its size for, inside there were ten warriors as well as what Marcus took to be Ferdia's family busily preparing the food. There was a space left for the chief and Marcus and after a nodded approval from Ferdia he sat down.

"Thank you for your hospitality Chief Ferdia."

"I am not chief. Our chief died in the raid." He looked carefully at Marcus. "He was the warrior who attacked after our king surrendered."

Marcus remembered it well for the blow had ended the career of Flavinius Bellatoris, a former prefect. "He did not think the terms were honourable."

"He did not but I will not speak ill of the dead for he has passed over."

"And your king?"

"He died in the battle on the other side of the river. There is no king now. For all his family were killed at the battle and we have not chosen our new one yet."

Gaelwyn entered and, after a nod from Ferdia he sat down next to Marcus. An older, very small woman, Marcus took to be Ferdia's wife brought him a bowl and spooned a stew into it. Before she gave some to Gaelwyn she looked him in the eye for even sat down Marcus was almost on eye level. "Do you come for war Roman to kill the last of our children?"

Ferdia shouted, "Woman know your place. You have disgraced me."

Marcus smiled, "No mother. I have come to end the wars so that your children's children can have peace." She nodded and served Gaelwyn. They ate in silence for a while, Marcus realising from the glance given by Gaelwyn that the custom was not to speak whilst eating. In truth, he was enjoying the stew which, like much of the food in the area was gamey and tasty. He could not identify all of the game animals but from the tiny bones there were many small creatures in it. When he had finished Marcus said, "Thank you for the food."

"Now we have eaten, we can talk."

Marcus looked each man in the eye as he spoke for he saw that this was more of a council than a gathering of warriors. "My general wants nothing from your people but peace. He wants to give you buildings for trade and for education. He wants to give you roads and he wants to give you protection."

"We have given you peace without being asked. We need neither buildings nor roads. Why should things change?"

"All things change Ferdia. Neither you nor I are the same boys who played in the fields and hunted rabbits. The buildings we bring are warmer in the winter and cooler in the summer. Our education means you will be able to make more of the things you need. The roads we bring will enable you to travel and trade with other villages. All of this means that you will prosper. The protection we offer means that our ships will stop the Irish raiders coming for your children. Our forts, to the north and to the south, will stop the raids from the Pictii and Caledonii and will stop your children being taken as slaves."

Drinks were brought and Marcus used the opportunity to let the men talk amongst themselves. He noted with satisfaction that Gaelwyn was leaning to one side, the better to eavesdrop. Marcus took a swallow of the liquid which was a honeyed beer. "Good", he said to Ferdia's wife, who this time smiled and nodded.

The conversations petered out and although Marcus had not understood much of what they had said he had not heard raised voices which made him optimistic. "We accept your peace." He stood up, as did all the other men and held out his right arm. Marcus stood up and clasped his arm.

"You are a wise man. For now, we will leave you but, in the spring we will return with men to build and to find what you need. What of the other villages, there are two close by?"

"Briciu is close by and he is a good man, he walks the way of peace these days. He will listen but Sulian; he calls himself chief, likes war and likes power. He has attacked us many times. He has a stronghold."

"Thank you Ferdia for your honesty and your hospitality."

As they rode back to the Roman camp the prefect turned to Gaelwyn. "It looks like Briciu must be the next village along the valley and this Sulian the hill fort."

"It makes life simpler for you prefect for you now know when to war and when to talk." He grinned up at the prefect. "At least the food is better than the camp."

"It is that Gaelwyn."

The following day Marcus called a meeting of his decurions. "Yesterday went well. They want peace, which suits the general and it suits us." Seeing Macro's face, he added," Don't worry Decurion Macro, some of them will be stupid enough to fight."

"Thank you, sir,"

"Today I will take Gaelwyn and the signifier. Decius send out one turma to scout the hill fort and another to be out of sight of the next village but within buccina call. We scared them a bit yesterday. Gaius must have given them a dirty look." The ever affable Gaius started to protest and then realising it was a joke he joined in. "The rest of you can remain in camp but I would like a crew for the bolt thrower, we may need it. Assemble it and hold a competition to see who can fire it effectively. The reward can be no sentry duty for the team during this patrol. Right let's get on with this campaign."

As Marcus rode away Decius turned to Gaius. "This general is the best thing to happen to our prefect in a long time. He is like a new man."

"Aye Gaius, he is as he was when Ulpius gave the orders."

"You are right, you are right. Let's get the patrols out. Agrippa, scout the hill fort. Julius baby sit the prefect."

The village was almost identical to that of Ferdia. Perhaps they had had word sent or the three men posed no threat; whatever the reason the headman, Marcus assumed was Briciu. He too was short and squat with a tonsure of red hair cascading over his shoulders. In his youth, he would have been a powerful man and Marcus could see the scars from battles and combats. "Welcome Roman. What can my humble village do for you?"

The second delivery of the speech was easier and by the end Marcus was convinced that there had been contact between the two villages for there was almost instant acknowledgement that they too would cooperate.

"Sulian now, he is different. He will fight you and if he beats you Ferdia and I will suffer."

"You need not fear, Sulian will not beat us. We have taken hill forts before and we have beaten bullies before. Briciu we are here to stay."

Decius was surprised to see him return so quickly. "We have only had half the turmae training with the bolt thrower. Most are bloody useless but there are a couple of likely lads. Agrippa isn't back yet."

"I wouldn't have expected him. Decurion Demetrius your turma is mounted. Gaelwyn scout the next valley. We'll deal with Sulian tomorrow and then move on."

"Well that is at least three days in the same camp. The lads'll be happy."

Agrippa arrived back shortly before Julius. "We will hear your reports while we eat. Macro went out hunting when he found he was worst bolt thrower in the ala. We have some fine deer and some salmon."

"That lad is a good provider," added the quartermaster licking his greasy lips after having sampled the quality of the venison. He was so happy he provided an amphora of wine to wash it down.

"Right Agrippa. How does the land lie?"

"It won't be easy. The hill fort has a good site. There is a ditch and a palisade. There is just one gate with two small towers. When they saw us they hurled a few insults, manned the walls and began to fill the ditch with spikes. I think we can safely say that they are belligerent."

Macro looked at Julius, who just said, "They want to fight." Macro beamed and continued gnawing on the leg bone.

"We rode around the site. It is quite large but because they only have one gate it makes assault a little easier. The only way out, apart from the gate is to climb over the palisade and we could run any of them down."

"How many warriors?"

"There seemed to be quite a few. I would estimate six hundred or so."

"A large force. We outnumber them but winkling them out is always expensive in terms of losses. It is a good thing we have been training on foot. It will come in handy." An involuntary groan emanated from Decius. "You'll be so fit when we finish Decius you'll be able to enter the running race. How about the crew for the bolt thrower? We will need that."

"We have two sir, the actual team and a backup in case they get hurt or we manage to build another one."

"Build another one?"

"Yes sir. I have a couple of lads in my turma who reckon they could knock one up."

"Good man Vettius. Two would be handy. You might see if they can manufacture bolts. We may be out on patrol for some time. Now Julius what did you and the cheerful Gaelwyn find?"

"He listens well sir." Julius looked around as the decurions fell about laughing. He had not intended it as funny.

"Ignore them lad, they are just plebeians. No sense of dignity."

"Well sir there are two villages in the next valley. I took the liberty of speaking to the headmen." Marcus raised an eyebrow. "Gaelwyn gave me the gist of what you said. I thought it might save time…" he tailed off lamely.

"Don't apologise son. Initiative is a good thing. I approve. And…?"

"They are happy to cooperate. Seems the wars cost them crops and people died of hunger; women and children mainly. They seem very family orientated sir."

"Good. Anything else?"

"They did warn me about the next valley. They said the clans there were very bell… warlike and I got the impression they were looking forward to us pacifying them."

"Excellent. Tomorrow is an important day. Our men will be using new weapons and new tactics. Do not berate them for mistakes. Anticipate where they will make mistakes and eliminate them before they happen. I am hoping to take it tomorrow but whatever the outcome we will return here tomorrow night."

The next day the prefect led his column the short distance to the fort. The bolt thrower was kept a discreet distance away for Marcus wanted to try diplomacy first.

Armed warriors lined the defences and a large man shouted, "What do you want Roman?"

The manner and tone of the question left all who could hear it in no doubt, these Novontae were up for a fight. The palisade bristled with armed and armoured men. "We have come to bring peace to this part of the Roman Empire."

Marcus got no further. "This is not part of the Roman Empire and never will be. You may have been the women who call themselves Brigante but we are Novontae and your bones will bleach white on the green grass of my stronghold."

"Know this Chief Sulian that if you fight us you are dooming your people to servitude. If you embrace us we will provide baths, schools, building, indeed all the trappings of civilisation."

"The only thing I will embrace that is Roman will be the dead bodies you leave in my valley and we spit on your civilisation." With that he dropped his arm and a shower of arrows flew towards them. Every Decurion shouted shields in the same instant but the troopers were well trained enough to protect themselves. What they could not protect was their horses and a few fell, pierced by the barbs. Marcus heard the gasp of anger and knew that it was Sergeant Cato.

"Fall back." They fell back to the jeers of the villagers. "Agrippa take your turma and Vettius' guard the rear and sides. Keep out of arrow range. Just stop them escaping. Decius get some men to bring forward the bolt thrower. Gaius and Lentius get your turma to form a shield wall within bow range of the gate. Metellus and Domitius bring forward your archers behind the shield wall and clear that gate. The rest of you assign horse holders for the turmae and bring the rest in a line one hundred paces behind Gaius and Lentius." He turned to see the assembled bolt thrower being manhandled into position. "Let's see what our new artillery can do. I want you to batter the gate. If you can hit in the same area it will weaken it. When the gate is destroyed then target the towers."

"Yes sir." The men raced off eagerly and placed their weapon in the centre of the shield wall. Already the superior Roman bow was having an effect for they were able to fire not only at the palisade but beyond it. They could hear the cries of pain as the arrows found targets. All the while the barbarians were taunting and jeering but it was noticeably less confident after a few volleys. The jeering stopped altogether when the first bolt whizzed from its thrower. The gate shuddered as the bolt went straight through. The men gave a minor adjustment and the next one landed almost next to the first and this too went through.

"That's got the buggers thinking," smirked Decius. He was correct for they could see the defences they thought had been effective crumbling before their eyes. Four bolts later and the gate was a ruin. As the bolts targeted the towers the archers began to fire directly through the gate and soon the inhabitants learned to avoid showing themselves.

Decius rode up next to Marcus. "Agrippa's in place. This is the easiest assault I have even seen."

"Don't get ahead of yourself Decius we still have to climb the ditch. Are the logs in place?"

"Yes, my lads brought them up."

The plan discussed late into the night was to demolish the tower and gate, keep the defender's heads down, run up with logs to fill the ditch either side of the gate and race in. It had all seemed very easy when they were in their cups. Decius and Marcus were now looking at the slope up which their men would have to run and brave the missiles which were bound to be hurled from the fort.

A very self-satisfied voice said, "Towers gone. Both of them."

"Well stop feeling so proud of yourself and start on the walls either side of the gate." Turning to Marcus Decius said, "Better get the lads in position. You lot go and get the logs."

The middle part of the fort had been turned into a charnel house filled with the limbs and bodies of those hit by the bolts as they carried on through the walls and into people. The palisades on either side of the gap were still filled with the angry barbarians but the middle sixty paces were defenceless.

"Archers and shields move left and right to clear those palisades."

As soon as the troopers moved the defenders increased their rate of fire but the Romans still had the protection of their shields, wood reinforced with leather and metal; the barbarians had no weapons which could penetrate them. The log carriers were moving up the hill preceded by two turmae with shields and javelins. They were under strict orders to keep their javelins and not throw them; once they came to the palisade they could be the deciding factor. The crucial time was when the troopers with the logs had to throw them into the ditch for when they did so they were defenceless. Fortunately, either the archers had run out of arrows or they were not in the right place for only a couple of troopers suffered wounds. As soon as the logs crashed down onto the sharpened stakes they rendered them useless as a defence. The two turma ran at the palisades and hurled their javelins. At the same moment Decius ordered the rest of the ala, including the shield wall and archers to attack. The demoralised defenders were overwhelmed. The troopers ruthlessly hacked down the last of the defenders and then made their way through the stronghold butchering anyone they found who presented opposition. They had learned in Wales and Stagh-Herts that women could be just as deadly as any warrior.

Marcus remained with the bolt thrower, confident that his ala could deal with the tribesmen. A rider raced towards him and Marcus recognised him as one of Agrippa's men. "Decurion Agrippa would like to report that the barbarians tried to escape over the wall. We killed a lot of them and a lot more surrendered. They are women and kids mainly. He wants to know what to do…sir"

Smiling the prefect could understand the decurion's uncertainty. Killing warriors who surrendered was one thing but he knew his men, they would baulk at women and children. "Tell the decurion to secure his prisoners."

Inside the fort the last of the warriors who remained had retreated into the central part near to the chief's hut. The chief stood there with his last few guards around him. Decius signalled to the archers who drew back their bows. There was no point risking his men when they could kill them at a distance.

"You cowards is there no one who will face me alone, man to man!"

Macro caught Decius' eye and nodded. Decius just said, "Kill his men." In an instant, every warrior lay dead and Chief Sulian looked stunned.

Marcus stepped out his spatha held easily in his hand. Behind the chief the remaining women and children cowered as they watched their leader face the huge Roman. Roaring with rage Sulian threw himself forward slicing his two-handed sword at Macro's head. The decurion's head moved just before the blow connected and Macro punched the chief, who was off balance, in the side with the boss of his shield. He fell in an undignified heap on the floor which made him even angrier. He stabbed forward and Macro deflected it, slicing into the top of the chief's leg as his guard dropped.

"Macro! Stop pissing about and kill the bastard!"

Looking like the cat who has had had his mouse taken away from him Macro seemed to dance forward in a series of punches from his shield and stabs with his blade. Suddenly it was over and the chief lay there riddled with six or seven mortal wounds.

Patting him on the back Decius said, "Glad you are on our side old son."

Later that afternoon as the stronghold burned a sorry stream of prisoners was herded by Agrippa towards their camp. Marcus sought out Julius. "Find that marine. We have some orders for him. Decius, hobble them and make sure they can't escape. Get a corral or something built. Cato should be able to help you. Gaius give me a casualty count. Lentius collect up all the weapons and take them to the two friendly villages. Say it is a gift."

Decius stopped giving instructions to Quintus Augustus and said, "Are you sure that is wise? Arming them? They could turn nasty."

Marcus shook his head, "No I have met them and they will not besides can you think of a better way of showing that we trust them? They have no defences if they did rebel Macro could take them with one turma and not suffer a casualty. Trust me Decius this is the right way."

"Sir?"

The marine stood before Marcus. "Sorry we haven't got to use you before but we need a message sending to the fleet. Can you do that?"

"Yes sir. They will be off that point," he gestured to the south, "tomorrow morning."

"Good I want you to go there and ask them to take these slaves off my hand. I'll send the prisoners and guards with you."

"Yes sir."

Later that night Marcus wrote up his report for the general. So far it had gone better than expected; if the fleet could take the prisoners off his hands then that would free him up to continue his pacification of the Novontae. Decius joined him with two beakers of wine. "Think we deserve this sir."

"What was the butcher's bill?"

"Six men dead. Twenty wounded, two seriously."

"Too many Decius, too many."

"But sir we killed over four hundred warriors."

"We may have to do this ten, twenty times. Do the sums, that would mean we would lose one hundred and twenty dead and four hundred wounded. Could we operate effectively then?"

"But reinforcements sir."

"You know how long it takes to train a recruit and that is when we are in a permanent camp. Here we are on campaign we can't afford the time. Next time we use two bolt throwers and double the archers. It might take us a little longer but the barbarians are not the most patient of enemies, I suspect they would not bother to wait for us to attack, they would attack us."

"Perhaps you are right sir. It just seems a funny way to win the war."

The next day after Quintus and Vettius had escorted the prisoners to the fleet Marcus and the rest of the ala headed west. As they passed the four villages which had accepted the peace Marcus was pleased to see them waving. It was a good sign. He suspected that word would have spread from village to village about Sulian's demise. In one way that was good for it gave out the right message about opposing Rome, on the other hand it warned the two hill forts in the next valley of their imminent arrival. They could have more time to prepare for the Romans and create more problems.

Chapter 11

They had just finished the camp when the two turmae returned with the marine. "Any problems?"

"No, it went well. We got some supplies from the captain and we gave him your reports."

"Good get yourself some food and then come to my tent afterwards to discuss the next phase of the campaign."

The prefect looked round at his decurions. They had grown into an efficient team. They each had friends they preferred to work with, Agrippa and Lentius, Gaius and Macro, Julius and Decius but they could work with any other decurion. They all deferred to Decius but he never took advantage of that. He saw that they were easy in each other's company. They joked and laughed and took the ribbing which was inevitable in a male society. He could not ask for better officers.

"Gaelwyn has scouted the two hill forts and it seems that they have got wind of our little incursion. Warriors are pouring in to help defend them. The good part of that is that when we defeat them," his decurions all grinned at each other when he used the positive words, '*when we defeat them*'; it was another sign that they would win, "there will be few enemies left to fight and we should be able to negotiate as young Julius so ably demonstrated the day before yesterday. I will not attack until we have another bolt thrower built and while it is being built I want the willow we saw down by the stream cutting and making into man sized shields, not to hold as a shield but to be a barrier to protect the archers and artillery. If we weave the willow we can still see though it but it should stop the arrows that they use. If we get them finished tomorrow then we attack the day after. Any questions?"

"Sir?"

"Yes Decius?"

"You did mention to me about more archers."

"Good man! Of course. I want one in two of your men armed with a bow. We know they can use them and it demoralises the enemy. In addition, Gaelwyn said that the two hill forts are close enough to support each other which means we will have to watch one while we attack the other. We will have fewer troops available." He was delighted that the idea did not affect them. They were confident enough that they would succeed, no matter what was thrown at them.

The following day the prefect took Decurion Demetrius and Gaelwyn with him while he confirmed the negotiations at the villages which had acceded to the Roman demands. Decius chivvied and chased the men manufacturing the bolt thrower and spare bolts. The rest of the ala practised with their bows.

"Thank you for taking me along sir."

"You deserve it Julius. It was a good idea to offer them peace. The sooner we can pacify this area the sooner we can move on to the harder nut which is Caledonia."

It was a pleasant day to be riding with a pleasant breeze from the south bringing the tang of the sea. The birds were busily singing and everything was green and lush. The three men found that they did not need speech to fill the silence. Eventually Julius ventured. "Sir do you think I have a future in the auxiliary?"

"You have had a letter from your father."

"How did you know sir?"

"I knew you had had a letter and you have been a little quieter of late as though debating something."

"Yes sir. He thinks I ought to return to Rome and take my place in the Senate or perhaps join one of the Emperor's legions in the east, where I will attract more attention."

Marcus pondered this for a few moments. "Both good choices and were you my son and I was an important patrician I might make the same suggestions. The east and the Emperor is where the glory is. Rome is where the power is. Here we are a backwater at the end of the civilised world. If you were in the east or Rome you would be amongst civilised peoples with all that attends its, fine food, comfort and the potential for great glory. Here you will never find glory for who cares about Britannia, apart from the general of course. The divine Claudius used it to get himself a brief moment of glory and then promptly forgot about it."

"So you are saying Rome or the east is a better choice?" Julius was confused. He had expected the prefect to try to talk him out of a move; perhaps he was not bothered if the young man stayed or not.

"No Julius I am saying if I were your father I would suggest those choices. As a father, you want the best for your son in your world. This is my world Julius. I was taken from my family before my eighth summer. I have never lived anywhere which is civilised. I have never sought glory, fame or power. For me the First Pannonian Cavalry is all I aspire to. Had my family still been alive I might have said that this was part of my journey to a quiet life raising horses with my son but that can never be." Julius was touched by the sadness in Marcus' voice. "As for your question which was have you a future then I will give you a totally different answer. I will give you the answer I would give to any of my young decurions, Gaius, Macro, and Domitius, any of them. You have a future in this ala because this is my family. You especially could rise to the highest rank, you could be prefect but that will never bring with it the status of a legionary posting or the glory of the east nor the power of the Senate. But you do have a future here Julius. A future with comrades who would fight for you, bleed with you and die for the ala." He looked at the wide eyed young man. "Does that answer your question?"

"Yes sir. I will write to my father and tell him I am staying in Britannia."

"Good for that is the answer I wanted."

Gaelwyn riding behind them smiled. For a Roman Marcus had much of the Brigante about him. He admired the prefect's sense of family, not just blood but comrades. He admired the fact that he fought so hard for what he believed in but most of all he admired him because he cared about everyone.

Late in the afternoon they rode back into the camp. Decius had worked hard and they could see the second bolt thrower being assembled next to a pile of bolts. The Decurion Princeps wandered over to the prefect as he rode in. "How did it go sir?"

"It went well. Young Demetrius had done the hard part. They seemed to quite like him. Perhaps it is his young innocent face."

"Good job you didn't send me then. One sight of this ugly gnarled tree trunk of a face and we would have had a war."

Marcus laughed. "One thing you will learn as a leader is use the weapons you have to their best advantage. When we attack tomorrow it will be your ugly face which leads it. I hope to terrify them into submission."

"Did you visit their fort?"

"Aye. They are about two miles apart. It will be difficult for when we attack one the other can attack us."

Julius was still with them. "Like Vercingetorix and Caesar at Alesia."

Decius looked up at him, "What? Where?"

"Julius Caesar was attacking the Gauls at their stronghold and he was surrounded by another Gaulish army. He had to fight on two sides. You know your history Julius."

"Having been given the name Julius my father made me read the Gallic Wars until I could recite it."

"You have given me an idea. The two forts face each other. They are like the one we destroyed yesterday, one way in and out. They must have had conflict at some time because the gates face each other. If we make our camp and siege works between them we can turn the bolt throwers to repel attacks. Well done Julius. I had, to my shame, forgotten Caesar." Julius blushed, a habit he wished he could lose. "We will also have to dig some ditches to slow down any counterattack."

Decius groaned. "I long for the days when we just rode around on our fat arses admiring the scenery."

Winking at Julius Marcus said, "Funny that."

"What do you mean?"

"Well Decius that is what young Julius and I did today and it was very pleasant!"

The column took most of the day to reach the belligerent hill forts. Rather than try the diplomatic route straight away Marcus instead, set half the ala to building a camp equidistant from the two hill forts. The other half remained in readiness for any sortie. The barbarians did indeed jeer and shout but the armed warriors kept them at a distance. With this incentive, the troopers worked twice as hard and had the camp erected in a time which impressed even Decius. "Looks like the threat of a Novontae arrow up the arse makes them work harder than my vine staff."

"I want one in three men on duty tonight Decius. I know we will have tired men tomorrow but we cannot risk a night attack."

"I'll rotate them sir. If we use the hourglass we can make sure that everyone gets some sleep."

It was while Agrippa and Lentius were on duty, just before dawn that the attack came. Their attackers came from the hill fort to their left, the one with a chief called Moffat. The warriors approached silently and would have made the vallum had one of the attackers not fallen in the ditch, crying out as he fell. There were many alert defenders and the attack was easily beaten off in a shower of javelins. Later when questioned by Decius about the lack of an alarm for the camp Agrippa explained, "It happened too quickly and they just took off when they found their sneak attack had failed. Sorry sir. Our hands were full but they never even looked like they would get over the ditch let alone the vallum."

Marcus was pleased that they had repelled the warriors. They took the fifteen bodies from the ditch and slung them on the backs of mules. Marcus and Decius led a turma as an escort for the bodies. They approached Moffat's hill fort and, outside arrow shot they unloaded them. As a trooper led the mules back Decius, Gaelwyn and Marcus approached the gate.

"No further Roman."

"We have returned the bodies of those foolish warriors who attacked us last night. It was an unprovoked attack."

The voice bellowed from the tower. "Unprovoked? You build a fort next to our home and you say you are not provoking us?"

"It is our custom to build camps wherever we travel. Our friends do not find it worrying."

"We are not your friends. Take your customs back over the river to the cowards who like you. We do not and we want nothing to do with you."

"Many villages nearby believe we are friends. They have welcomed Rome."

"Did Sulian welcome Rome? No and where are his bones now? I do not trust you Roman. Now leave my land before we destroy you."

"I will give you the same warning I gave Sulian. Join with us and become part of Rome; receive the benefits civilisation brings or fight us and all your warriors will be destroyed and your people sold into slavery."

"Brave words from a handful of horse soldiers. We will fight you and we will keep our freedom."

"I am sorry to hear that Chief Moffat for this will be the last time we will talk. You have just signed your own death warrant."

As they rode back they heard the gates open and their warriors race out to claim the bodies of their dead.

"Well you warned him fair and square sir."

"They will fight prefect. While you were talking I could see warriors arming and preparing to attack."

"Thank you Gaelwyn. Decius as soon as we get back I want two turmae as a mounted response. The rest can dig a ditch, about here. That should be out of arrow range. When that is complete bring up the bolt throwers, wicker protection and the archers we will start the bombardment as we did at Sulian's. You can then dig another ditch four hundred paces from the other side of the camp just in case Caolan's warriors decide to take advantage of our assault. Let Lentius watch that side."

The barbarians had never witnessed siege works before and they did not know how to react. Inside his stronghold Moffat was having an argument with his headstrong young warriors. "I have seen Romans fight before and they are well organised. They do not fight as we do. Keep to the plan. When they attack us Caolan will attack them while they attack us."

"Can we trust that cattle thief?"

"Cian, you are bitter. You have a blood feud filling you with such thoughts. We have to forget such things until we have beaten our common enemy."

"Yes, I have a blood feud but look they are busy digging. If we attack now we will kill some of them."

"I listened last night to Quinn and now we only have their bodies and no dead Romans."

"Let me take my oathsworn. We are young and we are fearless. Let me kill some Romans."

Moffat could sense the mood of anger. Cian was a rival if he held firm now he might lose his life with a knife in the back. Letting Cian loose would appease those more aggressive and his failure would diminish the threat to his power. "Very well but just kill a few and get back here we cannot afford losses."

"Watch a real warrior Moffat and you will see that we will have no losses."

The fifty warriors gathered behind the gate. At a nod from Cian the gate swung open and the warband raced out. The men digging were Quintus' men and as soon as they heard the roar they dropped their tools and took up their shields. Behind them they heard the buccina and. felt immediately more confident for Vettius and his turma were already racing to their aid. Although the wedge of warriors hit them hard and managed to push them back a few paces their shields and mail took the brunt of any blows which the barbarians managed to land. Cian's war hammer did smash through the skull of a young trooper but the eager barbarian's joy was short lived as an arrow thudded into his arm. Realising they were now outnumbered the oathsworn grabbed their leader and ran back as quickly as they could. By the time they had made the safety of the stronghold eight bodies littered the patch of earth between the trench and their walls.

Moffat looked down at the pale face of Cian. "One Roman dead and eight less warriors to defend our homes. Next time you will listen to me not young pups who are barely weaned!"

At the ditch Quintus, clasped Vettiius' arm. Thanks, Vettius for coming to our aid. Take Gaius Vetriculus' body back to the fort we will bury our comrade later."

By the time the noon break had arrived the ditches were built and the bolt throwers were in place. The Romans could see the heads of the barbarians as they peered from the towers and palisades at this strange style of warfare. The rear trench still had to have its stakes embedded but apart from that it was finished. "Let your men have a break. They all lost sleep last night. Make sure they get a good meal. It is going to be a long afternoon."

"Yes Decurion Princeps."

Inside Caolan's stronghold they had to peer in the distance to see what was happening. "Lugh, you have younger eyes what can you see?"

"They have finished their ditches and now they look to be eating and drinking."

"These Romans wage war in a strange way. Can you see their mounted men?"

"Yes, they are just behind the wood to the left."

"It is obvious that they want to ambush us if we attack. Well we can counter that." He turned to his lieutenants. "Before we attack them we will slip a small band around the rear of the woods then they can attack the horse warriors with arrows, spears and stones. After they have been destroyed we will attack them while they are busy attacking Moffat. Take them over the furthest side of the stronghold and follow the burn. That way they will not see you."

"What about those ditches?"

"We will bridge them with the logs I had the men prepare."

His lieutenants were far more confident about Caolan as a leader than Moffat's were. He was a cunning and careful warrior who had survived the debacle of the Taus. Many felt he would be the next king of the Novontae when the Romans were eventually beaten and his men looked forward to slave raids once more.

"Ready Decius?"

"Yes sir, the rest break helped."

"Begin the assault." Just as at Sulian's the inhabitants hid in terror as the bolts screamed into the gates. The arrows rained death on those who had neither shield nor shelter and soon Moffat directed all to move from the walls save those with armour and shields. It was almost identical to their first assault, the main difference being the extra bolt thrower which added to the devastation. The two bolt throwers destroyed the gates and towers in a very short time.

"Ready for the assault sir?"

"Not yet. I will take two turma and join Lentius to watch the other fort. I will sound the buccina when it is time."

While the prefect made his way to Lentius Decius continued to demolish the walls. With two bolt throwers, it was a far more efficient and deadly process. Decius wondered what carnage ensued for when they had sacked Sulian's the bodies had been mangled so much that they did not appear to be human. With two in action the results would be twice as horrific.

Marcus arrived close to the woods with the two turmae of Julius and Domitius and greeted Lentius. "Any sign of movement?"

"Not yet but they have been in the towers watching our movements so they know what we are about."

"Right. Sound the buccina." The strident notes of the buccina echoed over the hillsides and they heard the roar as the troopers advanced up the hill.

"Look sir." Julius pointed to the other fort. The gates were opening. "You were right sir."

"It is one thing to make the right decision and another to ensure you benefit. Form line."

His turmae formed an oblique line from the woods and he waited for the barbarians to emerge. He needed them in the open and far enough away from the safety of their own stronghold for he wanted this [part of the campaign over with quickly. If he could destroy these two then the rest of the Novontae might fall into line. As the force emerged the prefect could see them glancing over to their left. They knew there were Romans there. "They know we are here. Watch out for tricks. Ready your weapons."

It was as they were preparing to advance that the ambush was sprung. Slingshots and arrows rained down upon them striking them on their unprotected right side. "Lentius, Domitius wheel! Julius advance on the warband."

It was as they wheeled that Lentius was struck. First, a slingshot cracked into his skull making a noise like an egg breaking and at the same time, an arrow slammed into his chin as his head was jerked back. He was dead before he hit the ground. "Follow me!" Marcus drew his sword and headed into the woods. They could not afford an enemy in the rear and Julius would have to manage the best that he could. The barbarians took to their heels and began to outstrip the horsemen who found the confines of the woods difficult. "Domitius keep after them. Turma three follow me."

The enraged turma were desperate to avenge their leader and they wheeled in a tight line behind the prefect. As they emerged from the woods they saw that the barbarians had reached the ditches and laid logs across them. This meant they were in single files and Julius had wisely taken his turma to the other side of the ditch where his men were picking off the warriors as they gingerly came over one by one. Those who rushed found themselves impaled on the sharpened stakes. Marcus led his turma around the right of the warband to encircle them. With only two turmae they could only slow down the advance. "Use your javelins and bows. Thin them out."

Half of the warriors who had not crossed the ditch formed a wedge and began to advance towards Lentius' turma. They had equipped themselves with shields and the barrage on them was not as effective as it might have been. It was necessary to destroy them. "Reform!" His men thought him mad for they had to withdraw to get into line. The warband thought it was a retreat and began to hurry forwards, eager to get to grip with these horse warriors who had thinned their ranks so much. Once in their line Marcus shouted, "Those with javelins throw them at ten paces the rest draw your swords." Yelling, "Lentius!" The line roared forward like a tethered sapling which is released. The warband looked in horror as nearly forty horses and a wall of iron raced towards them. They huddled closer together to give maximum mutual protection and they braced themselves for the impact. Suddenly the front ranks were thinned as javelins thrown at the closest distance ripped through them making holes in their defensive wall. The horses naturally went for the gaps that appeared before them and, with the sword of Cartimandua singing as it sliced through the air the turma broke into the shield wall.

Julius was struggling to hold the barbarians who had forced his turma back with arrows and spears. Caolan himself led the band and he had smashed one trooper who had gotten too close to him with his war hammer. He then sprang lithely on to the back of the dead trooper's mount and his men roared as they charged towards the bolt throwers now less than eight hundred paces away.

The bolt throwers themselves were being rapidly turned to face the new threat for the rest of the ala was inside the stronghold. The only force which remained to help them was the beleaguered turma of Julius now down by four troopers.

Turning to his troopers Julius shouted, "We will have to charge them in the flank! Close order, knee to knee."

One of the veterans laughed and shouted, "Just like your brother taught us."

"Yes Livius, just like my brother taught us! Charge!"
It was a forlorn charge for they were outnumbered three to one and the barbarians had their shields to protect their sides; in addition, the charge was uphill but still it was a glorious charge. The momentum carried them into the heart of the warband just as the first bolt thrower managed to turn and fire its first bolt. It sliced through six warriors killing three and badly wounding three. As the second bolt screamed through them the effect was instantaneous, they turned and ran back to the safety of their fort.

Caolan was apoplectic with rage. "Come back you scum! You cowards." He could see that they were not heeding him and, as he was mounted he took off towards the west. Julius watched impotently as he escaped them for he and his men were still engaged in a frantic combat with those who remained before them.

When those fighting Marcus saw their comrades running they followed them and soon there was a horde returning to the stronghold, from the battlefield and from the woods. "Sound pursuit!" Tired though they were every trooper obeyed the order and the remnants of three turmae pursued an enemy twice their number. Those who still remained in the stronghold of Caolan vainly tried to close the gates but those fleeing the carnage burst through. Soon the troopers were in the settlement with those being pursued and the slaughter began. The leaderless Novontae saw that it was hopeless and one by one threw down their weapons, the trickle became a torrent and soon the exhausted troopers who remained found themselves in control of the stronghold. They looked around in surprise when they heard a cheer in the distance and saw troopers waving from Moffat's stronghold. Both citadels had fallen at almost the same moment.

Later as they herded the prisoners into two groups, the warriors and the women and children, Marcus surveyed the battlefield. He had hoped to finish it quickly but he had not expected to do so in one day. Nor had he expected to lose so many men, good men. Looking down at the body of Lentius he suddenly realised that the only two left from Ulpius' turma were himself and Gaius. He knelt down to touch his old comrade's body as though by touching it the death would be gone and Lentius would laugh and joke with him once more.

"He looked after me." The prefect looked up to see Gaius, tears streaming unashamedly down his blood streaked face. "When I first joined, I knew nothing then, just a little kid really; he made sure no-one took advantage of me. Him and Drusus they were like big brothers. They taught me how to be a trooper and when he became decurion he still made sure no-one took advantage of me. He showed me how to become a warrior that men could respect and follow and now he has gone."

"As we shall all go one day. Our band of brothers is becoming fewer. And Gaius you too do what Lentius does, I have seen you with Julius, which is why this ala will survive stronger and more powerful because no matter which of us falls, and it could be you or me just as easily as Lentius, we know we have trained better men to follow us."

"Sir?"

Marcus looked round as Gaius wiped his face with his neck cloth. "Yes trooper?"

"Decurion Princeps compliments sir and he has secured the field. Decurion Macro has returned. No sign of that Caolan."

"Thank you, trooper, I will rejoin him shortly." Gaius turned to face him. "Are you ready to face your men?"

Giving a sad smile, he murmured, "Yes sir."

It was late in the evening when the decurions not on duty managed to congregate in the prefect's tent. They all had sombre, reflective faces. Lentius was not mentioned but the empty space between Gaius and Decius spoke volumes. "How many the Decius? How many did we lose?"

"More than we wanted sir. Sorry about that. I know you wanted to keep the casualties down."

"Perhaps I should have told the enemy and not you. How many?"

"Thirty-eight dead and forty wounded six seriously. And…" he tailed off superstitiously not naming Lentius as though naming him made him finally dead. "The good news is that we captured more than we hoped." He looked anxiously at Marcus. "The general won't be unhappy that we let the warriors live will he? I mean I could get the lads to go around and slit their throats."

Marcus flashed his deputy an angry look and then thought better of it. “No there has been enough killing. Julius, I want you to go with the marine tomorrow and signal the fleet. I suspect the warriors will be bound for Rome either the ludos or the salt mines. Either way they will die soon enough. I intend to keep the camp here and use it as a base. It will prevent the re-occupation of the forts and save our depleted numbers from having to build a camp each night. Besides Gaelwyn has told me that we are no more than half a day’s ride from the coast. You might as well know that I think there will be no more fighting. Instead I want all of you to adopt Julius’ style of negotiation and persuade the villagers to accept Roman rule. If anyone does not wish to accept the Pax Romana then we fight but I think they will acquiesce. Anyone we are uncertain of we take hostages. Tomorrow I will assign you all a patrol area except for Macro, I want you to find this Caolan, take Gaelwyn with you. He has pretensions of greatness according to the prisoners and fancies himself king. If you find him…kill him.”

Chapter 12

It was drawing towards the short days of the year when the First Pannonians finally negotiated a peace with the whole of the Novontae. As they headed for their meeting with the fleet Metellus and Agrippa were discussing the pleasures which awaited them in Luguvalium. "Well I am looking forward to the baths and warm barracks. This is a bleeding cold country."

"Me? I just want a woman."

"A woman? What about the prisoners, you could have one of them."

"I want a woman who smells nice and does look like her husband without a beard."

"Too choosy you are that's your trouble. Too choosy."

They were both in for a disappointment. After he had boarded the bireme with the last of the hostages Marcus came back with a wry smile on his face. Summoning the decurions he held a short briefing. "Well gentlemen we will not be returning to Luguvalium."

"Not back to Novontae country. It's too bleeding cold there."

"No Decius we are going east to Coriosopitum."

"Where is that?"

North of here, actually north west in the land of the Votadini. It seems the general has built or is building a fortress there and we are going to join him. Seems he is impressed by our work here, a single ala to pacify a whole tribe. We are the victims of our own success."

"Well there goes your bath Agrippa."

"And the women there will make the Novontae looked like goddesses. There is a saying about the Votadini, that is where men are men and so are the women!"

The ala once again suffered the deprivations of northern winters with winds which whistled in from the east bringing biting, savage winds to discover every gap in clothes no matter how tightly wound; the rain which came not only vertically but horizontally. The fogs and mists ate into a man's bones until his very teeth ached with the cold. The only difference between this trek and the others they had endured was that they at least had won peace and did not need to worry about Brigante and Carvetii armies. The general had subdued the land between Dunum Fluvius and Tine Fluvius by a mixture of diplomacy, hostages and, where the locals were totally belligerent, ruthless warfare.

"The thing is sir he has done that with a legion and six or seven auxiliary units."

"I know Gaius but he had more enemies to deal with. The furthest north we travelled was Morbium. Where we were we had been grinding down the opposition for years. We had it easy. Don't look down in the mouth I am more than proud of what we achieved and I know the governor will feel the same. We are one army each doing its own part."

Gaius was, in fact, speaking for the ala for they felt he did not get the credit he deserved. Gaius knew how long Marcus Aurelius Maximunius had served and how many campaigns he had fought. There was not another leader who had given as much to Britannia.

When they reached Coriosopitum they cared not that it was half finished nor that it was occupied by the Ninth; they only cared that they had reached their destination. What worried Decius was that he could not see any other auxiliary units. "Why is that? It does not bode well for us. I bet the general has something special in mind."

"Something special Decurion Princeps?"

"Aye and probably nasty too. Mark my words."

When they arrived, the general asked them to build a marching camp next to the fort. "See that means we aren't staying. What did I tell you?"

Decius had nearly organised the camp when Marcus returned from his meeting with the general. He was smiling which did not put Decius at his ease."

"Well sir?"

In answer to your question about the other units, they are spread across the frontier. Seems this is the narrowest part, so far as we know in the whole of Britannia. We can control this neck of land with the legion and our auxilia. We will have a proper camp for the winter. We are the last to arrive. The other prefects will be coming tomorrow and then we leave for our camp the day after. Happy?"

"Behind every black cloud is a bloody bigger one ready to piss all over you. That's Britannia for you."

After a night in another cold camp the ala was not in a happy mood. Having just spent the best part of half a year subjugating a land almost as big as Brigantia with less than fifty losses their reward was to build another camp in the middle of winter and spend the rest of the winter freezing in the most desolate land the gods created. The prefect however seemed positively cheerful. When they saw the prefects beginning to arrive, Gaius drew the prefect's attention to the fort. "Shouldn't you be getting over there sir? You don't want to be late."

"Don't worry Gaius I won't be late and I have lots of time."

Marcus was just checking the store situation with the Quartermaster and Attius his clerk when Decius came racing into the store tent. "Sir, the general and the prefects. They're here, they're coming here now. From the fort sir."

Marcus smiled for he had never seen the Decurion so flustered. "Better call out the guard then hadn't you Decius?"

"Yes sir. Will do. Right away."

Turning to the other two Marcus said, "We'll finish this after the general's visit."

The whole camp turned out to see the most senior panoply of officers they had ever seen. Marcus was amused to see decurions coming on parade with their best armour and polished swords. Agricola dismounted and clasped Marcus closely around the shoulders. "Good to see you prefect, good to see you." Those close enough to the two men were perplexed to see the general wink at the prefect who seemed very relaxed for such a high-profile visit. The general turned to address the whole camp. "First I would like to thank all of you in front of the other prefects and your able commanding officer for the incredible work you did in the land of the Novontae. To have taken so vast a land, with so few men and resources and to do it with such a small loss of life is miraculous and I salute you." Theatrically he took off his helmet and gave a small bow.

Gaius immediately regretted all his churlish thoughts. Here was the credit which the ala and the prefect deserved. However, the general had not finished. In recognition of this and bearing in mind that there are very few Pannonians left in the ala due to their lengthy and valuable service in Britannia, we have decided to rename this ala, Marcus' Horse."

The unprompted and universal cheer took even Agricola by surprise and he turned to Marcus and said, "Popular decision eh?" Holding up his hand for silence he continued. "I know you will all continue to go from strength to strength and continue to do such magnificent deeds. From now on all cavalry volunteers from the Brigante, Carvetii and other native tribes will be recruited into Marcus' Horse." He remounted his horse. "Well prefect if you would care to join the other prefects and myself in the Praetorium we can have our briefing and perhaps a small celebration."

Sergeant Cato brought out Argentium looking resplendent and groomed. Decius flashed a look at Cato. As Marcus left he smiled at Decius and said, "Carry on Decurion."

"Sir." When the entourage had left Decius and the others turned on poor Sergeant Cato." You were in on it, weren't you?"

"I only knew this morning. The prefect said there would be a parade and he wanted Argentium to look his best. I was sworn to secrecy. I didn't know about the name honestly Decius."

"Yes well," unable to contain his joy he then beamed a smile at all of them. "Well tonight Quartermaster the best wine I think and Macro go out and hunt us something special. Marcus' Horse is going to begin as it means to carry on with a real feast!"

In the Praetorium Marcus' back was becoming sore with all the backslapping. His two Batavian friends were particularly overjoyed. "Gentlemen let us get on with the briefing before poor Marcus' back breaks. "First I would like to welcome Centurion Aurelius who is the training officer for our new unit the Usipi. Once they are trained the centurion will command them. They are a new unit from Germania and the centurion can speak their language. The rest of you know each other." He pointed at the map on the wall. "We have done very well since we began our advance; in fact, far better than I would have expected. However, if the rest of the province thinks we are going to rest they are mistaken. During the winter, I want all of you to continue to patrol and offer Pax Romana. If there is opposition either take hostages or defeat them. Speed is of the essence. The tribes seem to think winter is a time when we do not war they are wrong and they will find out soon how wrong they are."

The following day both men and officers had thick heads which did not make their move west along the road that would soon be known as the Stanegate comfortable. This almost took the sour look from Decius' face for it meant they did not have as much mud as usual. The land however did not suit him for it was an open windswept heath which just rolled north into the country of the Selgovae. "I told you a bloody cold billet and knife wielding bollock stealers within spitting distance."

Marcus turned to his friend and said caustically, "Good to see the temporarily happy Decius was just aberrance."

The winter was indeed cold and the new force of Marcus' horse was worked hard as they gradually increased and enlarged the territory controlled by Rome. As Decius said the country did have the advantage of being flatter than Wales. Agricola wisely avoided using the horse in the vast forests which split the country in two. Instead they patrolled the eastern coastal plain dotted with fishing villages and small hill forts. Ill-prepared for any kind of winter fighting the inhabitants acquiesced to the Roman demands with almost ridiculous ease. The odd chief who appeared belligerent was made to offer up family hostages and the Agricolan war machine rolled ever northwards.

Agricola called a conference of all his prefects at the coast where the Classis Britannica was gathering for a final push around to the Bodotria Fluvium. "This is going far better than we could have hoped. The fleet commander has drawn a map of the river and he believes, and I agree with him, that the river would be a perfect site for a string of self-supporting forts. To that end the infantry will continue to push northwards. I would like the Gaulish cavalry to maintain their patrols along the east coast."

He turned to Marcus, "Prefect I have something different in mind for you. I would like you to return to the land of the Novontae, partly to show our presence there, partly to ensure that peace still remains but mainly to continue up the coast as far north as the Clota Fluvium for I believe that is where the string of forts will end." The other prefects shared a look which told Marcus that they thought his task one that none would envy. "It is a difficult assignment I realise but you have shown an affinity for that country and people. You will have the sole support of the Classis Britannica on the west coast and you should be well supplied."

"What do I do if I encounter opposition greater than I can handle?"

Agricola smiled at the prefect, "That would indeed be a mighty army if Marcus' Horse could not deal with it. However, you are right and we should make contingency plans." He turned to the centurion of the Usipi cohort. "Centurion your cohort can build a fort," he pointed at the map, "here that should enable us to communicate across land should the prefect require support and it will also give you the opportunity to train your men." The centurion had confided to Marcus that the Usipi were the most obnoxious and arrogant bunch of auxiliaries he had ever trained. The building of a fort would give him the opportunity to knock some of the edges off them. "I will send a cohort of the Ninth to assist you and, er help with the training."

The centurion sighed and said gratefully, "Thank you sir."

"Any further questions? No? In that case, Prefect, I hope to see Marcus' Horse in the spring."

The journey through the trackless lands of the north was a hard ride but one which Marcus knew they had to do. He chose a route which approached his friendly villages from the north rather than the south. This was mainly because he had missed them out the previous year and he felt it important to get the feel of the land. The chiefs were more than pleased to see Marcus and, as he shared their food he discovered that life had improved since the eradication of the warlike chiefs. "Where did Caolan go?"

"We heard that he fled to the Dumnoni and he had joined a warband there. They live to the north west close to the wild islands."

Thanking them it gave Marcus food for thought. He had hoped to use the same strategy as the previous year using negotiation rather than force, the fact that Caolan had found sympathetic tribesmen meant he was more like to have to fight. At least when he fought the next time he would have naval support which meant increased artillery support.

The next few weeks saw them cross the trackless lands to the sea. They were further west now than any Roman soldier had ever been and although the Novontae there did not offer any opposition Marcus had to spend longer than he wished negotiating peace. They were camped with the tiny settlement of Girvan when the local chief, an ancient warrior called Keir drew Marcus to one side. "The Irish often raid us here and take our young as slaves. This is why we have a high place in the hills for there we can wait out their raids and return to rebuild. Now that you are here be believe that the raids will stop."

"They will chief. We will patrol the seas with our fleet."

"One of their kings has fallen out with his family and he is living with a small band of warriors in the hills to the north. He came to my village in peace and asked for shelter. We gave him shelter for a short time but his men liked my women too much and he wisely took them north."

"Do you want them destroyed?" Marcus asked bluntly.

"No for he was courtesy itself and paid for the food that they took. I mention it only to prevent you stumbling upon him. There has been too much bloodshed in these lands."

"I can see that your people are lucky to have such a wise leader and I thank you for the warning which I shall heed."

As the column moved north Marcus summoned Gaelwyn and Decius to ride alongside him. "It seems there is a band of iris ahead."

"Good, the lads need a good fight."

"No Decius this is not a warband but displaced warriors from Ireland. They may prove useful." Decius looked disappointed. "Gaelwyn I want you to go with a turma and find these warriors. Decius detail Julius, he appears to be the diplomat, tell him I would like to meet with these Irish."

Julius was honoured to have been chosen. He was still the youngest decurion but he had formed a real bond with his troopers. Gaelwyn, unusually also liked the affable and unpretentious young man. He always deferred to the old Brigante warrior and he listened to all the advice he was given. Gaelwyn felt, as with Marcus that this was a Brigante born to another tribe. The hills were rolling hills and both Gaelwyn and Julius knew that the turma would be easily spotted by a sentry. The scout, therefore took a circuitous route some way inland where he could spot the Irish before they saw him. Just before noon the scout appeared next to Julius. Julius shook his head in disbelief; the man seemed to have the abilities of a ghost or spirit.

"They are around the next headland in a small camp. There are thirty warriors. They have three sentries, one to the north, one the east and one facing us south."

"Thank you. We shall carry on this track and just come upon them. As though by accident." Turning to his troopers he shouted. "When we meet the Irish don't get excited. I don't want any reacting aggressively to them no matter belligerent they appear. One false move from them and we can bring up the whole ala." His men smiled; the young man had a presence and inspired confidence.

As they came over the rise to the small camp Julius counted ten warriors. He held his hand palm out in the universal sign for peace. A huge red-haired man, mailed from head to foot and resting his tree like arm on the top of a double headed war axe spoke in passable Latin. "Welcome Roman I am King Tuanthal Teachtmhar. What brings you to my camp?"

I am Decurion Julius Demetrius of Marcus' Horse in the army of General Gnaeus Julius Agricola and I was sent by my prefect to discuss your intentions but before we do so would it not be more polite to ask your other twenty warriors to join us. I wouldn't want them to be uncomfortable squatting in the bushes." His men fought to control their smiles and the King nodded and shouted something in a language which even Gaelwyn did not understand and a sheepish band of warriors emerged from behind the troopers who just sat, faces immobile showing nothing although their eyes showed their glee.

"For someone so young you are wiser than many greybeards."

"Others have made that mistake." The young decurion dismounted in one fluid movement and stepped forward to clasp the arm of the King. The King had not expected such confidence and looked perplexed although he did take the arm. "Your Latin is excellent King Tuanthal Teachtmhar where did you learn it?"

"A Roman ship foundered on our coast some years ago and one of the slaves we took taught us as children."

"Yes they do say the younger you learn a language the easier it is. Would you find it easier to talk with my prefect, he is within a few miles?" He leaned forward confidentially. "And it will save you repeating you repeating yourself."

"Er yes. Can we offer you food?"

"No, we have many supplies with us for we are a large ala. Gaelwyn find the prefect and bring him and the ala here and now King Tuanthal if you don't mind me excusing myself, the men and I would like to start building our camp. Right men, Macro lay out the lines for the camp. Drusus tether the horses. Excuse me."

The king had been totally thrown off balance by the Roman's calm and confident manner. He had expected the troopers to be intimidated by their martial appearance and had not expected his prey to have seen the ambush. He had not intended to actually attack the Romans but he wanted to impress them with his men. It had all turned rather sour and the king sat like an uninvited guest at a wedding as the troopers busied themselves with their camp.

It was only an hour later that the ala rode into view. Julius could not help but admire the column as it rode in mail and helms sparkling in the late winter sunlight. He glanced at the king and saw that he also looked impressed, glad, perhaps that he had not chanced his arm and attacked the tiny turma. Julius nodded to his chosen man to continue the building of the camp and strode over to greet the prefect and make the introductions. He did so a good forty paces so that he could speak without being overheard if he needed to. In a louder voice than was necessary he said, "Welcome prefect we have met with King Tuanthal Teachtmhar who wishes to speak with you." Dropping his voice, he added, "There are thirty men and I think they had an ambush planned but thought better of it." In a louder voice he said, "I took the liberty Decurion Princeps of starting the camp as the day is drawing to a close."

Carrying on with the charade Decius said, just as loudly, "Well done Decurion and you have picked a good spot. I taught you well."

"Come with me Decurion." Marcus winked as he led Julius to the king. After the greetings Marcus summoned some chairs. "I think we would be better seated eh King?" The move was not lost on Julius; by seating all of them it made them equals negating the claim to be king. "How came you to these lands?"

"I am king from over the water in Ireland and I had my throne unjustly taken from me by usurpers. I was forced to flee and we came to Britannia to offer our services to Rome in the hope that she can reinstate me in my kingdom."

Marcus recognised the lie for what it was. Until the Romans chanced upon him he had had no intention of seeking Rome's help but he was obviously an opportunist. "I am sure that the general will look favourably on your request. Rome ever needs allies especially in the far reaches of our Provinces such as this one." Julius could not help but admire the prefect. Despite his humble origins he had picked up the art of negotiation and diplomacy better than some patricians. He had effectively said they might help the king but only in return for a piece of their land. What the king said now would determine the success of the ploy.

"That is what I wanted to hear."

"Good." He turned to Julius. "Send for the marine."

The king looked puzzled. "My teacher did not tech me the word marine, is it a sailor?"

"A military sailor yes. We will contact the fleet and inform them of your request for an alliance. The message will get to the general much quicker that way."

The king looked around. "You have a fleet? Here?"

"Yes they will sail along here shortly and we will send them a message. Might I invite you and one or two of you men for a meal? We will, of course, provide food for the rest of your men but space in our small camp is limited."

The king looked at Marcus with grudging respect. He obviously didn't want thirty armed Irishmen loose in his camp. He would have done the same. "I will be pleased to accept your invitation."

After a heavy night's drinking, even Decius had found it hard to keep up with the Irishmen although the Quartermaster had still been drinking long after the last of them went to bed, the prefect met with the king. "Now this is a delicate problem King Tuanthal for, until I receive orders from my general I just can't let you wander off around the country." He saw the king flush a little. "No, no you misunderstand me. The people around here have had problem with Irish pirates stealing their children as slaves and I know that is not you but some may fear you and get their retaliation in first. I do not think my general would like to lose a new ally because some local people mistook you."

"What do you suggest then prefect?"

Perhaps if you would accompany us for me are meeting my general just up the coast. You would then have my protection and of course hospitality."

'And,' thought the king, *' we would effectively be your prisoners, with ropes of linen but prisoners nonetheless.'* "Of course, we accept your hospitality although you Porcius may have to get more supplies of that fine wine."

"That is why we have the fleet. We want for nothing."

It was early spring when Marcus' column reached the shores of the estuary. Macro and Decius had been disappointed that all of the tribes had accepted Roman rule with such equanimity. Marcus was pleased. His ala had grown thanks to remounts and recruits. His losses, Lentius and the other troopers had been made good. On the ride north he had come to know the Irish king. Whilst he might question his nobility he could not doubt that the man was a fine warrior and believed that he had been treated badly. Macro had enjoyed the nightly combats for, for the first time, he had found an opponent who challenged him. Macros still won each time but it was not easy.

The reports from Agricola indicated that the invasion along the east coast was going well. The Usipi in the centre of the country were less than impressive but Marcus' Horse had, again performed the wonders expected of him and his ala. He camped at the juncture of the sea and the estuary. The fleet was close by and Marcus knew that the ships could easily contact Agricola who, he assumed, was not far away.

As the men built, for the immeasurable time, their fort the king, Tuanthal Teachtmhar drew Marcus to one side. "Prefect, I have to compliment you. Your men are superb. The warrior Macro, he would be a chief in my land. They love you, you know that?" Marcus nodded in an embarrassed way." Had I had the love of my people the way you have from your men I would be king, not only of my kingdom but the whole of Ireland. How do you do that?"

The prefect considered for a moment. "The man who trained me was a great man. This unit should be Felix's horse for he made it what it is. He taught me to value every man, no matter how lowly, how base as an equal. He taught me to give every man respect until he disrespected me. It is as simple as that."

"Is your general a similar man?"

"Yes, he is as great as Ulpius but he has a greater vision." Marcus turned to look directly at the king. "He could conquer the whole of your country as easily as you might spar with Macro but I believe, King Tuanthal Teachtmhar that it will be you who conquers your island for I have seen a change in you since first we met."

"Will you come with me? With your ala, we could make Ireland part of Rome."

"I would be honoured, but only if my general sanctions it."

"It has been a privilege to ride with you and your men."

The witch had finally reached Calgathus. The king was not the old man she expected but a young man with piercing eyes and a highly charged nature.

"So you are the witch who fermented such discord in Britannia?"

"I am High King and I would that I could carry on my work here in Caledonia."

"These Romans are as fleas, annoying but you can rid yourself of the pestilence."

"Do not be so sure. The Brigantes, the Carvetii, the Novontae and the Ordovice all thought so and now they lie rotting in fields the length and breadth of Britannia."

"What would you have me do, if you were to give me advice?" the threat was implicit in his voice.

"Join with the other tribes and fight him as one army. You will outnumber him. Rally your people so that all, men, women and children feel part of the fight. Finally, you choose the place of battle not this Roman peacock."

"The words you speak, though from a woman's mouth speak of a man's mind. And what will you do?"

"There are many auxiliaries fighting for Rome. Some of them are not enamoured of Roman ideals. I will find their weak spots and turn some of their units against them. They have few enough soldiers available anyway. One or two traitors could turn the tide."

"Very well. I will seek my brother kings and find a place where we can destroy this Roman beast, once and for all.

Agricola's camp.

"You have done well Marcus. You constantly amaze me. I give you tasks that Hercules would baulk at and you exceed them." He put his arm around his shoulder and spoke quietly. "This Irish king, what do you make of him?"

"He may not be a king but he likes Rome and what we do. It would seem to me that if we a support him we might gain a land the size of Britannia for the cost of a couple of cohorts and an ala."

"When we have finished out work on the mainland we will visit his island of Ireland. In the meantime, he might make a useful unit in battle."

"He and his men are brave and cunning. They could turn many battles. They can fight on foot or horse."

"Good you have done well. Go back to your men and leave the king to me. In seven days' time, we will see what opposition is in the western isles. Perhaps we will see how the Irish are in combat."

Chapter 13

"I hate the sea."
"I know Decius."
"And it upsets the horses."
"So Sergeant Cato has told me."
"Well, we should be on land."
"Has this anything to do with the fact that you have emptied the contents of your stomach six times since we left the mainland?"
"It stands to reason. If the gods had meant us to travel on the water he would have made it so that we could walk on it."
The isle grew larger as they approached. The general had told them that it would give them an idea of the problems of invading Ireland. The King had spent many nights trying to persuade the general to support him. As they approached last island the king turned to the general. "General. We have almost finished the conquest in which you have not lost a single man. My island, Ireland is there." He pointed to a smoky hump in the distance. "Give me but his ala of cavalry and I will give to you the land that is Ireland as a present."
"A generous offer. But with this ala alone I hope to conquer Caledonia which is a more pressing issue. I cannot give you men but I can give you money and I can give you horses and arms. Finally, I can give you the ship which will return you to your land. Just promise me that you will be an ally of Rome."
The king extended his arm. "You have my word."
Agricola smiled and walked away. The king turned to Marcus. "Should you ever leave this general, and I accept he is a fine man worth following, I will offer you a kingdom in Ireland." Decius, standing nearby raised his eyebrows.
"Thank you, king, and I would happily serve you, once we have completed the task of taming Britannia and with this general I think we have a chance."
"You are right prefect. Tell your men, and especially Macro that it has been an honour to serve with your ala." As though rehearsed all of his men raised their swords and roared, "Marcus' Horse ha!"

Feeling more emotional since the night his wife had died Marcus raised the sword of Cartimandua and said, "May the Allfather protect you King Tuanthal Teachtmhar of all Ireland."

That was the last they say of the enigmatic king but word crossed the oceans that he had indeed conquered the whole isle and named it as an ally of Rome. This was long after Agricola had been withdrawn to Rome and the charismatic general never knew that he had conquered a land by proxy.

They were soon busy dealing with the effects of Caolan's defection. He had stirred up the tribes of the islands and the ala had to spend more time than it had to winkling out the resistance on the small islands which littered the coast. Most galling was that Caolan had disappeared from sight. "Mark my words sir, that bastard will be back. I can feel it in my bones."

"I fear you are right Decius."

Summer saw the army busy building a series of forts along the line from the Bodotria to the Clota. Decius was mildly surprised when Marcus' Horse did not have to build any forts but, instead, were given the honour of accompanying the general as he scouted north of the line. Marcus was amazed that Gaelwyn, who had never been north of the Taus, should be considered such an expert but, incredibly he seemed to have an instinct for knowing both the land and its people and the general came to rely on him almost as much as Marcus.

Marcus was riding next to the general as they rode in the hummocky, hilly land north of the Clota. "You know Marcus I am surprised we have not met a force of the enemy yet. We have gained a remarkable amount of land with little effort."

"I think that the advances in the winter took the people by surprise. They do not wage war in the winter up here and they could not feed themselves and fight. We are coming to summer and I fear it will not be as easy."

"You are right. I will send for the Ninth. If we can build a fort in the middle of the Northern lands we can control them."

"Gaelwyn has spoken to the prisoners and he believes that the land to the west is too hostile for our men and there are not many people there. Perhaps to the east?"

Agricola nodded. "Your scout is wise. I agree. We will build our line of forts and when the Ninth arrive we will push north east. I do believe Marcus that we can do this. I will leave skeleton garrisons and bring every unit north. When we defeat them, it must be complete and final."

That summer saw a war of attrition. The general suppressed minor revolt after minor revolt but eventually the line of forts was built and the land south of the Clota, Bodotria was secure. The Ninth were ready to fight; they had spent most of the campaign so far building roads and forts. As Decius said, "If you want a villa built then you send for the Ninth. When you want a country conquered you send for Marcus' Horse." When Decius returned to camp after a night in the local tavern, sporting a black eye Marcus discovered that his Decurion Princeps had made the mistake of mentioning this in front of five of the ninth's centurions. The following night Macro, Gaius, Agrippa, Metellus and Julius had asked for a night's furlough. Whilst they sported the injuries sustained in a heated discussion, their smiles told Marcus that the centurions of the Ninth understood the viewpoint of the troopers.

The general's only comment to the prefect was, "Marcus do have your men take their aggression out on the natives. The Ninth are our only legion, we may actually need them."

The winter was a duplicate of the previous winter with Agricola aggressively sending out vexillations to invest settlements and accept their support for Rome.

Caledonia

In the heartland of Calgathus' kingdom, his war chiefs and princes were beside themselves with rage. Let us throw this upstart south of the Taus where he belongs."

"How would you do this cousin in winter when we barely have enough food to feed ourselves? Would you take the men from protecting their families to fight the Romans and return to a hearth full of the dead?" The cousin dropped his head. "No, we wait for the summer. All out warriors will gather for I have promises from all of the kings to support our endeavour. When he has put his head too far into our land we will strike it off. Be patient. For this Roman has strayed too far into our land and will soon pay for his mistake."

The Usipi were trudging up the roads built by the ninth. Their centurion, Centurion Aurelius, was heartily sick of them. His handful of legionaries, detached from the ninth, were desperate for the day they could sign them off and return to the ninth. The ringleader of the Usipi malcontents was a warrior called, Adelmar. He had been captured close to the border with Gaul, he had been a raider but had hidden the evidence of his raiding. Press ganged into the Usipi he quickly realised what whining sheep they were and, through bullying and coercion had established himself as their leader. Unlike the other auxiliary units, the Usipi felt no allegiance to Rome. They hated Britannia and they loathed their centurion whom they saw as a symbol of Rome. Adelmar advised them to bide their time.

Adelmar was in a tavern in Trimontium. The centurion could never work out how Adelmar managed to persuade so many of his comrades to exchange duties but he did. He was drinking the flat tasteless beer they brewed which only made him miss his homeland even more when the woman sidled up to him. He did not look up at first, he just said, "Piss off whore."

"I will do, plaything of a Roman who takes you each night from the rear. But I thought you might like to be rid of your oppressor." His hand went to his pugeo but he suddenly felt a sharp blade at the base of his groin. "It is only a small manhood but soon it will be mine and I will make a soup of it for my sisters to enjoy." It was the word sisters which made him drop his weapon. Glancing down at her amulets he recognised her for what she was a priestess, a witch.

"I am sorry how can I help you?"

"It is how I can help you that is the question. You would like to rid yourself of the Romans?" He nodded. "You would like to return home to Germania?" Again, he nodded. "Then I will contact you again and show you how. Do not antagonise the centurion for he is the key to your escape. Ingratiate yourself and appear friendly. Soon I will meet with you again."

He glanced down and she was gone. But now he had hope, freedom was at hand. Soon he and his men might make a return to Germania.

The land through which they now travelled was far more threatening and dangerous than any land since they had fought beneath the foothills of Wyddfa. Marcus' Horse was strung in a wide arc travelling on tiny deer tracks through forests and seeking ways through impossibly boggy quagmires and marshes. The land was alive with insects, all of which seemed to take great delight in attacking and biting Macro. Each night as they made their camp his face would have even more red blotches and spots, marking the site of a bite of some voracious insect. "I can fight men. How do you fight these little bastards? Look at you Gaius and Julius not a bite to be seen. How do you manage it?"

"Garlic. Chew garlic or wipe the bulb on your face. They do not like it."

"I'm not surprised! It stinks."

"There is your choice Macro. Do you wish to stink or would you rather continue to be bitten?"

Julius' words made sense, eventually to Macro. "Have you a spare bulb?"

"Here. Ask the quartermaster for some more or look for the wild garlic in the woods."

"Wild garlic? How will I find it?"

"By the smell Macro. It stinks."

The fighting was just as difficult as it always had been in these remote parts of Britannia. The tribesmen had the advantage of terrain and would make forays when the men camped attacking the foraging parties as they sought water and wood. Soon the foraging groups were sent in increasingly large numbers.

Calgathus was pleased with the way the campaign was going; the Romans had slowed their advance and, whilst his men were not causing huge casualties it was a war of attrition. The Usipi were not the only auxiliary unit which was disenchanted. There were even grumblings amongst the legionaries of the Ninth. Fainch had spies everywhere; her network of witches constantly reported to her. She met secretly with King Calgathus who respected her information. "The Romans are more vulnerable than they think at night."

"How so?"

"On Mona, the Romans built one of their camps and some Ordovice stole into the camp at night and kidnapped the man who now leads the horse warriors."

"Why is he still alive then?"

"That was my mistake and I will not make it again. My point is that your men can get into the Roman camp. There the Romans cannot fight as they do on the battlefield. The Ordovice managed it and you have more warriors."

The king thought for a moment about the suggestion which had the merit of risking few of his warriors and yet could achieve much. "The legion is the largest of their forces; if we could destroy or badly damage that one then the others would lose heart. I can see, Fainch, why the other kings valued you and your opinion. I will order an attack."

Marcus smiled to himself as he briefed Decius knowing as he did the dour and pessimistic nature of his deputy. "We are moving out of our camp today Decurion Princeps."

"Oh, that's wonderful. That means we have to build another camp with these tiny insects chewing away at us. The general needs to sort himself out. Put us in one place and then we would be able to fight and not have to build every day."

Marcus nodded. "Good point and as the general is accompanying us perhaps you can tell him yourself."

"This day gets better and better. That means we will all have to be on our best behaviour as well." Mumbling to himself the grumpy decurion left to order the dismantling of the camp.

Agricola rode at the head of the column with Marcus. Gaelwyn and Vettius' turma were scouting ahead. "It is good to be away from headquarters for a while." The general looked over his shoulder. "Although it seems your Decurion Princeps is less than happy with the situation."

"Don't mind old Decius. If he had nothing to moan about he would worry too much."

"You have a good ala here Marcus. I would that all the alae were as efficient. Tell me how is it that your ala is so proficient with the bow? It is unusual."

"It's the Pannonian part sir. In Pannonia, the warriors fought with a long lance and a bow. When they were drafted into the army they adapted the lance to a spear but they had to learn how to use swords. Ulpius Felix told me that his men still practised their archery even on service and the old prefect encouraged them to use it when in action. It sort of evolved and now we train the new recruits, the ones from Britannia, in its use. The sad thing is no one knows how to use the long lance anymore and that is a shame. I could never use it but Ulpius Felix once showed me how they trained with hoops hung from trees."

"Hm. Well I don't know about the long lance but I have requested some Syrian archers. They would not be as versatile as your ala but they are, apparently, deadly when used well."

"Yes, I have heard. I am from Cantabria and the archers there have a manoeuvre where they ride in a circle each man firing in turn, which is also highly effective."

"Really? Well I shall have to find out if there are any Cantabrian archers."

Sadly shaking his head, Marcus said, "I fear not. My village and most of the others were destroyed to prevent rebellion and insurrection. I have never heard of any such units in the Roman army."

"Nor have I but Marcus tell me, do you not feel resentment that we, Rome, killed all of your people?"

"I have lived too long amongst Romans to feel Cantabrian but I do worry when we are asked to slaughter whole tribes."

"You mean as I did with the Ordovice?"

Realising he might have overstepped the mark Marcus looked up at the general trying to gauge his mood. "Well yes sir. Killing whole tribes means that others are more likely to fight to the death and that means we lose more men."

"You may be right prefect for your conquest of the Novontae made me reassess how we deal with the tribes. However, the Ordovices had been a thorn in Rome's side for too long and since their demise there has been total peace in that part of the world."

"Possibly because there are no people there now sir?"

"Perhaps. Now this Cantabrian Circle, when you get the opportunity do you think you could train a turma in its use and demonstrate it to me?"

"I don't see why not. My weapon trainer, Decurion Macro, loves a challenge."

"Good. Now the reason I am accompanying you, apart from the refreshingly honest conversation, is because I want to get to the edge of the frontier. We need to find a way to bring Calgathus to battle and I will not do that at headquarters. The Ninth has a camp a few miles from here if we camp close to them we can send out joint probing patrols, and perhaps antagonise the enemy into attacking."

The spot they found was a good site for a camp. It was on a hilltop which overlooked the woods and forests surrounding it. Marcus ensured that his men cleared back the undergrowth and the trees to give them clear lines of sight. It was also close enough to the Ninth's camp for them to be neighbours. Accompanied by Macro and his turma Marcus and the general explored the land to the north east.

"There are few settlements in this part of the land Marcus."

"Yes sir but there are many valleys which are hidden." Agricola looked up with a question in his eyes. "Gaelwyn had been scouting already and he has found many smaller settlements."

"Then we need to make a larger fort, a permanent fortress for the Ninth. If we cannot find all the people at least we can manage their movements. We will visit the prefect of the Ninth."

They headed east and soon came upon the camp of the Ninth. While Macro saw to the horses and the general went to find the prefect Marcus went to visit his old friend Decius Brutus, now First Spear.

"Good to see you Marcus, sorry, prefect. I should say sir and kiss your arse now that you have been promoted." Decius was grinning as only old friends can do when they insult each other.

"Decius, it is good to see you and I am pleased that you too have been promoted." First Spear in a legion was the highest promotion a legionary could hope for. "It seems such a long time since Glanibanta."

"Yes, they were interesting times. I wonder if the fort still stands."

"It does. My ala spent some time there. It is still a beautiful place."

"Of course, your ala. Marcus' Horse. It has a good sound to it. Ulpius would be pleased and proud."

"Yes, Decius for you knew the man and I would have preferred it to be called Ulpius' horse but the general insisted."

"Do not be modest you deserve it. I have heard great things about the deeds of Marcus' Horse." His face darkened, "Would that the general would allow the Ninth to have a chance of such glory."

"I think he hopes to but this land does not suit the legions. It is a little too much like Teutonberger Forest and we know what happened to Varrus there."

"Varrus was an arse. Besides he did not use auxiliaries and this general is wise enough to use you horsemen and those Batavians."

Marcus laughed. "He has also used us as infantry in Mona. Decius is almost half the man you knew with all the running up mountains."

"So the old fat goat is still alive."

"And what of your men?"

"I think that they are trained enough but they have not seen action since the battle of the Taus. The odd skirmish does not make you a warrior and I worry that they are becoming a little soft. Where are you based?"

"Decius is building a fort just three miles that way. We will be within singing distance of you."

"And the general is with you?"

"For the moment. He is formulating a plan to bring the enemy to battle. They are behaving like seawater in your hand the moment you think you have it, it slips through your fingers."

"I would ask a favour of you."

"It is given whatever it is."

"I would like my cohorts to train with your turma. If we are to fight in the forests then cooperation is vital. We need to know how each other fight."

"Done. I will mention it to Agricola while we ride back."

The general emerged from his meeting and Marcus took the opportunity to mention Decius Brutus' idea. "I think that is a sound plan. How do you know First Spear?" On the ride back Marcus told the general of the joint vexillation years before. "You see," he said slapping his leg enthusiastically; "I knew that we could find ways for the legions to fight alongside the auxiliary effectively. Well done Marcus. You and your predecessor were obviously visionaries. We will continue this successful close liaison."

Three days later and the fort was finished. The very next day Agricola and Marcus took two turmae to the Ninth's fort and began manoeuvres in the forest. At first the legionaries found it difficult to understand how they would fight alongside cavalry but when Marcus dismounted a turma and showed them it became much simpler. Although exhausted they returned to the auxiliary fort pleased with their first attempt at joint action.

The Venicone warriors gathered in the eaves of the forest. The witch Fainch watched from a distance; Calgathus wanted to present himself as the master planner for, as he said, the Venicones see women as something a little higher than beasts of burden. Fainch accepted this for she knew of the folly of many men. Her reward would come when Calgathus destroyed this Roman army and reversed their fortunes.

"The Romans think they are secure in their walls of wood. They think that we are afraid to take the war to them. Tonight, warriors of the Venicone you will do what no tribe has ever done before; you will enter a Roman fort and destroy a whole legion."

Some of the warriors looked sceptical. They might outnumber the five thousand legionaries but everyone knew how well the legionaries fought. Calgathus could see the doubt on their faces. He pointed to Fainch, "What if I were to tell you that the priestess over there witnessed far fewer men than you enter a Roman fort and spirit away their leader what would you say then? Are the Ordovice braver warriors than the Venicones? Your chief says you are the bravest warriors and I believe him."

One bearded warrior with streaks of grey rippling through his hair stepped forward. "But they have walls and ditches."

"Are the ditches deep? Are the walls high? The answer is no. If we attack at the same time, if we climb the walls at the same time, making not a sound then we can succeed. There will be but forty men on the walls. Can we not silence forty men? When you are inside the fort where will the legionaries be?"

One voice shouted, "In their tents asleep."

"And do the Romans sleep in their armour? No. Do they sleep holding their weapons? No. Tell me, "he said looking directly at the warrior who had questioned him, "do you fear sleepy men with no armour and no weapons?"

There was a roar of, "No!"

"Then tonight we attack. Tonight, you will destroy the Romans as they sleep."

Decius Brutus was just finishing his rounds. He turned to the duty centurion who was following him. "Keep your men on their toes. The cohorts today were made to look useless by the auxiliaries. They need to be sharper. They are getting complacent."

"You are right First Spear but it is hard to make then care when they never fight."

"Don't worry I have spoken with the prefect and the general. They will fight and soon." First Spear's words would come prophetically and ironically true even as he slept blissfully unaware of the nightmare which was about to erupt.

The Venicone warriors slithered along the ground towards the fort. The smallest and fittest warriors were in the fore. They had covered their bodies in natural dyes and mud which darkened their skin. The ones who would scale the walls were armed only with knives. Along each of the four walls four warriors carried slings to stun any sentry not silenced by the knives of their comrades. Reaching the ditch was the hardest part of their assault but once there the sentries' attention was drawn further away. The warriors quickly crawled to the foot of the palisade. One man squatted while another crouched on his back. The signal had been practised back in their camp and as one the squatting man sprang up and the crouching man jumped. The effect was astonishing for the Roman sentries suddenly saw sixty men descend from the skies. The knives flashed as the sentries struggled with the sight they had witnessed. Even as they died the next sixty were springing their way into the air. Sling shots buzzed and struck targets. The Venicone chief, hiding in the tree line began to believe that they would succeed.

Centurion Ballus had, fortunately for him been on his way from one the south to the north wall when the attack began. He suddenly saw his men began to topple, the centurion a fifteen-year veteran knew they were under attack, "Alarm! Alarm!"

Realising that speed was of the essence the Chief ordered all his men to attack. While inside the fort men struggled awake as they heard the shouts and screams of the attack. Decius Brutus was awake and out of his tent before Ballus got off his second alarm. "Grabbing his gladius, he shouted, "Sound the alarm." The strident screams of the buccina awoke even the deepest sleeper and men grabbed spears and gladii to face the unseen enemy.

Decius suddenly found himself facing two warriors, one armed with a knife and one with a war axe. The man wielding the axe was more dangerous and he dropped to his knees as the axe scythed over his head and he stabbed the warrior between his ribs. Even as he died his companion slashed at Decius with his knife, slicing through his upper left arm. The gladius continued around in an arc and the warrior with the knife slid to the ground his throat cut. Decius had time to glance around. His men were fighting for their lives but they had no armour and were outnumbered. "To me! To me!" Grabbing the axe in his right hand and holding the gladius in his left hand the centurion became the rallying point and the training of the ninth took over. Men ran to him, automatically forming ranks as though armed, armoured and on parade. Suddenly they had a chance for they were a unit once more. Decius nodded his satisfaction. They might be going to die but they would at least take many barbarians with them.

Vettius raced to Marcus' tent. "Sir, Sir. Come quickly! We heard a buccina."

Awake in an instant Marcus leapt from his cot. "Sound the alarm." As he emerged from his tent pulling his mail shirt over his head he saw Agricola similarly dressing himself. “Sir a buccina…”

“I know I heard it. The Ninth must be in trouble.”

“Marcus Saurius guard the fort. Decurion Princeps follow the general and me to the Ninth’s fort.” Leaping on their horses bareback the two leaders raced from the fort.

“Shit!” murmured Decius, “Just charge off don’t wait for us.” He turned to Macro who was also on his horse with three of his turma. “Macro get after the Prefect stop him from taking on all the bleeding barbarians all by himself.” Macro grinned and took off like a greyhound. “Come on ladies otherwise the general and the prefect will kill all of the barbarians without any help from us.” It was a testament to their training that the troopers of the ala were only a few heartbeats behind their leaders, all of them bareback but all armed.

Marcus, Macro and the general had to slow up because of the terrain in the thick forest. “Sir we are going to have to leave our horses in the tree line.”

“I know Macro.”

“You!” Macro pointed at one of his troopers. “You watch the horses and don’t let any barbarian steal them or it comes out of your pay.”

Agricola and Marcus grinned at each other. They both dismounted at the tree line and they could see Venicone warriors still climbing over the walls although the gates were just being opened. The four Romans were all ready to charge alone when Gaius and his turma arrived. They were fully armed having been the sentries on duty. “Gaius leave someone to watch the horses and then follow us. Wedge formation.”

Even though some of them were shield less they went into the classic wedge formation with Marcus as the point and Agricola on the right. Macro turned to Marcus, “With respect sir I have a shield,” and he unceremoniously pushed Marcus to the left.

The forty-man wedge raced towards the gate and before the Venicones knew what had hit them they had killed those trying to enter. The wedge smashed right into the heart of the fort and Marcus shouted, “Form line!” His well-trained troopers immediately formed a solid line of shields and javelins, a wall of death for the Venicones.

Hard pressed with men falling all around him Decius heard the Roman voice and felt the pressure slacken slightly as warriors found themselves assaulted from the rear. "Come on lads. They are Roman voices. It is Marcus' Horse! Rally and hold!"

Suddenly their situation was no longer hopeless and men who had been about to accept death now fought for life. The Venicones turned to face the new foe and the general found himself, for the first time since Wales, fighting for his life. Fortunately, he was next to the killing machine that was Decurion Macro. As more and more of the ala rushed in to back up their comrades the Venicones found themselves pressed between two mighty sets of foes. Soon the battle became a series of individual conflicts and in that situation, there could be only one winner, the Romans. The Venicones were brave and they believed the words of Calgathus but gradually the heart went out of them and they began, where possible, to flee over the walls or through the gaps in the clumps of men engaged in a deadly combat. Those who remained died. Eventually, as dawn broke with a sad, grey drizzly morning the only living creatures in the fort were Romans.

Marcus saw, across a bloody, mangled sea of bodies, his friend Decius Brutus. "Hail First Spear. A good joint exercise I think but next time a little warning might help!"

As the two leaders began to laugh, uncontrollably Agricola shook his head in disbelief. With soldiers like this how could any tribe stand against them? As much as he hated the loss of Roman life the incident had been invaluable for the Ninth and Marcus' Horse were now entwined as brothers who had fought for each other. The bond would last and grow stronger. He now knew that, against all the odds, he would conquer the whole of Britannia.

The face of the witch Fainch grew white with hate and anger as she viewed the debacle the attack had become. The Venicone had been on the brink of success when her nemesis, the Roman with the sword of Cartimandua, had once again intervened and snatched victory from the jaws of defeat. She had missed her chance on the island of Mona she would ensure that she would not miss her chance here in Caledonia. The next time she would ensure that he died and at her hands.

As the legionaries began to clean up the fort Agricola spoke to Decius Brutus and Marcus as the two senior officers, for the prefect of the Ninth had perished along with more than a hundred and fifty legionaries. “I had thought to do so before this attack but now I am certain of my strategy. First Spear, we will move north and we will build a permanent fort. Not a temporary camp which can be assaulted so easily.” He held up his hand as he saw the expression on Decius’ face. “I know, you are sick of building but this fortress will show the barbarians that we are here to stay.” His voice became gentler. “First Spear, does it matter which soldiers have the victory as long as Rome prospers?” Decius hung and shook his head. “We all serve Rome but you know First Spear that we, “he put his arms around both men, “serve and aid each other.”

Decius looked at Marcus and held out his arm. “Thank you, Marcus. The Ninth Hispana will never forget this day. There would be far more brave men lying there but for your speed and bravery.”

“Decius, had our roles been reversed you would have done the same for me. We formed this bond in the bloody fields of Glanibanta, we are bound by blood and by honour.”

Chapter 14

The new fortress of Inchtuthil was strategically sited in the Valley of the Tava. To the north the high mountains were like the spine of this land, the backbone of the country rising like some giant prehistoric creature. No army could descend into the valley of the Bodotria without passing the fortress. The pass to the north west was also within striking distance for the legionaries. Around it smaller forts dotted the land providing the auxiliaries with their own bases. Agricola used his time well to ensure that they were stoutly built. The naval supplies continued to arrive bringing men and material to bolster his army. The barbarians could only stare impotently at the burgeoning Roman presence. Their attack on the Ninth had so nearly succeeded but all it had done was to make the Romans more alert and to increase their defences. Ditches were now double and deeper with sharpened spikes in the bottom. Walls were higher and sentries were doubled. Any complaints from the men disappeared as the stories of the night time assault were told. The security of their home was more important than the loss of a little sleep.

Marcus' Horse found themselves up the valley from the Ninth at Cardean. Less than two hundred paces away was the Batavian fort with the first and second Batavian cohorts. Agricola was taking no chances, he wanted his most experienced forces at the front to give adequate warning and to repel any assault. Although other auxiliary cohorts were arriving none was as reliable as these three and some, like the Usipi were a liability.

The Quartermaster Porcius Verres scoured the local area for supplies to supplement his ala's diet. This was not altruistic he could buy more, with less money locally than he could from their bases further south. He found a small fishing village south of the fort on the wide estuary of the Tava which provided him not only with fish but game as well. The clan there although at first wary soon welcomed the silver the business brought. It was close enough that he could also buy some of their bread which was of a better quality than his own ovens could provide. In fact, the portly Porcius became quite fond not only of the bread but also the sweet honeyed cakes which they produced.

Fainch was not unaware of both the forts and the Quartermaster's expeditions. She remembered a former Quartermaster, Gaius Cresens; she had been able to subvert him for he was corrupt and evil. This quartermaster was not. She needed another plan. The woman who produced the honey cakes worked and lived alone, her husband having died some years earlier in an inter clan strife. Fainch insinuated herself into the woman's company portraying herself too as a widow. The woman needed help as the ala was demanding more and more of her breads and cakes. As a priestess, she was not without culinary skills and she persuaded the woman to allow her to live and work with her. This strategy was crucial to the witch's plan for revenge. She took to chatting to Porcius when he came every few days for his delicacies. She bantered with him and gave him tastes of new treats she had cooked.

"You must tell me what your men at the fort like to eat, I am sure that I could make them treats which they would enjoy."

"For myself I love the honey cakes Ailsa makes. But these are very pleasant too. What are they?"

"They are oatcakes with dried berries and honey in them. I also have a few spices in there which I think gives them a little heat."

"I will take some of them back for my officers. Some of them like a change from their normal diet."

When he returned a few days later he sought out Fainch although she now called herself Una, and asked her about her oatcakes. Some of my officers liked your oatcakes. In fact, the prefect told me they were the most pleasant food he had eaten since arriving here. They reminded him of the spicy food of his childhood. I will buy some for him." He leaned over confidentially, "he is a great leader and a warrior of renown. The general himself often visits our fort to discuss great matters with him."

"In that case when you return I will bake a batch just for him."

Porcius looked downcast. "Have you none ready?"

"The spices are expensive. I only use them when I know I have someone who likes the cakes."

"I will return the day after tomorrow. Ailsa have you my treats ready?"

"Of course, Quartermaster." She eyed his rotund frame. "If you continue to partake you will be twice the man you are now."

He laughed, "And that is no bad thing is it eh Una?"

"No Quartermaster it is not."

The batch that Fainch intended to bake would indeed have spices in them, in fact they were vital to disguise the taste of the poison she would administer. She had two choices wolfsbane or white baneberry. The white baneberry was deadlier and she had used it to kill Queen Cartimandua but it had more of a taste; it had only worked with the Queen because of the alcohol and spices in the pudding. It would be the wolfsbane. This time there would be no escape for Marcus Aurelius Maximunius.

Agricola and his three prefects were studying the map of Caledonia. "I think that a push up this valley," the general indicated the valley running north west, south east from the Ninth's fort, might be useful. It seems to be the only route into the highland area."

"Ambush country sir." Prefect Strabo tended to be a little blunt in his observations.

"You are right Furius but we need to find out who is out there and in what numbers. You three prefects are experienced and you work very well together. Remember Mona and Wyddfa? We had worse country there to manage and we succeeded."

"True sir," Cominius was far more reflective than his friend, "but we have never really faced these warriors in battle. These are the Caledonii and the Vacomagi. How do they fight? What are their numbers?"

"Which is why, prefect, we are sending this expedition to gauge our enemies." The general turned to Marcus who had remained silent so far. "Prefect you have said little. Have you an opinion?"

"I have kept silent general because this is not horse country. It would not be my men who would have to come up with a strategy. Those hills and forests prevent my troopers from using their speed and impetus. We could be fighting as infantry."

"That is true. The horses would only be useful if we had to pursue an enemy."

"Which may well occur."

"Ah, this is a problem for I do not wish to send just two cohorts, it would invite ambush. I would prefer an ala and two cohorts but you have a point prefect. You have presented me with a dilemma."

"Perhaps some refreshments might help us to think a little more clearly?"

Furius beamed, "An excellent idea. You do have a good quartermaster prefect. Any man with a girth to rival mine knows his food."

"He has procured some excellent food from the local area. I think you will enjoy it. Atticus."

His servant entered, a dour look on his ancient face, "Yes prefect?"

"Bring us some wine and a selection of those sweet cakes he promised me."

"Yes prefect."

"We could have a turma as scouts and then the rest of the ala as a rear guard. That way they could fight on foot or horse as circumstances dictate."

"Good idea."

Cominius still foresaw a problem. "From the scout's report, it is going to be difficult to find good sites for camps and, bearing mind the problems the Ninth suffered I would want secure camp sites."

Just then Atticus returned with the food. "These look interesting Marcus what are they?"

"They are sweetened breads from a village by the coast. Our quartermaster has procured them for me. These, "he picked up the berry and honey bread, "are my particular favourite and before you devour the lot Furius I will eat one." He pointed to the small breads, golden and appetising. "Those are also really good but they have neither berries nor spice in them."

"They will do for me." Furius tucked into the breads so favoured by Porcius. Marcus chewed on his delicacy whilst Agricola and Cominius sipped their wine.

"I think you are right about the secure camp sites. It is a ticklish problem."

They all looked at Marcus who had suddenly stopped eating, dropping his half-eaten cake to the floor. "What is the matter Marcus?"

"My mouth feels numb, feels strange and I am hot even though it is cold I…" Suddenly he started coughing and spluttering, the three men could see that he was struggling to breathe. Atticus heard the commotion and rushed in.

"Master what is it?"

Agricola picked up the half-eaten cake. "It was this. Strabo how do you feel?"

"Fine. I had three of these and I have no ill effects."

"The prefect has been poisoned." Atticus ran from the tent and Agricola and the others began to loosen the prefect's clothing.

"What do we do?" The three men so confident and competent in war knew not what to do. It was obvious that the man had been poisoned but what could they do?

"Get the surgeon."

Cominius ran from the tent just as Atticus returned with a black power and some water. Throwing the wine from the untouched beaker of the prefect he poured the black powder in and then the water. He began to stir, flicking his eyes constantly at the prefect. "Hold him up he must drink this." Agricola and Strabo were too stunned to wonder at a mere slave ordering them around nor could they even begin to question what concoction he was giving the obviously dying man. "Put his head horizontally," ordered the slave who began to pour the black, viscous liquid down the prefect's throat. Suddenly Marcus's body began to contort and Atticus had to hold his mouth shut and pinch his nose. "Hold his arms and legs! Stop him from thrashing around." The two Romans easily controlled his arms and legs and the prefect had to swallow. Cominius had returned with the surgeon as Marcus began vomiting a black and yellow liquid.

"What did you give him Atticus?"

"Ground charcoal and water sir!"

"Good. Is this the poisoned cake?" Stunned, they all nodded. The surgeon sniffed it and put a tiny morsel on his tongue. He immediately spat it on the floor. "Either monk's bane or wolfsbane. Well done Atticus you may have saved your prefect's life." He went to the tent's entrance and shouted. "You two troopers come here." A moment later the two men entered the tent shocked at the sight they beheld. "Take the prefect to his tent. Take off his armour and cover him. Atticus, you must stay beside your prefect and give him more of the charcoal and water. When the vomit is purely black you may stop," As the four men left Agricola spoke for all of them. "We need to find the quartermaster. This was an attempt on the life of the prefect. An attempt which may well have succeeded. Prefect Strabo go and find the quartermaster, Sura bring Decius."

By now the whole camp had heard of the attempt and Agricola found a flurry of decurions at the tent. "Decius order your decurions to bring the ala to readiness. Then join the quartermaster in the prefect's tent!"

The Quartermaster was white. "Sir I…"

"You are not a suspect in this Quartermaster. I need to know where you bought these cakes."

"I have been using an old woman in the village, Ailsa. She made those." He pointed to the cakes left by Strabo.

"The general pointed at the cake being examined by the surgeon. "And those?"

"No those were made by a new woman in the village. Una."

Decius had returned to hear the last words. Agricola considered the cake as though it could speak." Why did you acquire these for the prefect?"

"She made them especially for him. He had one last week and enjoyed it."

Decius spoke his voice hard and quiet. "This woman, Una? When did you first see her in the settlement?"

"A week ago. She helped Ailsa and…"

"Describe her."

"She is small, not young and yet not old. Her eyes…"

"They are the colour of young violas and you felt your loins ache when you saw her?"

Agricola and the two prefects turned to stare, along with Porcius at the Decurion Princeps who suddenly had second sight. "Decius how did you know?"

His face drained of all colour he turned to the general. "The prefect described her to me when they were travelling back from Mona. It was Fainch the witch. The woman who murdered the Queen and caused the death of the prefect's wife and child has tried to kill him again for it was she who tried to burn him in the wicker cage."

"Decurion Princeps take four turmae and turn that settlement inside and out. Porcius accompany them. I want this Una taken and Ailsa, she may or may not be an accomplice but we need to find out." He turned to the two prefects. "Get back to your commands until we get to the bottom of this I want everyone on full alert. Tell Decius Brutus at the Ninth what is going on."

Agricola struck the desk with his fist in anger. This was the kind of warfare he did not care for. Barbarians could try sneak attacks, they could ambush his men but to poison and kidnap went against everything Agricola held dear. What galled him the most was that it was a woman, a druid; the rest had died but the last remnant of a foul, decadent and evil religion was wreaking havoc with this war. The woman would have to be found and when she was found there was only one punishment, crucifixion.

Decius was in a grim mood when he and Porcius confronted the baker, Ailsa. "But sir she was just a woman who offered to help me. I did not know her. I swear."

"Listen you piece of vermin, my prefect has been poisoned and the poison came from here. I care not that you are a woman. If I don't find that woman then you will suffer her punishment, crucifixion for I will have revenge and my general will have revenge. Whether you are innocent or not does not matter. The poison came from this hovel and before we leave here this hovel will be ashes and, if I do not get the answers I want so will you."

Porcius put his arm out as though to restrain Decius. "Decurion Ailsa is a good woman."

Decius grabbed the portly Quartermaster by the throat and put his face close to him. "Listen, you fat piece of shit! You were the one who bought the food! You were the one who gave it to the prefect. You are so close to having my dagger rip out your throat that I would keep quiet if I were you."

Gaius stepped forward and pulled Decius off. "Decius this will not get us Marcus' poisoner. The witch will be found but stop attacking everyone. We know how cunning the witch is. Don't we? Would the prefect have threatened an innocent woman?" Decius began to turn on Gaius. "She is innocent Decius. Would she still be here if she were guilty? The Quartermaster is innocent. All that he did was to get those things which pleased the prefect. Like getting the wine, you liked, the food we wanted and all those things we have taken for granted. I know that you are Decurion Princeps but if you continue to rant and rail believe me I will have you arrested." Decius looked up angrily. "You are not yourself. You are not thinking. Now go outside and kick something and let me question the woman. Macro, see the Decurion Princeps outside."

It was a tense moment; Decius was torn. Inside him something told him that Gaius was right but his heart told him to kill everyone and that would cure the Prefect. Macro looked at one of the three men he admired in the world and, catching Gaius' eye nodded and put his arm firmly around the Decurion Princeps. "Come on sir a bit of fresh air will do us both good." He added affably. "You can hit me if you like."

Ailsa was a quaking, quivering wreck sobbing uncontrollably on the floor. Porcius Verres was as white as Gaius had ever seen another human. Gaius looked at him. "Quartermaster I need you to focus. You know this woman and I need to know what she knows."

"Yes Decurion. You are quite right."

"Ailsa when did the, when did Una leave? Calm down and tell me."

Between sobs she blurted out her answers. "It was last night sir. She said she had to get some more herbs and berries." She spoke haltingly and the tears coursed down her cheeks.

"Which way did she go?" The woman pointed over her shoulder. "North west. Good. That makes sense she is heading back to Calgathus. Is there anything more you can tell us about her? Anything to help us identify her?" The woman shook her head. "Think, a mark, a scar anything?"

Suddenly she sat up. "A scar sir. She has a scar. I saw a scar."

"Where is it?"

"It runs from her wrist to her elbow." The woman used her finger to show, on her own arm where it was."

"Good. Now Ailsa. I believe you are innocent and the quartermaster believes you are innocent but the Decurion Princeps is a bitter man. He will hurt you if he can and that would hurt him. Have you anywhere you can go away from here?"

The woman looked around as though Decius might come in with his pugeo and kill her. Decius stroked her head to calm her. "My sister she lives south of here. I could go there."

"Then go, slip out of the back now and go. Porcius go with her and then return to the fort. I think it best if Decius does not see you right now."

By the time Gaius got outside Decius was a little calmer. "She went north west up the valley yesterday."

Decius said dully, "Towards Calgathus."

"Towards Calgathus. Macro take your turma and ride up the valley, take Gaelwyn with you and try to find her trail. Be back before dark."

"Sir."

When they were alone Decius looked up at Gaius. "Sorry about that son. I made a bit of a dick of myself."

"That's alright Decius we all share your anger but sometimes you have to be cool. Remember the prefect when he found his wife and son had died, he didn't rant and rave. He was calmness itself. We couldn't understand it then but you know Decius I do now and I think I admire him all the more for it."

"But he was poisoned."

"Yes, like the Queen and by the same woman. The thing is we have more of an idea now. If Marcus or you had described the witch do you think that Porcius might have recognised her?"

Understanding suddenly dawned on the Decurion Princeps. "Yes. I can't believe what fools we were. We kept it to ourselves, privacy I don't know what. We should have told you all. He would still be alive."

"First off he isn't dead yet. From what I understand Atticus has given him the chance of a life Secondly, we now know even more. She has a scar running along her wrist. We tell others of the scar and the eyes."

"Who?"

"Everybody! You know how the auxiliaries and the legionaries feel about Marcus. Ten thousand men looking for the witch! Decius, we have a chance. Now let us go and report to the general."

"Excellent work gentlemen. And I agree we tell everyone what this witch looks like. I think we will return to Roman rations for the rest of this campaign."

"How is the prefect sir?"

"He appears, Gaius, to be holding his own. I think that concoction has helped. There was less yellow material in the last vomit but he is still not awake. Decurion Princeps until he recovers please take command of the ala. All we can do now is see if the remarkable Gaelwyn and the redoubtable Macro can find any clues."

As soon as Gaelwyn and Macro appeared at the fort, long after dark, it was obvious that their quest had been in vain. "Found her trail sir. How he does it I have no idea but Gaelwyn must be part hound. Followed it right up the valley but there was a hill fort and her trail led right up to it. The ala might have taken it with siege engines but not one turma. Besides Gaelwyn reckoned she wouldn't have stayed there. We know where she will be now. With Calgathus."

"Then the sooner we meet that bastard in battle the better."

Atticus once again mopped the prefect's brow. The vomit had become black the previous day and the surgeon had said that the worst was past. After four days Atticus hoped so. He believed that but he wanted a sign that the prefect would return to life. The prefect was sweating heavily and Atticus remembered a saying from his mother, 'feed a cold, and starve a fever'. Perhaps his old mother knew best for the prefect had eaten nothing for more than four days and he still had a raging fever. His cloth was soaking wet and the old man picked up a dry one. As he leaned over the prefect opened one eye and said, "Atticus, I am starving. Have we any of those honey cakes left?"

Atticus was so relieved he burst out laughing and crying at the same time. "Sorry, prefect they are all gone."

Chapter 15

Centurion Aurelius was heartily sick of the Usipi. They were the most unpleasant and uncooperative cohort he had ever trained. The only consolation was that now that they were close to Inchutil he could at least share his woes with the auxiliary prefects Strabo and Sura as they drank in the small beer house close to their camps. Its owner had quickly realised the potential of selling barely brewed beer to Romans who just wanted to be out of their camp and talking. "The trouble is they don't actually want to be here. Your Batavians how do they feel about Britannia?"

"They actually quite like it. They get fed well, they enjoy the discipline and they enjoy the fighting."

"That is what I don't get. These bastards volunteer and then decide they don't like it and the worst is Adelmar. He was always a bastard but in the last year he has become a sneaky bastard."

Vettius had just wandered into the beer house and ordered a beer. "Who is a sneaky bastard? There are hundreds of them round here." He took a sip of the beer and looked sourly at the owner who just shrugged and wandered off to another customer, the Romans always spent well and there was no other choice for ale.

"The centurion here has some Germans who aren't working as they should and they have a ring leader, Adelmar."

"Tell me Decurion do you have problems with your recruits?"

"No centurion. The Decurion Princeps scares the shit out of them and then we have a seriously good weapon trainer, Macro."

"He is one hard man centurion."

"You are right Cominius I wouldn't want to face him."

"They are both right and, to be honest, most of the lads quite like being in Marcus' Horse. I could have a word with the prefect; we are having a bit of a slack time at the moment building up to the final push next year. Without blowing our own buccina we have a good set of trainers, Agrippa, Cato, Decius and Macro."

"He is right centurion. We would both like them working with our lads and ours are good cohorts."

"Well I have nothing to lose. If you can swing this Decurion I will see you right. Some more of that gnat's piss you pass off for ale you robbing bastard." The landlord wandered over shrugging off the insult. Soon these Romans would be gone and he would have profited from their short occupation.

Marcus was not fully recovered but he was improving. The general happened to be visiting and he heard Vettius' request. "Well Marcus if you can spare them that would help me. I have fourteen thousand auxiliaries but these Usipi are a thorn in our side. If Decius and his men could improve them it would bring this campaign to an end quicker."

As soon as Decius saw Adelmar he identified him as trouble. Still rankling over the poisoning of Marcus, Decius was in no mood for the sulky ways of the German. "Right you German twats. I am Decius Flavinius Decurion Princeps of Marcus' Horse, the finest auxiliaries not only in Britannia but the whole of the Roman, bleeding, Empire. These decurions train my men and they are good. You, on the other hand are the most useless bastards in the whole of General Gnaeus Julius Agricola's army." He took a breath and gave them the thousand paces stare. "But we are going to change that. Right we will start with a little run to the coast in full armour, now move."

The coast was ten miles away and Decius knew that when they got there they would see the whole of the Classis Britannica. He had wanted a show of force to intimidate them. He winked at the centurion as he jogged past him. Macro smiled, a year ago and the Decurion Princeps would already have been out of breath, now he moved as easily as any of the troopers

By the end of the day the Usipi were exhausted but, surprisingly some of them had a satisfied look on their faces and Centurion Aurelius drew Decius to one side. "It is only a small change but I think we are winning. Some of them actually look like they feel better for this; more like soldiers. Thank you, Decurion Princeps."

"Don't thank me I enjoyed it but a word of advice. Get rid of that bastard Adelmar. He is a bad 'un and you are not going to change him. A little training accident perhaps?"

"I know Decius, I know but I have been given a duty and I must carry out that duty."

Later that night the bad 'un met with Fainch in the sand dunes close to their camp. "I fear that the Romans are turning my men, some of them wish to please the centurion."

"It is time to do something about it. When you run to the beach are there ships there?"

"Yes, the whole fleet."

"Are some of them close to the shore?"

"Yes. The marines are cleaning the things that cling to the bottom of their hulls."

"Then the answer is before you. When you go there and you rest, kill the Romans, capture the ships and sail away to your homeland."

The idea seemed so simple that Adelmar said, "Yes." The problems of sailing a ship across the ocean did not occur to him for he had become accustomed to ruling his men and this Decurion Princeps was undermining his influence. Within a short time, most of the Usipi would be happy to serve the Romans. He would have to take his chances when the opportunity arose.

The opportunity did not arise for a few days for Macro took over the training and gave them sword and combat practice. This also made more of the Usipi want to follow Rome for they enjoyed the easy manner of the affable giant. Finally, a few days later Decius and Vettius turned up to take them for their training run to the coast. The cohort ran much more easily and Decius and the centurion at the rear nodded to each other. "It is working Decius, I can feel the change."

"Me too. I will have to leave you half way to the beach, I left a horse there, I have a meeting with the prefects and the general but Vettius will chase their arses, he is a good man. "

"Thank you. You cannot know how much I owe you."

"We stick together don't we? All for the general and bloody Rome." Laughing they jogged on.

Later as Vettius halted them on the beach they slumped to the ground. The marines from the ships laughed at their exhaustion and ate their noon food happy that they were not the auxiliary tramping around this bleak land. Adelmar waited until Vettius and Aurelius were relieving themselves before he initiated his plan; he wanted to take no chances. He needed the two officers to have their backs to him and his killers. Twenty of his chosen men raced to the two officers, stones and daggers in their hands, the other two hundred, whom Adelmar trusted, ran for the ships. Vettius and the centurion died ignominiously with no chance of defending themselves, hacked and crushed to death by the savage Germans. The marines also died almost to a man as the two ships were flooded with fierce warriors. Adelmar was careful to try to retain some of the marines to help him sail the two small ships. Many of the Usipi stood on the beach looking at the mauled and mutilated bodies of the two officers and watched the perpetrators scrambling aboard the ships. They honourably decided to take their chances with Rome and Adelmar cursed them as the ships were wedged off the beach." You spineless dogs. I hope the Romans crucify you!"

The rest of the fleet were too surprised as they witnessed the two ships heading north. By the time the commander had given orders to chase, the two ships were heading for the squall which lay in the distance. As with all the weather in this part of Britannia it was unpredictable and the centurion soon gave orders to anchor for he knew that the weather had beaten them.

It was Decius who found the bodies of Vettius and Aurelius. The Usipi prostrated themselves on the ground before Decius. His anger was so great he wanted to kill every man of them but then he remembered Gaius' words when he had last been angry. It was not these men who deserved his rage it was those who had fled. Part of him felt proud that two hundred men had chosen to stay rather than take the dubious freedom offered by Adelmar. He swore that if he got the chance Adelmar would die the slowest death imaginable. As events turned out that happened without Decius raising a finger.

Agricola listened to the report of Decius with growing frustration. "Just when I think I have enough men to bring this Calgathus to battle something happens to rob me of the very men

I intend to use." He looked up at the other prefects who were in the tent, Marcus, the Batavians, the Gauls and the two Tungrians. "What do we do with the Germans who survived?"

"Well sir," ventured Decius, "these lads could have run. The fact that they didn't might mean that they want to fight for Rome. Couldn't we split them up in the other auxiliaries? I mean we are all short of a few troopers and if any can ride we can train them. It would strengthen the cohorts we already have."

The Tungrian prefect Quintus Verenus shook his head. "They are Usipi how could we integrate them? Our men would object."

Cassius Bassus snorted, "My men will do as I tell them. Give me some of them. I guarantee that they will fight as well as my men."

"Of course, if we integrate them as two centuries and a turma then there will be less friction. If Cassius wants eighty and I have eighty that leaves forty for the cavalry."

"That is a reasonable idea Cominius. Any objections? Good now I have to decide what to do about the two ships they stole. I suppose I will have to send some of the fleet after them. Are the Usipi sailors?" The prefects shook their heads. "Well they may catch them. This also delays my attack until the spring. The Emperor had hoped that this adventure would have been over by now for he needs the legions in the East."

Marcus spoke up for the first time. "Then who will control the land if the legions leave?"

Agricola looked up at each of the prefects. "Why you of course. Look at the string of forts we built. They house auxiliaries not legionaries. Here at Inchtuthil the Ninth will control the North; the twentieth in the west and the second Adiutrix in the east. We only require three legions and eventually the Second and the Twentieth can be withdrawn. Since we pacified the lands south of here and Wales has there been any trouble?"

"No sir. Not that we have heard"

"Apart from attacks on our forces in our camps we have not had to fight a major battle here yet. When we do, we will win, you will win, for it will be the auxiliaries who fight that battle not the legions." Decius Brutus looked angry. "First Spear, it is not because I do not value the Ninth or any legion but the auxiliary can move quicker and react in a more flexible way and that is what is required in this land. We will have one chance to end this and I intend to seize that opportunity."

As they left the general to return to their forts Marcus rode next to his Decurion Princeps. It was the first time that the prefect had ridden since he had nearly lost his life. "Thank you for running the ala while I was indisposed."

"Indisposed? Is that a better way of saying nearly joined the Allfather?"

Marcus laughed. "It was a close thing but it has at least cured me of my sweet tooth and made me appreciate the dull rations prepared by our own cooks."

"We should have brought those cooks from Glanibanta then Porcius wouldn't have to procure food for us."

"Decius I understand you exchanged words with Porcius?"

Decius hung his head. "Sort of."

"He is a good man and he did not deserve to be threatened. You will need to speak to him. You know that?"

"I know that it is just… well I haven't had time what with training those Germans."

"Well the Germans are not an issue now are they?"

"As soon as we get back."

"The other detail we need to attend to is twofold, the German recruits you acquired for us and a replacement for poor Vettius."

"We will need another decurion for those recruits. There is always Cilo and Galeo. They are experienced and good lads."

"Excellent choice Decius. See to it."

Marcus Maenius Agrippa urged his sailors on. "Those barbarians murdered your shipmates in cold blood and stole two of my ships. I'll not rest until they are caught."

"What I can't work out sir is why they went north. No-one has ever sailed that far. It is like sailing to the end of the world. We have no idea what to expect."

"They aren't sailors, are they? They will just follow the coast and that is what we will do. If it were not for that squall we would have captured them by now." He scanned the sea to the east and he could see the line of biremes keeping the same distance between them. If the Germans tried to slip past them they would be seen, not only seen but caught and crucified.

The Germans however were having a hard time of it. Adelmar had allowed his men to kill all but one of the sailors and the only man he had left was an old sailor. Fortunately, he had plenty of rowers. The squall had been sent by the gods hiding them from their pursuers. But he needed to turn to the east, which was where Germania lay. He went to the sailor and told him to turn the ship to the east.

"But the wind is from the east. We will have to lower the sail."

Adelmar looked up at the sail and to his untrained eyes it looked far too complicated. He would have to wait until the wind changed in their favour. "Well at least we will outstrip the Romans this way."

The days grew and still they had not had a wind from the west. Worse they had had no food and little water. Every time it rained, which in this part of the world was frequently, Adelmar had them collecting rainwater in every container they could lay their hands on. His men's attempts at fishing had ended in failure and they were starving. Suddenly they noticed the wind was no longer coming from the side but from their stern. They took it to be a good sign that the wind was shifting; what they did not know was that they had turned the coast of Britannia and were now heading west towards the advancing western Classis Britannica.

Agrippa however had noticed the change in the coast for he had charts which he was compiling for the Governor. "It appears we have not gone over the edge of the world but turned the edge of the land."

As the days turned into a week, it was the weaker Germans who suffered. One of the younger Germans had been ordered aloft by Adelmar to see if he could spy their pursuers from the top of the mast. He had just shouted down in the negative when the wind shifted a point or two and, in his weakened condition, he slipped. He hurtled to the deck where he broke his neck and instantly died. His friends were about to throw the body over when Adelmar intervened. “We are hungry, aren’t we? This is food, isn’t it? Let’s eat.”

At first only those who were absolutely starving joined in the butchery of the corpse but as the smell of cooking flesh permeated the ship, reminding many of the Germans of the pork they had eaten at home, they relented and soon the corpse was devoured. It staved off hunger for a few more days.

The following day disaster struck for the leading German ship suddenly saw five biremes heading for them. The quickly turned their ship but as they were heading into the wind they almost came to a standstill.

At first Adelmar cursed his companions for he could not see the Roman fleet approaching. When he did he could not fathom out how they had got ahead of him. What he did not know was that they were the western fleet sailing up the west coast. “Head North.”

Adelmar had worked out that they could not sail into the wind but they could if it were coming from his right side. He received an even greater shock when he saw heading from the south east another fleet. His only hope was that he could outrun. One advantage of his overloaded ships was that they had more rowers than they needed and their rowers could be changed frequently. Adelmar knew that if caught he and his men would be crucified. They rowed as though their lives depended on it; which it did.

Agrippa saw his western fleet. “Well now we know that Britannia is an island. The general will be pleased for he will have almost conquered the land. First we catch these barbarians.”

Once again nature intervened in the form of the wind direction. The two captured biremes began to pull away from the fleet. The captains were all better sailors than Adelmar but until he turned towards one of them they had no chance of catching him. Their only hope was that the Germans would tire. And they were tiring and they were beginning to panic as the coastline receded behind them and all that they could see was the ocean stretching out to the edge of the world and if they sailed too far they would fall off the edge. Adelmar used the haft of his spear to hit his men, “Row you bastards. They will crucify us if they get us. Are you cowards? We fear nothing. This is not the edge of the world for there would be fire. "Adelmar didn't know if there was fire at the edge of the world but it seemed reasonable and as there was no sign of fire it encouraged his men.

"Land!" One of his lookouts spotted land to the north east.

"See I told you."

The frightened helmsman suddenly spoke up, terror in his voice, "The wind is coming from the south we could end up wrecking on those rocks."

"The wind has changed, has it? Let's see who is the stronger. Men we are going to turn east and head home." There was an almighty cheer and roar which carried across the water to the leading Roman ships. "But first we have to outrun these Romans. Night is falling and I want to lose them in the dark so every whoreson of you will have to row as though two men and I will row as three! Head east." Clambering down the mighty German took the oar and as he pulled it he called out the beat. Soon the whole of the boat's crew was roaring out the beats and the bireme almost flew through the water. As men failed they were hauled from their benches and replaced. One of them an older warrior collapsed and went deathly white. It was Adelmar's oldest companion Baldar. The ruthless leader ignored his distressed friend and took his place, snarling his anger as he pulled on the oar.

The following day the biremes were in the middle of a landless ocean exhausted from their rowing but they had lost the Romans. As dawn had broken they had been relieved to see they were alone. "Now we head south east and the next land that we see will be home."

"But how do you know where south or east are?"

"The sun rises in our homeland and sets in Britannia. That will give us direction."

One of his lieutenants came up to him, "Baldar is dead."

Laughing grimly Adelmar said, "Well at least we eat."

Three days later Agrippa reluctantly gave up the chase. The ocean was too big to spend a long time seeking out the two rogue ships and he was needed for the campaign. He did not know if the enemy survived or had been wrecked. He would have to return to the Governor empty handed but at least with the valuable information that Britannia was an island and was close to being conquered.

Some weeks later some Frisian fishermen discovered a drifting, half sunken bireme. When they approached they found on board thirty skeletal Germans who begged to be taken to land. Of Adelmar there was no sign nor of the other boat. The Usipi had escaped from Britannia and discovered that it was an island however the handful of survivors were all sold into slavery and never again saw their homeland.

Agricola was phlegmatic about the failure of the fleet to recapture the mutineers. "True we have lost two ships but we have made the discovery that we have almost reached the limits of the province. We will bring the enemy to battle and bring them soon. Send for the prefects. It is time to make plans."

The prefects had worked together long enough to have an easy relationship with each other. They all recognised the qualities the others possessed as leaders and as auxiliaries. The Tungrians were the best swordsmen Marcus had ever seen and Macro had taken to visiting their camp to spar with them. They in turn were impressed by this giant of a man who had the most affable nature they had ever seen. "Marcus we might finally beat these people."

"I hope so Cominius. My men have had as much training and building of camps as they need and a battle will relieve much of the tension."

"You are right. It is the waiting for the ambush, the night attack or… Have you fully recovered?"

"I have now but the first few weeks I was as weak as a baby. Thank the Allfather for Decius he was a rock."

"You have a good deputy there. What is even more remarkable is that he appears to have no ambition to usurp you."

Marcus laughed. "Decius was promoted late in life. He was the biggest moaner and whiner in the ala until he became a decurion. He has no ambition. He will take any promotion which comes his way but he will not seek it. Besides he will soon have his twenty-five years in."

"I cannot see Decius on a farm."

"Me neither. But if you suggested running a tavern..."

Furius joined in the conversation. "Now that is a dream worth pursuing!"

"If you are quite ready gentlemen? Good. "The general unrolled a map. "Here is my plan of campaign. Marcus and the Batavians will scour the north-west valley. Find out where the enemy are and drive them like game towards the north east. The Gauls and the Tungrians will do the same along the coast. The fleet will scout ahead and send us reports."

"Do we go all the way along the valley sir?"

"No Marcus. I believe two weeks should do the trick and that along with the other column should make them fight us. I don't care where it is but wherever it is we will win. You should be able to come north east and join with us."

"And what of the Ninth sir?" Decius Brutus had an unhappy look on his face.

"You, my dear Centurion, will be the rock upon which we base our attack. You will follow the Gauls and Tungrians. If they pursue small bands you will continue north east. I want to catch as many fish in my net as possible for by doing that I will ensure that my successor will have an easy task."

"Your successor? Are you leaving us?"

"The Emperor has summoned me to Rome."

"But your work here is not finished."

He looked at them all one by one. "But when we defeat Calgathus in the last battle I will have finished my task. I will have conquered Britannia."

Chapter 16

As Marcus and his ala made their way up the valley he was surprised by the terrain. Once they had left Inchtuthil it began to broaden out more than it had appeared from the fort. The upper levels were heavily forested and, as the sun suddenly cleared the grey cloud to reveal a blue sky, he could see the huge forests rising in the distance. Perhaps cavalry could travel in this land. "Gaelwyn, take Decurion Demetrius and his turma; you are to scout that settlement up ahead."

The settlement could be seen by the smoke rising above the forest tops. Marcus could only assume it was close to the valley for there were so few places to build in this rocky land.

"What do we do if it is a hill fort sir? Send for the bolt throwers?"

"No Decius that is why we have the Batavians. They have artillery and they will assault. Our role is to find them and, if they run, pursue them. Prefect Demetrius would have liked this task. More like a hunt. It would have suited his patrician ways."

"I can't get over how different his son is. Where his father was aloof, he is friendly; where he was cold he is warm. It's like a different person."

Gaius piped up, "He must take after his mother."

"There may be some of that Decius but you two should take some credit. He wasn't as friendly or as warm when he first arrived and he was arrogant too; not as bad as his brother but he still had an attitude. You two helped to show him the right way to do it. Remember that when you are running the ala."

"I can't see that sir. I have no connections. I don't expect it."

"Gaius, I had no connections but I received the promotion and I didn't expect it."

"You thinking of retiring sir?"

"No Decius. What would I do? I am no farmer. No, I expect I will go out as Ulpius did with a sword in my hand, his sword, the sword of Cartimandua."

"Sir, sir."

"Yes trooper?"

"Decurion Demetrius says it is a hill fort and they are not friendly."

"Thank you. Signifier ride back to Prefect Sura and tell him we have some work for him."

The hill fort was similar to those in the land of the Novontae but this one had a raging stream racing around one side of it. "Well Marcus that means they won't be escaping that way."

"You are right Cominius. I will hold my ala to the north west on the track. With the stream to the west and the gate to the east that leaves them north east as their only escape."

"Just where the general wanted them to be."

"Metellus take Gaelwyn and scout ahead. See if there are any more settlements."

Marcus and Decius found a nearby hill top from which to watch the Batavians attack. "It will be good to see how it should be done won't it sir."

"I think we did well but these boys have been doing this a lot longer, there must be things we can learn."

"We may not need to learn them if the general is right one more battle and it is all over. We could find ourselves in the east."

"Don't get your hopes up Decius. The legions might go but they have plenty of cavalry in the east who are better than we are at what they do. We will still be here long into the peace. This will always be our home."

The Batavians had onagers as well as the bolt throwers and the barrage of stones and bolts was intense. The palisade crumbled as though made of papyrus and the Batavians charged up the hill keeping an open formation. The onagers began to hurl their stones into the fort itself and from their vantage point Marcus and Decius could see the damage that they caused. They continued to crush and maim even after they had crashed into the first warriors and villagers.

"That's what we need next time sir. They can fire over their own men. Look it is all over."

Sure enough, the remaining villagers and warriors were fleeing north east to where Marcus assumed Calgathus was gathering his warriors. "We might as well go down to the fort. This looks like a good place for tonight's camp. "

The camp was already built by the time a weary Metellus and a seemingly indefatigable Gaelwyn returned. "Nothing sir. There is barely a sheep track. Gaelwyn could find no sign of any warriors or people. The hills are steep and covered in forests."

"Good well done Metellus." He called over the two prefects and Decius. "This is as far as we go. We drive them towards Agricola."

Calgathus was in his heartland in the Correen Mountains. His warbands had been arriving for the muster but increasingly there were refugees driven there by the Roman sweep. He had a huge number of mouths to feed for there were more women and children than he had expected. Fainch had kept in the background as he spoke with the other chiefs who had arrived. She had heard strident voices and knew that there was disagreement about their next course of action. She yearned to be involved but, unlike the Ordovices and Brigante the Caledonii did not listen to their women. Calgathus was a pragmatist and he would hear her out but she was frustrated because she had to wait.

Eventually the chiefs left and he summoned her to his side. "What will you do oh mighty king?"

"We will fight. This general has forced my hand. We have to fight for his forts are strangling my country. We cannot raid south and his army is squeezing the life out of my people. The question is where we fight. Some of my chiefs want to charge down and attack him where he is right now. Others want us to choose our battlefield to suit us. What is your opinion?"

"I think you should choose your battlefield. You want a hill with woods nearby for the legions fight better on the flat in open country. A hill means his machines cannot kill as many of your men. A hill also means your chariots can kill more men."

Calgathus nodded. "What you say makes sense and I know of such a place not far from here."

"How many men can you field?"

"As many as six Roman legions."

"And they only have one."

"You were right witch."

"Right? When?"

"When you advised us to join together and fight in the land of the Brigante. Here our families suffer as well as the warriors. This general has chewed us a piece at a time. Tomorrow I will lead my army and people north to Raedykes it will stretch the Roman army and the field will help us to win. When we are there I will speak with my people. They must know why we fight and why we must win."

His people gathered at Raedykes. It was a rounded hilltop with forests streaming away to the north. There was a smaller hill opposite and a plain between. In the distance, the sea could be seen, grey and threatening. The king stood on his chariot at the top of the hill to address his people. "We are going to fight the Romans here in this place of our choosing." His men roared their approval and beat their shields with their swords. "We will wait at the top of this sacred hill and we will wait for the Romans to come to us. Some of my warriors say that these Romans cannot be beaten. Remember they have never fought the Caledonii. They do not have their women watching them, encouraging them as we do. Warriors fight better when their women are close by. When they fall on the field they are left. They do not have their families to honour their glorious death they are thrown in to a hole in the ground and forgotten. We know why we are fighting. We are fighting for our land. Their land is far away. If we are strong and remember our families are watching, we will prevail and win. If we remember that this is our land and no one can take it from us then we will prevail. We will win and the Romans will die." There was an enormous cheer at this statement and the women screamed their approval. When they had quietened down the king finished, "Then we can return to our homes and our lives and remember this glorious day when we defeated, finally, the Romans."

The Roman army eventually all met up at the coast. Marcus noticed that the fleet was in close attendance. The General waved an expansive hand in its direction. "Although it is unlikely that we will be able to call on naval support, I felt that we should take every advantage available to us. Should the barbarians try to out flank us the fleet can use their artillery. Agrippa is not happy about having his ships on what he calls a lee shore, whatever that is but we need their artillery. Centurion we will build our camp there." He pointed to an area behind a small knoll. "Prefect if you could send out your scouts we shall see where the enemy is."

"Yes General. Gaius take Gaelwyn, Julius and Macro; make a wide sweep and find out they are. It will be hard to hide almost forty thousand wild warriors."

As they rode off Decius said, "Forty thousand? I hope the general knows what he is doing because all I can see here is twelve thousand auxiliaries and less than six thousand legionaries."

"Don't forget the thousand marines."

"Oh, they will be really useful." Decius had a poor opinion of the marine service.

"Don't underestimate them Decius. They are just legionaries who fight on ships. Anyway, let's get this camp built."

They had barely started when Julius Demetrius rode in. "We have found them sir. They are about two miles away at the top of a hill. There is a wood behind it."

"Good lad, go and tell the general."

"Are we attacking uphill again?"

"Decius, we have fought with this general for seven or eight years. Has he ever disappointed? Has he ever made a decision we felt was a bad one?"

"No but if you keep sticking your chin out sooner or later someone is going to smack it."

"Tomorrow we attack. Decius Brutus, the legion will be in reserve before the camp."

The unhappy centurion shook his head in frustration. "Well I hope you enjoy your fight tomorrow because we are caretakers again watching the general's baggage."

Agricola flashed an impatient look which was enough to silence him. "The Batavians and the Tungrians will advance up the hill and after a volley or two of arrows charge. Marcus' Horse will be stationed on the extreme left flank, the Gallic Horse on the extreme right. "He looked at the two prefects. "Your role is to prevent our being outflanked. If the attack looks like it is slowing we will release some of the legionary cohorts from guarding the baggage and they can bolster any flagging attack." The prefects all turned and grinned at the red-faced centurion. "We have never fought a pitched battle against the Caledonii and we know not how they fight."

Marcus stood, "Gaelwyn, my scout said that they still use chariots."

"Do they? Do they indeed? Well we have all faced them before and we know they will not have the large horses we use but it is worth bearing in mind."

Cominius joined in the debate, "I suspect a wild charge, like the Ordovices used. If they have the advantage of the slope then it could be effective."

"Which is why you will need to keep your lines firm and support each other."

The Gallic prefect spoke up, "What if they don't try to outflank then what are our orders?"

"I will be watching from the small hill opposite. The buccina will sound cavalry charge if I think it would be appropriate. Any further questions? No? Then we will rise before dawn. I want to be in position early."

If Agricola thought he was going to catch Calgathus asleep he was sadly mistaken. The Caledonii were up even earlier than the Romans and when the Roman army arrayed itself, it faced an enemy completely filling, the side of the hillside. In front of them, engulfing the plain between the Romans and the foot soldiers, there were chariots already in position. Agricola stood with the prefects at the top of the small hill. "Clever, very clever. I can see that I have a worthy adversary this time. Do you see the chariots will slow up my attack and they threaten to outflank our cohorts? Very clever. Right prefects to your men. The attack begins with two buccina blasts."

Prefect Marcus Aurelius Maximunius led his ala away to the left. He was aware that the Caledonii were watching his movements. He planned to use a little initiative. Gaelwyn had spotted a small ridge which would give them a better view of the hill and some momentum when they set off. The hill was steep in places although mercifully without rocks and trees. His horses would not be able to gallop at full speed but they would not have obstacles and pitfalls in their way. Once in position he took his place at the front of the line with Gaelwyn on one side and the signifier on the other. Behind him Decurion Princeps Decius was next to the aquifer. The rest of the Decurions lined up before their respective turma. Marcus glanced down the line and felt pride. He slid his sword from its scabbard, the gleaming blade polished like silver. Ulpius would be with the Allfather watching him. He held the sword in the air and as one man his ala roared, "Marcus!" The Caledonii looked over nervously anticipating a charge.

Marcus smiled; anything which discomfited the enemy would help. He looked at Gaelwyn. "You need not be here Gaelwyn. You could remain behind with the scouts."

Flashing a disparaging look he said, "Am I a woman that waits to make the food? I am a Brigante and I am one of Marcus' Horse. My place is here with you." He glanced over his shoulder at Decius and said mischievously. "You need at least one warrior to watch your back."

"Cheeky bugger!"

The banter was interrupted by the two buccina blasts. The attack began. "I hope Cominius and Furius know how to handle chariots."

"Do not worry Decius the chariots will pose no threat but there are a huge number of warriors for the prefects to face". The auxiliary cohorts looked pitifully small as they stepped across the green hillside to face the warbands who made the grass invisible. The chariots raced back and forth, their archers shooting ineffectively at the advancing Batavians. Suddenly the Batavian line halted. The Tungrians still went forward. The whole of the front line of the Caledonii seemed to lurch forward in anticipation of a swift victory for surely the Roman line was crumbling.

"Should we go in sir?"

"No Gaius, the prefects know what they are doing." Suddenly the sky in front of the Batavians was covered in arrows which plunged down on to the chariots. Every arrow found a target as the archers had aimed all across their front. Some horses crashed dead whilst those whose drivers and archers had perished ran back and forth in panic. Some escaped east or west but most of them ran up hill rather than face the wall of iron that was the auxiliary line. The Caledonii suddenly sprang aside to allow the frightened beasts to escape; some of the warriors were too slow and were trampled underfoot by the terrified beasts and their chariots.

Still the auxiliaries came on, although because the Batavians had halted, the line was oblique and the Tungrians were the first to strike the Caledonii. These warriors of Belgae descent were mighty swordsmen, armoured as they were and protected by shields their opponents stood no chance. It was like a farmer scything his corn as they cut swathes through the Caledonii. The wounded fell to the floor to be trampled by hob nailed caligae. When the Batavians hit the line, the effect was the same.

"They should have charged down the hill."

"You are right Decius although even then it would have taken a powerful body of men to crash through three lines of Batavians."

"And don't forget the Ninth; it looks like Decius Brutus is just itching to get to grips with them."

The eight thousand auxiliaries made relentless and inevitable progress up the hill. In their wake, the ala could see the writhing bodies of the dead and dying and almost to a man they were Caledonii. "Looks like this will be over before noon."

"Don't be so confident Decius this Calgathus has shown himself to be a cunning commander. This battle has some way to go."

At the top of the hill Calgathus and his war chiefs watched with dismay as the Romans cut down their warriors with impunity. "We have more men, oh king but they cannot get to the enemy for our own warriors."

"Send them around the side and we will attack them in the side and the rear."

Within a few moments two warbands, with four thousand warriors in each began to move swiftly east and west to outflank and destroy the Romans. The attack on the hill had slowed down mainly because of the slope and the mass of bodies. The hill was slick with blood and the auxiliaries were fighting the hill as much as their enemies.

"Prefect."

Gaelwyn pointed to the north to where they could see warriors flooding west. "I see them Gaelwyn. Ala form column!"
"What is the plan sir?"
"They plan to outflank our friends. We will go further west and outflank them. They may be faster than us in those woods but in the open they stand no chance. If we can catch them from the flank or rear we can drive them back into their own men."

Standing on the small knoll the general was itching to be amongst the fighting. He saw the outflanking barbarians and was gratified to see the two cavalry units respond. He turned to an aide, "Send a message to Decius Brutus and ask him to move forward a thousand paces." When the man had gone he turned to one of the tribunes. "Just in case the cavalry fail to halt this attack. Actually, I have no doubt that they will but the poor Ninth need something to do."

The Caledonii to the west of the battle were totally oblivious of the cavalry threat. Marcus had taken the ala below the skyline, confident in his men's ability to make up any lost ground. The tribesman ran in a compact group; their leader Lulach determined to hit the Romans hard in their flank. His warband was made up of huge warriors armed with long swords and war hammers; when they struck the whole battlefield would hear the sound.
Strabo's First Spear was the first one to see the threat. "Prefect Strabo, look!" He pointed to their left where, in the distance they could see a dark shadow moving swiftly across the green hillside.
"I see it. Second and third centuries form a line to the left. First Spear take charge."
"Sir." Calmly and efficiently the one hundred and sixty men turned and formed two lines at an oblique angle to the main line. They still managed to march forward while keeping their attention on the approaching barbarians.
"Keep it steady lads. I don't want anyone falling over."
"There's a lot of them sir." The voice came from one of the Usipi recently drafted in to the Batavians. He had never stood in

line before and was intimidated by the horde approaching at great speed.

"Quiet lad. I know there are more of them but they are all piss and wind! Shield and sword, shield and sword. Look for the weak point trust the man next to you and we'll be on the top of the hill before you know it."

Gaelwyn waved from the top of the ridge. "Halt. Right turn!" The column instantly turned into two lines. "Forward."

Moving forward at a walk they rode to the top of the ridge. A thousand paces below them the warband was rapidly approaching the left flank of the Batavians. "Trot"

As soon as the ala began to trot down the hill the Caledonii became aware of their presence. "Do not worry about the horses we will be upon these foot warriors before they strike."

"Gallop!" The hooves thundered, making the ground shake and some of those warriors on the extreme right began to glance nervously over their shoulders. They heard the buccina sound just as the warriors at the point struck home. The Batavian front line sagged under the pressure. First Spear yelled, "Third Century, put your backs into it and lock shields!"

The second rank did as they were ordered and the line bowed but did not give. In the front rank the second century was fighting for its life. Their swords sought out the bare flesh of the enemy and hacked and slashed creating savage wounds if not deadly ones. The war hammers and swords beat hard upon the shields and helmets of the auxiliaries but for all their noise they were largely ineffective.

Marcus' Horse thundered down the slope their swords and javelins a glittering sea of death sparkling in the early sun. Each trooper was leaning forward extending his sword or javelin. Marcus and Decius had decided to forego their bows as they need impact. The Caledonii began to turn to try to halt the avalanche that was descending upon them. It was hopeless. The horses and riders rode over the front ranks as if they did not exist. The warriors behind the front ranks had their backs to the horsemen who took every advantage they could. Javelins and swords instantly created a corpse and soon the pressure on the front slackened. First Spear saw it and decided to go on the offensive. "Push! Heave! Send these barbarians to Hades!"

The ala was now inextricably entwined with the Caledonii but they had the advantage of height, training and the belief that they could defeat any enemy. The decurions and Marcus led the line; they were the first to strike blows. The sword of Cartimandua ran red with blood and seemed to sing in the prefect's hand. Behind him guarding his flanks rode Decius and Gaius. They became a wedge driving deeper into the shrinking mass that had been Lulach's war band. A huge warrior ran towards Marcus' left side for the prefect was fighting a war chief on his right. Even as the warrior lifted his war hammer above his head to strike a fatal blow Decius had hurled his spatha, striking the warrior in his throat. He fell dead in an instant. Decius reached down to retrieve his spare gladius from its scabbard. "Who is next?"

Agricola was regretting not joining one of his forward cohorts as he saw the mêlée developing. Both of his cavalry units were engaged and he had no doubt that they would win for already warriors were streaming back from the flanks. In the centre, the Batavians and Tungrians were still making progress albeit slower than hitherto. To no one in particular the general said, "One more ala and I could ride around their rear and we would destroy them all."

Marcus was tiring but he suddenly saw a red horsehair crest a few paces from him; a centurion! "Come on Marcus' Horse we have nearly done it!"

The sound of the exultant prefect's voice spurred them on and gave each trooper extra energy. Suddenly the resistance seemed to crumble as the ala and the Batavians met in the bloody battlefield littered with barbarian bodies. "Well done First Spear."

"Well done yourself. That was as neatly timed a charge as I can remember."

"My compliments to your prefect. Sound the recall!"

As the strident sound of the horn echoed on the battlefield the ala began to form lines and decurions quickly checked casualties. "Not many missing sir."

"Thank you, Decius. Marcus' Horse, pursue the enemy."

Every decurion grinned and the troopers all whooped. The turmae would all fight any enemy they found. Like huntsmen chasing their quarry they raced up the hill after the fleeing warriors. In the centre, the Caledonii saw that they had been outflanked, not the enemy and they began to stream back with the cohorts in hot pursuit. "They are heading for the woods."

"Macro and Gaius cut them off from the woods."

It was a difficult task he had given his two best officers. They had to negotiate bodies, pockets of warriors still fighting and the fleeing remnants of the thirty thousand warrior army. The two decurions formed the tip of an arrow formation as their troopers streamed behind them. The edge of the woods was less than two hundred paces from them but there were still thousands of men in their path. Somehow, they cleared a path and reined their mounts in under the eaves of the trees. "Dismount! Horse holders."

In a well-practised manoeuvre, they dismounted and stood in a line facing the enemy. The training they had received from Macro now came into its own. The Caledonii had fled for the safety of the woods and now they were barred by the heavily armed and armoured Romans. Worse some of the Caledonii had flung their shields away and faced them with only a sword or dagger. The two turmae were like a rock upon which the sea of warriors crashed and died. The ones following ran further north to enter the woods at some point past this deadly obstruction. This brought them within the range of the rest of the ala and soon the bodies began to pile up. By the time Marcus arrived the majority of the barbarians had either died or entered the woods.

"Well done Gaius, well done Macro. Decius, we will need to rest the horses."

"But sir they are getting away."

"I know but look at the horses; they have charged and then run up the hill they will need to rest."

"Sir our horses have had a rest we can pursue."

"Very well Gaius and Macro take your men and follow. We will join you shortly."

"Sir the enemy are on foot can I take my turma on foot."

"On foot Julius?"

"Yes sir, my turma is fit we can do it. We can seek out those who are hiding from our horsemen."

Very well."

Roaring with delight the turma of the popular young decurion spread out through the woods. "Keen, isn't he?"

"I think we all were when we were young."

In the woods, the horses of the ala had to tread carefully along the trackless woodland. Julius and his men soon began to catch them. "Keep your eyes open and look up as well."

"Look up sir?"

"They can climb trees."

It was only moments later that their caution was rewarded. Gaius and his men had just passed a thick patch of trees when warriors began to drop on top of the warriors whose eyes were looking downward. "Come on!" With a roar, the men of the tenth turma raced forward to assist their fellow troopers. The shock and surprise now changed and the warriors tried to disengage.

As the troopers finished off the odd survivor Gaius came over to Julius. "Thank you decurion. A timely attack. I think we will look up and not just down from now on."

As Marcus and the rest of the ala began to sweep through the woods little knots of warriors were found and despatched. It was slow going as the exhausted Caledonii tried to catch their breath and still avoid the pursuing Romans. By the time the recall had sounded the ala were deep in the woods and reluctant to return. "Sir we could have them all."

"The general knows what he is about besides I am worried about the horses." He gestured at the limping and lame horses littered around the trees. "There will be another day."

Chapter 17

"So, gentlemen that nearly worked perfectly. How many men did we lose?"

His aide had spent the last three hours talking to prefects, counting the wounded and counting the corpses. "Five hundred and thirty-seven dead and five hundred and ten wounded forty of them seriously."

"And the enemy?"

"A little harder sir as there are many bodies in the woods and it is now dark. We estimate ten thousand."

"That is disappointing."

"Disappointing?"

"Yes, Prefect Bassus for it means that there are still twenty thousand Caledonii out there. The war could have ended today but I fear it will continue and without me. Had I had another ala of cavalry we could have ended it today."

"Or more infantry sir. We found it hard to pursue on horse in those woods. One of my decurions took his men on foot and they were just as effective as those mounted."

"And our men were exhausted."

"I know Prefect Sura."

Decius Brutus had an '*I told you so*' look on his face. "With respect sir had you used the Ninth the Batavians would have been free to pursue."

There was an awkward silence and the general reddened slightly. "Quite. At least you can spend the rest of the year proving that you were right Decurion as you and the auxiliaries hunt down Calgathus." There was almost a sigh of relief as the prefects realised that Decius, a very popular man, was not to be censured for saying what all of them had thought. In saving the Ninth from involvement to use later on he had in effect lost the opportunity to win the war in one last battle. At the end, the gambler had played cautiously.

"I can understand it Decius. Our lines of supply are over extended. We have not secured the lands through which we came and the north and Wales are barely settled."

Decius nodded but Gaius said, "The thing is sir we still have all of that to do and we have a powerful enemy up here to defeat. I would have gambled." He looked at the prefect. "And I think you would have too."

"Well I am not the general so we will never know."

"I will tell you one thing, that king of theirs won't risk a battle again. It will be back to night attacks, ambushes and murders. It is going to be a bloody war."

Deep in the forests to the north Calgathus and his army were licking their wounds. "It seems that an open battle is not the way forward. Perhaps we should now listen to the wise words of the witch eh?"

"Women!"

"I know Lulach. I know. Your men fought as well as any but how many Romans did your men kill?" Lulach angrily turned his head away. It was not for want of trying. His men had bled and died but the Romans seemed impervious to the blows landed by his men. "We have to accept that although any of our warriors could defeat a single warrior of theirs when they fight together, no matter how many more men we have, they will defeat us. We have to find a way. I think we killed more when we attacked their camp than we did on the field of battle."

"Then that is what we must do oh king. Night attacks."

"There are many things we must do but first we must head north east away from them so that we can plan in safety for they will follow us and we have our families with us."

"And as long as their fleet is there we cannot go near to the coast."

"I will seek out the witch and ask her advice."

"But King Calgathus she is a witch!"

"I will use anybody to rid my land of these Romans."

At least one Roman was leaving. Gnaeus Julius Agricola stood on the beach saying his goodbyes. "Well Prefects, and First Spear. We have travelled a long journey since first we fought at Stanwyck. We have travelled to the westernmost extremities and now the northern most and we have done it together. I cannot think of any other men who could have done better than you and your soldiers. There are now among you greybeards where first I saw the lean and callow youths. We have fought and defeated every enemy of Rome who has dared to challenge us. It is sad that we have not, as I had hoped, completed the task but that will be your duty and honour to complete. I truly believe that we have broken the back of these barbarians. It is forty-one years since the first Roman stepped ashore and in a mere eight years we have conquered more than all of our predecessors in thirty-three years. That is something to tell your grandchildren as I will tell mine." He clasped each man's arm in a soldier's salute; he spoke not a word for there were tears in his throat. When he came to Marcus he clasped his arm and then embraced him. In a quiet voice he said, "Marcus Aurelius Maximunius you embody Britannia. Keep it safe and finish my work."

Barely able to speak he said, "I will my general."

The impatient captain pulled up the gangplank and ordered the rowers to back water as soon as Agricola stepped on board. The prefects watched the sail become an indistinct blur and disappear south around the headland.

They walked silently back to the camp until Decius said, to no-one in particular, "Isn't it typical? You get one general trained up so you know what the hell he is thinking and they take him away and give you a new one."

The tension broken the senior officers all laughed. Furius said, "Anyone know who the new Governor is then?"

"Sallustius Lucullus."

They all looked at each other blankly. "Well we will have to wait and see then. I suppose until then we carry on with the general's orders. I daresay the new governor will make himself known to us before too long."

The new Governor was indeed landing, even as they spoke at Rutupiae. He had looked forward to this posting his whole life, for he was returning to his homeland. He was Lucullus son of Prince Arminius who had fled to Rome with his father King Cunobelinus, the only true King of Britannia and now his grandson was returning to rule a land even greater than that of his grandfather. Admittedly he was not a king but he wielded more power than a king. The petty princes and kings who had driven his family from their land would pay for their past treacheries and insults. The first thing he would do was to finally destroy the Caledonii and complete the work of Agricola.

The Caledonii themselves were not idle. Long into the night the king sat with Fainch as they discussed strategies which would evict the Romans from their newly won land. "Now is the time to strike King Calgathus. The general who led these men has departed. They are leaderless. Believe me I have fought the Romans since I was a young girl I know how they fight. They have order and discipline but it all comes from one man. The Romans will patrol and build but they will not attack. We have a free hand until a new general comes."

"What could we do against these Romans?"

"They are building roads and forts are they not? That is a perfect opportunity to attack. They cannot build and fight. Yes, after the first few attacks they will increase their guards and we will have to try a different strategy. As Lulach said we could attack their forts at night. We lost fewer men in that attack than the battle."

"But I do no not have the numbers I did have."

"You know how you build a dam? You divert the water and then you put stones in the bed. You build up the big stones and then you fill in with smaller stones and finally very small stone. Then you allow the water to flow again."

Impatiently he said, "This I know! I do not need a lesson from a woman."

Ignoring the insult, she said, "It takes much work to build a dam as it has taken many years to build their Empire but to destroy it you take out the small stones, one at a time, little by little eventually the whole thing becomes unstable and it collapses. Our attacks will be as the removal of the small stones, in themselves not powerful but, taken together, they will work."

"I will order my warbands to target the road builders. There are many roads and forts being built. It may have success. The attacks on the forts I will consider if the first attacks are successful."

The vexillation from the Second Tungrian cohort hated road building. The two centuries were warriors first and foremost, it was their life. They enjoyed the benefits which roads brought but they believed there were many inferior cohorts to their own who could do such labour. At least building this road to Alavna meant that they were many miles south of the land where the Caledonii were hiding. The other advantage was that they did not need to wear the Lorica segmentata which was vital in war but heavy and uncomfortable in peace. Like every other soldier they too wished that they had finally seen off the threat of Calgathus. As long as he and his not insubstantial army remained it was like a toothache which won't go away. It might calm down for a while but you know that eventually it will flare up.

Lulach had brought his warband south over the Vorlich mountain. It had been a hard trek but it had the beauty that it avoided all Roman patrols. They had only to cross one valley and Lulach had chosen the middle of the night at spot two miles from each of the camps sited along the valley. His four hundred warriors were eager. They had had to draw lots to decide on the warband for so many had wanted revenge for the defeat at Mons Graupius. Even as Lulach and his men got into position other bands were doing the same further north on the road being built to Inchtuthil.

He peered over the mound behind which he squatted; twenty of the men were on sentry duty while the other one hundred and forty toiled on the road. He signalled his smallest warriors and they ran south and north to encircle the Romans. The other three hundred warriors began to filter down. The sentries had already been targeted and two warriors were approaching each one. It mattered not if they raised the alarm for Lulach was convinced his men could cover the distance before the Tungrians could arm themselves and, more importantly put on their armour.

Eight of the sentries had been killed before one made a sound. With a roar, the warriors leapt over the ridge and raced down the slope. Although taken by surprise the Tungrians training took over and they quickly picked up swords and shields. By the time the Caledonii had reached them they had formed a shield wall. The Tungrians were angry and fought back ferociously but, without their armour and helmets they were more vulnerable to the blows of their opponents who, for the first time almost fought them on an equal basis. The smaller warriors who had encircled them began to hurl slingshots at them and soon there were casualties. It would have turned into a disaster had not the signifier remembered his buccina and sounded a blast. A blast which caused him a crippling wound to his leg as a warrior threw a spear at him but it had the desired effect. Lulach roared his command. The Caledonii disengaged and fled back into the forest taking with them any swords and shields they could from the dead Tungrians. When the relief column made their way down from their section of road building most of the wounded had been made comfortable and those too severely wounded had been despatched. It was the Tungrian way.

The prefects met at Inchtuthil to plan their strategy. "Any word from the new governor?"

"He sent a message with the fleet. He is in the south, then he will visit Deva, across to Eboracum and finally to us."

"No hurry then?"

"I think it is up to us. "

"You are right Cominius. We lost over a hundred Tungrian dead."

"We lost the same," added Strabo.

Bassus nodded, "Two hundred. No signal was given and two centuries perished. The bastards."

"The first thing we do is an obvious one, we double the number of guards on the roads."

"That slows down the building."

"So does dead auxiliaries."

Marcus looked at the map. "If the Gallic cavalry patrols from Alavna to Inchtuthil and my horse patrol the road from Inchtuthil to the fort at Marcus only then any attack can be thwarted because there should always be a relief force of forty cavalry nearby."

Metellus, the prefect of the Gallic cavalry, nodded, "It is a good plan but it means we cannot hunt the Caledonii."

Cominius looked up, "It seems to me that we know where the Caledonii are, attacking my men. In the absence of any better plan we will try this."

"To make it more efficient I would suggest that one turma camps with each cohort. That will mean less travelling. We can rotate the turma."

Decius of course, was overjoyed. "Looking after the bleeding infantry again."

Gaius smiled, "Yes Decius but think of the lovely road you will have to show for it."

"We don't need to patrol on the road. In fact, it may be better if we patrol along the forest edge for that is where we are likely to find them. Use your scouts and keep your ears open. One of the Gallic cohorts was almost killed to a man because they didn't get the chance to sound the alarm. I think we all know what the sound of battle is like. Gaius, you take the road closest to Inchtuthil and Decius the one closest to Marcus."

"That means I sleep in my own cot each night."

"True but remember we are the frontier. North of us there are no friendlies, not even ships since the general left."

Decurion Agrippa was feeling his age as he led his young troopers along the banks of the Isla. He was coming up to over forty summers, he was not exactly certain of his age but his body told him that he had had enough of riding for up to twelve hours a day. His mind still wanted war but his body didn't. He would have to discuss it with the prefect one of these days. He smiled. The prefect was a man you could approach. He knew of other ala and cohorts where the prefect was aloof and distant, not Marcus. "Sir?"

"Yes, what is it Cassius?"

"Tracks sir, crossing the river."

"You have good eyes, for I had missed them. Right lads be ready we may have found a warband. Cassius take the lead, I may miss something; you won't."

"Yes sir."

The raiders were already crawling through the tree line, slithering along the ground and hidden by the alder and elder bushes lining it. They could see the increased sentries but it did not worry them for they had been the warband to almost massacre the Gauls. They believed they were invincible. Even as the sentries were dying the warband leapt to their feet roaring their war cries. The Batavians had been prepared and were wearing their armour. Even so the speed with which they were attacked stopped them for forming a shield wall effectively. The

Centurion yelled, "Sound the alarm!" just a moment before the war hammer smashed sickeningly into his skull.

The Caledonii were not worried by the alarm. They would kill these foreigners and be gone before anyone could save them. Suddenly the warband at the rear started to scream as javelins and arrows poured down on them from the charging ala which sprang unexpectedly from the forest. Saoirse, their leader turned and yelled, "Run!" His men needed no further bidding and they disengaged quickly from their combat. Some of them rolled under the horses while others dodged under the bushes to avoid the cavalry and their steeds.

Agrippa saw the leader, recognisable by his armour and urged his horse on. A warrior tried to save his leader by thrusting a sword at Agrippa who swerved his horse and with a backhand slash ripped open the man's face. The swerve took him too close to Saoirse who, in desperation swung his hammer at the horse's head. The swerve of the horse and its instinctive reaction of self-preservation meant that the hammer did not connect with the horse but smashed instead into Agrippa's knee. The whole kneecap disintegrated and he screamed in pain. Dropping his sword, he had the instincts to hold on to this horse which leapt over the warrior crouching before him and came to an exhausted rest in the middle of the partly built road. Agrippa slid from the horse in more pain than he had ever felt in his life. Blood and bone were pouring from the crippling wound and, mercifully, he passed out.

When the decurion came to he found himself in the camp at Marcus. His knee was still giving him pain but it seemed to come in waves. He had no relief for the succession of shocks he suffered.

He looked around and saw the surgeon. "Awake at last. Your wound will hurt. We can give you more relief for the pain but I am afraid that the wound is serious. I will fetch the prefect. He wanted to know when you awoke. He has been most concerned."

Even in the throes of pain Agrippa smiled. He would have been surprised had the prefect not attended his wounded decurion. It was his way.

"You had us worried. You were asleep for a day and a night but, as the surgeon said, sleep is the best medicine."

"My men sir are they…?"

"Your men are fine. They all survived and they brought you in. I have never seen men so upset about an officer. They are good lads."

"I know sir. They are only lads but they are so keen. How about the Batavians?"

"You got there just in time. Sixteen dead including the centurion but it could have been worse and your lads accounted for thirty of their warriors."

"They did well then."

"That boy Cassius remembered where they had crossed the Isla and followed them. That is where they killed most of them. Including the chief who gave you that."

Agrippa looked down at the linen tent which obscured his view of the injured knee. I didn't want to ask but…"

"It is a bad one. You know that. The whole kneecap has gone. The surgeon says he can have the blacksmith make you two metal rods which will help you walk but you cannot ride again."

"It's funny sir. I was only thinking on the patrol today that I had had enough of riding and now that I have no chance of riding again I miss it already." He looked helplessly at the prefect. "Sir what will I do? What can I do?"

"I could get you a pension. You have enough service in. We can get you some land in the land of the Brigantes close to Stanwyck."

He shook his head. "I have only ever known the ala. All my friends, well you know sir, they died with Drusus. Since then you and the decurions, well you are my friends and family."

There is a post for you but to be honest Decurion Agrippa I am not sure you would want it."

"What is it sir? Let me make the choice. I can always say no."

"Well I need an adjutant. Someone to tell the clerks what to do and to manage the camp and, ultimately, the fort. I am not a desk officer and I need to be out and about." Agrippa was silent. "I told you it wasn't the best job in the world."

"No sir but it is a job and a useful job and I can still be here with the people that I need."

"Good that is settled. Welcome to the ala Adjutant Agrippa."

Later, sitting in the Praetorium drinking watered wine Decius asked. "It is a real job isn't it sir. I mean if it isn't I won't tell anybody but I just wondered."

"Yes Decius, it was not out of pity." He smiled at his deputy. "To be honest I was going to offer it to you."

"Me? Why me?"

"Well none of us are getting any younger and I know that the riding is getting to me you are older…"

Decius was indignant. "I am sorry sir but that is out of order. I do everything the younger lads do don't I"

"Yes Decius. I apologise. So to answer your question it is a real job and Agrippa will do it well."

"Looks like the plans worked."

"Yes, but they are still causing too many casualties. Now that Agrippa has the role of Adjutant I can ask the Gauls to patrol up here as well and we can take the ala and see it we can hurt the Caledonii. It's about time we took the offensive."

"That is good news sir. When do we leave?"

"I will see the prefect tomorrow. If he agrees, the day after. You had better detail a turma to guard the fort and get Porcius to give us supplies for ten days."

The morning of the departure Marcus held a briefing. He held it in the sick bay so that Agrippa would know what was going on. "Septimus you and adjutant Agrippa will stay here with your turma and the non-combatants. I want them all armed, surgeon, clerks, cooks, the lot. With us gone the last thing I want is this camp to be overrun. I have asked Prefect Strabo to extend his patrol rout to us here and he will send a century to help garrison it the day after tomorrow. The rest of us will head north. Our first camp will be at the site of the battle then I intend to push on to the north coast."

"Have you heard something then sir?"

"Not really but when I was talking to the fleet commander he said that between here and the north coast the land was gentler. Calgathus will need to feed and house a large population. Winter is coming and I can't see him living on the tops of those mountains. The land he described sounds like perfect winter camp territory. We will stay together. He has over ten thousand men but I want to hurt him, burn out any huts he has, destroy crops and, if we catch them, destroy any warbands. It may just stop him sending them to raid us. Any questions? No? Well then Decurion Septimus and Adjutant Agrippa, Camp Marcus is all yours."

Macro and Decius rode at the head of the column as it headed north east. Gaelwyn and the other scouts were beyond the horizon. It was a pleasant day to be riding with a fresh breeze from the sea. The land looked peaceful and, as Marcus turned to look at the ala behind him he could see the calm and peace reflected in his men. "Decius this is my last patrol."

"What do you mean last patrol? You just appointed Agrippa as adjutant. I thought that was because you wanted to be out of the fort more."

Marcus shook his head. "Decius, I have seen more than fifty summers. I know, you are older but you have been luckier than I, Mona and the poison have not only weakened me but made me realise that I am not getting any younger. The prefect of this ala should be a younger man, someone who is able to deal with the new problems facing us now that we have almost conquered this land."

"You are still young. You are too young to retire."

"When the new Governor arrives, I will ask him to appoint my successor. I will not be retiring for some time for one will need to be appointed. I can then consider what to do after the ala."

Decius began, for the first time to consider his future. He had never thought he would be Decurion Princeps, he had never thought he would still be alive. All those who had joined with him and most of the ones who had joined since were dead. It was a sobering thought that, Marcus apart, all his friends were the decurions and they were all at least ten years younger, young Demetrius was almost thirty years younger! What would he do? "Will you go back to Cantabria?"

"No, I left when I was but seven summers. I think I will settle, as Flavinius Bellatoris did in Britannia."

"He is dead you know?"

Marcus looked round, shocked. "I did not know. When did he die?"

"It was when we were in Mona, Aed's raiders burned out his settlement, crucified the old man."

"I wish I had known I would have made that bastard suffer at the end. Why did no one tell me?"

"You were still recovering from your imprisonment at the hands of Fainch and then, well other events took over and ..."

"I will offer a sacrifice for his spirit."

"Where will you settle?"

"Glanibanta is a beautiful place and away from the hustle and bustle of the rest of the province. I think I would be happy there and our people still live there."

Decius smiled. Only Marcus would think of the slaves as his people. "You are right it would be a good place. I just can't see you hanging up your sword."

They both looked at the sword, menacing even in its scabbard. "You know I hadn't thought of that. It should be used by a warrior, not an old man raising horses. I will consider what to do with it. Did I tell you of the story Macha told me about its origin?"

"No, I don't think so."

"It came from across the sea, made for a great warrior but as he was dying he hurled it into a lake and it was found by one of Macha's ancestors. The magic and its power go back a long way. I think the power and magic should continue to work for the land it belongs to, this land."

Not far away Calgathus and Fainch were considering the next strategies. Already the war chiefs had grudgingly admitted that Fainch was an asset rather than a liability. Her plans had worked out well and the Caledonii were striding around their camps with a spring in their steps. They were not remembering their retreat and losses they were dwelling on the success of killing Romans.

"The Romans have tightened up their defences and increased patrols. It is more difficult to attack them now."

"Here? Yes, but further south? Beyond the lines of forts in the land of the Selgovae? I think we need to send warbands further south. There are few Romans there and if we can cause them losses they will have to bring men from here, and weaken the frontier."

"Lulach would you like to raid south of the Bodotria?"

The young warrior's eyes lit up. "Give me a large enough warband and I will give you the land of the Selgovae."

"Good. If you leave now then I can send another warband to the land of the Votadini in a few days when my son returns."

Chapter 18

Lulach headed south with five thousand hardened and fierce warriors desperate to wreak revenge on the Roman invaders. They travelled in groups of a hundred to avoid detection and to increase speed. They went down deserted valleys, through uncharted forests and the only evidence for the Romans was the sudden drop in attacks on their road building for they left not a mark on the landscape.

Calgathus looked at the half empty settlement. "I will travel west to find my son and launch the second part of the invasion. Will you remain here or have you plans hidden even from me?"

The king was both cunning and wise and he recognised that Fainch used him just as much as he used her. He knew that she plotted but it was always against the Romans. His barbed comment was just a warning that he knew of her machinations and plots. "No oh king. I will remain here and brew up poisons for your warrior's bows"

"Excellent!" The king was delighted when Fainch had told him that she could use Wolfsbane to tip his men's arrows for it meant even a nick would incapacitate an auxiliary.

The king had furnished Fainch with some slaves. These were women captured in raids. Some had lived with the Caledonii for over twenty years; longer was rarer because of the harsh treatment they received. The women were particularly badly treated. As they were used by the warriors for sex the women of the Caledonii despised them, branding them whores. They took every opportunity to belittle and demean them. The five women who worked for Fainch had been pleased at first for it meant they were away from the Caledonii women. They soon found that their new bed was a far worse one for Fainch treated them as Roman collaborators. The eldest was Ailis, she had seen twenty-one summers. Strikingly beautiful she had learned to hide her beauty with dirt, grime and a downcast look. She had no desire to be the subject of sexual advances from the warriors of the Caledonii. She had been captured first by Venutius and then given to Calgathus when the two kings became allies. She was prized for she was a member of the Brigante royal family being descended from one of the old king's liaisons with a slave. The details of her origins were now lost in the seeds of time but her Brigante roots could not be hidden and Fainch knew that she had been captured by Venutius which made her the target of the worst abuses. The other four were just grateful that Ailis bore the brunt of Fainch's venom. The image of Fainch as a snake fitted their perception of her well.

Ailis shuddered when Fainch insinuated herself into their roundhouse. A dark and smoke-filled hut it was cluttered with the tools of Fainch's deadly trade. In one corner, there stood the wicker baskets containing the flowers, all members of the buttercup family, which appeared so innocent but, in the hands of Fainch became wolfsbane. The process was simple but potentially dangerous. The petals were first dried and then ground to a powder and mixed with water. The slaves did not mind the process at this point for the poison was not concentrated but the cauldrons were then boiled until it increased in potency. The fumes had been known to cause the slaves to pass out and they all feared touching the liquid once it was ready for use. Ailis was always given the task of stirring the foul liquid. She had taken to tying a piece of linen across her mouth and nose for she knew that if she passed out Fainch would do nothing to revive her.

As she stared, with only her eyes showing above the scarf there was pure hate in them. Her look was one of pure, unadulterated hatred for this witch. She longed to kill her but somehow, she never got the opportunity. The witch seemed to know what she thought and kept all the poisons out of her reach.

"I can see you, you know. I do not need my eyes to see the hate you are giving me." Fainch turned around. "Perhaps tonight I will punish you again. Perhaps tonight we will see just how much pain you can take."

Ailis shuddered; she had not believed one woman could do such unspeakable things to another woman. "I am sorry. It is the fumes; they make my eyes angry I cannot help it."

Apparently satisfied Fainch ordered, "Well get on with it. King Calgathus will need much poison for his warriors."

Marcus and the ala arrived at the scene of the battle. There were still remnants of the battle, discarded and broken pieces of armour. Any human remains had been devoured and scoured by animals. "Decius build the fort here."

"Macro, come here."

"Yes, Decurion Princeps?"

"You know I feel I have neglected your training of late."

"Have you sir?"

"You have seen me lay out a camp many times."

"Yes sir. Always the same way."

"Good, in that case you get to do this one. Build it over there."

Shoulders slumped, the normally ebullient Decurion wandered over to the site chosen. "Yes, Decurion Princeps."

Laughing Marcus said, "That was nasty, Decius."

"No sir, you said it yourself we are getting no younger and these lads will have to take over eventually."

"You are right. Gaius!"

"Yes sir."

"While we are building the camp, I want you to take Gaelwyn and scout the route north. Look for signs of large numbers moving across the land."

"Do you think they are close sir?"

"This is their heartland. They would not travel far. The general wanted to push on northwards and see an end to this campaign but then he was ordered back to Rome. The barbarians probably think we have given up."

"Right sir."

He noticed the two new decurions Cilo and Galeo. He waved them over as he dismounted his horse. Argentium was no longer a young horse and Sergeant Cato had been making noises about replacing him. Marcus knew that the sergeant was right but he had wanted to retire the horse when he did.

"Sir!"

"It is the first chance I have had to ask you, how it is going?" They both looked blank, almost worried. "The promotion? I remember when I made the move from trooper to decurion it seemed such a leap at the time."

They looked relieved, "No sir no problems. The turma is made up of good lads. They miss Vettius as we all do but they didn't make it difficult for me."

"And you Decurion Galeo? How are our German recruits?"

He laughed, "They found the transition to horses a bit difficult sir but now they have their arses a bit harder they quite enjoy not having to walk everywhere."

"They are big lads."

"They are that sir. Sergeant Cato struggled to get them big enough mounts. I have told them if they don't look after them they will have to walk!"

"Good. Remember, if you have any problems," he looked seriously at them, "and I mean ***any problems*** then come and see me."

Decurion Cilo looked at his friend and spoke for them both, "Sir, we owe you everything. When we returned to Morbium for the extra training we both thought about running but you sir, you looked after us, you and Decurion Macro. We'll never forget it and we'll never let you down."

"Let me down? Boys you could never let me down, now off you go, I think Decurion Macro needs some assistance." Decurion Macro was indeed becoming frustrated having watched Decius erect the camp it had looked easy, he now discovered it was not.

Calgathus met up with his son, Tully, close to the large lake north of the Clota. "Lulach is raiding south of here. I want you to take your warband east, cross the line of new forts and raid the Romans in the land of the Votadini."

His son, a bigger version of his father grunted his agreement. "Is this the witch's plan?"

"It is. Why"

"The plan to raid the roads worked at first but now I am losing more warriors. Will this plan end the same?"

"Once you have attacked the Romans then return north. With you and Lulach raiding down here the Romans will have to send the soldiers from our lands. Now do you see?"

"As long as we get to kill Romans. Who guards the camp with you and your oathsworn here?"

"Iagan, the king of the Taexali has brought his warband to aid us."

"I do not trust that man. He is not fit to be a king. He sent no warriors to fight with us."

"But he is the king and although they pay homage to me we need his support. When the time comes and the Romans are gone we will remind him of the duty he owes us but for now our families are protected and safe."

"This looks a good site for a camp Gaelwyn."

"Romans! Why you need to build each night I do not understand. We could cover twice the distances if we did not stop to build each day. We are like the snail who carries his home upon his back."

"It is safer. No night raids."

"Gaelwyn has told you there are no enemies close enough to attack us. Do you doubt my word?"

"No of course not, "the last thing Gaius wanted was to get the wrong side of the irascible old man. "But it is laid down that we have to build a camp. I will wait here while you fetch the column." Grumbling the Brigante scout rode off.

Marcus was delighted when he saw the site. "I think we will base ourselves here for a while." Away to the west the mountains rose to steep white tipped peaks but to the north, south and east the land rolled gently to the sea. There was adequate water and Marcus knew that Macro could supply the officers with deer for their table. It was, more importantly close enough to the area he knew the Caledonii and their allies would be.

The following day he sent out the turmae in pairs to scout the north west, the west and the east. The rest he retained at the camp. "Gaius, you take Julius west. Decius take Macro north west and Domitius you take Marcus Augustus south west. You are scouts. Do not engage the enemy no matter how easy they look. Once they know we are in the area they will flee and we will have to start all over again."

Gaius and Julius urged their mounts along the low valley sides. To their left the mountains rose like an impenetrable barrier. Gaius had seen a pass ahead which had woods nearby.

It would make perfect cover. Cavalry could travel further than the cohorts but they stood out along the skyline too easily. As they approached the woods he ordered his men to dismount. Leading their horses through the edge of the wood they found a track of sorts which indicated that men had used this for trade or warfare. Either way it could be dangerous and Gaius held up his hand to halt the column. Giving his horse to Julius he drew his sword and edged his way to the pass. Using the large, wide bole of a tree for cover he peered down into the valley below. Just behind a distant forest he could see tendrils of smoke rising into the sky. There were too many to suggest a lone traveller. It had to be a settlement. He quickly returned to the column and summoned a trooper. "Villius return to camp and inform the prefect that we have found a settlement. I am going closer to see how the land lies."

"Sir."

"Right men we are going to travel through the woods to avoid detection. We will walk on foot for a while," hearing a groan he grinned, "I think we need the exercise and it will minimise our chances of being spotted. Julius could you take the rear in case we stumble into anything I want someone to take charge."

Julius looked up in horror, "Nothing is going to happen to you is it sir?"

"No Julius, but as an officer you have to assume that bad things will happen and make plans to deal with them."

Their path took them downhill and soon his men began to realise how treacherous the ground was. The trees grew very close together and the canopy stopped light permeating this far. It was a dark Stygian gloom through which they travelled. Gaius also discovered that he had no way of estimating distance or time. He could be miles away from the smoke or about to stumble into the camp. It was his nose and then his ears which told him they were close for he could smell animals and smoke. It was only faint at first but the wind was coming from that direction. The wind direction helped to ease the decurion's anxiety for it carried their smell, their Roman smell, away from the settlement. As he stopped to sniff he heard the distant sounds which told him there was a settlement, dogs barking, shouting, children playing, cows lowing all the evidence he needed.

He gave his horse to a trooper and made his way back to Julius. "The settlement is up ahead. Come to the front and take charge. I will take Sergius, he has the best ears and eyes, and get closer. Have the men ready to mount and make a hasty retreat if we are spotted. Send two of your lads back to the pass in case the prefect arrives."

Sergius was a small wiry warrior who had been born a Brigante. Like Gaelwyn and before him Osgar, he had this ability to almost sense the enemy. "Right Sergius leave the shield, just take your sword."

The two troopers dodged from tree to tree checking for movement before advancing. It took them a while but soon they could see the forest getting lighter. They were getting close to the edge of the settlement. The two men dropped to the ground and, drawing their daggers, slithered up to the edge of the forest. A line of gorse bushes edged the forest and the two Romans slid underneath it, their mail and helmets protecting them from the thorny spikes and the dense foliage camouflaging them.

They found they had a perfect view of the settlement. There was a low palisade, obviously intended to keep out wild animals rather than attackers. There was a gate which was guarded on the south west wall. A stream ran along the north wall and turned slightly west close to where the two men hid. It was a large settlement and Gaius counted at least forty tendrils of smoke which he assumed meant forty fires and huts. He was busy attempting to see the sentries when he heard voices approaching. Sergius gripped his arm to warn him and they saw to their horror two warriors approaching the line of bushes where they had secreted themselves. The advantage of their nest was it was hard to see them the disadvantage was that it was almost impossible to get out quickly.

The two men lowered their breeks and began to urinate, the hot steaming stream raining down on to the two hidden Romans. "The sooner their king returns the better. My brothers and I want to do some of the raiding as well."

"And I just want to be away from that witch she frightens me. I will face any warrior from any tribe and I am not afraid of death but she terrifies me."

"And me. I have heard that she makes love to men and then consumes their body making herself more powerful by doing so." They had finished and were pulling up their breeks when, behind them came the noise of a breaking branch.

"What is that?"

"Could be a Roman spy." The two Romans could see nothing but they heard arrows being notched. Suddenly they heard, "There!" and the sound of two arrows flying through the air followed by the thud as they found their target finally there was the sound of the crash of a body hurtling through the undergrowth.

Gaius was incredibly frustrated. He could not turn around. Had one of his men followed him? Perhaps they had been away too long and Julius had followed. He dared not turn around.

"Well not a Roman spy but this deer will feed our hut tonight."

Waiting until the two sentries had re-entered the settlement the two men slid out backwards their bodies stinking of urine. "Sir when we pass that stream we saw do you mind if we bath? I am not going back to the turma stinking like a piss pot."

"Good idea Sergius, good idea."

By the time they made the pass Marcus and Decurion Cilo were waiting for them. "Found the settlement sir. It is a big one. Sergius reckons they are not Caledonii but Taexali an ally of them. But there are Caledonii in the settlement and," he paused, "she is there."

"She?"

"The witch. I think the witch Fainch is in the village."

Julius told Macro later that he had never seen the colour leave man's cheeks as quickly as it did from the prefect's.

"I hope she is Gaius. I pray to the Allfather that she is for then my quest will end when she dies."

None of the other patrols had sighted any combatants. From a distance, they had seen isolated huts and habitation but they had not seen a major settlement. "Decius will take turmae one, three, four five six and seven and approach from the north. According to Gaius the stream flows that way.

Gaius nodded. "It isn't a big stream you could ford it on foot."

"The gate is on the opposite side, the south west. We will leave Turma fifteen with the horses at the pass and the rest of the ala will go through the forest. As Gaius demonstrated that is the best approach to avoid being seen."

"But not being pissed on!"

Decius comment resulted in uproar as they all laughed at the hapless young man. Marcus let the laughter subside naturally. When we are in position we will attack along the south wall. Gaius said most men could leap the palisade."

"Decius might need a hand sir as he is a short arse."

"When we begin our attack, I want one mounted turma to chase down any fugitives and the rest can enter from the north. Questions?"

"Prisoners sir?"

"Thank you, Julius. No warriors or boys. Kill them. If you can take the women prisoners then do so but if any resist then kill them." He paused and looked around the decurions. "Gaius suspects that the witch Fainch is in the settlement." There were gasps and meaningful looks exchanged. "If she is in there she may try to disguise herself. No matter what she looks like she cannot disguise the scar running the length of her arm. We will then destroy the settlement. We can take any animals back that we can but I do not want us slowed down. We are doing what the Caledonii do, we are raiding. Speed is the key. I want us back in camp well before dark. Anything that holds us up must die."

Lucullus was in Eboracum when he heard the news. "Sir, the Caledonii! They have flooded across the border and started raiding in the lands of the Selgovae and Votadini."

Cursing the delays which had kept him in Deva longer than he had wanted the governor grabbed a map. "The trouble is all our experienced troops are north of this Bodotria River. Prefect I want two cohorts of the Second Adiutrix ready to move out at dawn. We can at least reinforce the border. The sooner I get to Inchtuthil the better. Send a ship to tell the cohorts and legions in the area that raiders will be making their way north. I want the area sealed so tightly that nothing, not even air can escape. Have we any auxiliary units here?"

"Just the Asturian horse and a new cohort of Batavians."

"Good I will take those as well."

"But governor that leaves us weak here."

"If we don't stop them at the border this will be the new border and Rome will have lost half a province. Half a province that it took Julius Agricola eight years to conquer. I am not going to lose it in my first year."

The forest seemed less dark to Gaius as they filtered down through the thick fine trees. Perhaps it was the presence of the rest of the ala that made it less intimidating. Gaelwyn was already on the edge of the forest scouting out the position of the sentries but the rest were only half way through the dense primeval woodland. The prefect had impressed on them all the need for silence. With nearly three hundred men in armour moving through woods it would be easy to make a noise and warn the defenders. Gaelwyn materialised from nowhere. "There are six sentries at the gate and one on the hill on the other side of the valley."

"Can you dispose of the single sentry?"

He held up the bloody knife. "He is already dead. They will think he is asleep."

When they were assembled at the edge of the forest Marcus sought out Numerius. "Your killers ready Decurion Galeo?"

Numerius grinned, "They can't wait sir." His Usipi had been desperate for the opportunity to prove how brave they were and the chance to storm the gate and kill the sentries appealed to them.

"It all depends on them silencing the sentries quickly."

"They have practised all night."

"Good then whenever you are ready."

The Decurion muttered something in German and the ten warriors grinned and then moved at incredible speed across the open ground. Six of them were spinning slingshots around the heads whilst the other four had their swords drawn ready. The swords were not needed as the lead shot unerringly found their targets and, with a roar, the troopers were through the gate and roaring their war cry as they fell upon the hapless defenders.

The cry was echoed as the rest of the turmae rushed forward and either climbed or vaulted the low palisade. Gaius just followed one of Galeo's Germans who simply ran through the fence as though it did not exist. The occupants of the settlement had been taken completely unawares. They had had no idea that there were any Romans within fifty miles let alone the fifty paces they actually were. A warrior emerged from a hut screaming his rage and Gaius sliced through his neck before he had time to complete his scream. The decurion rushed into the hut and quickly saw that its occupant was a half-naked woman. He ran back into the settlement and heard the sound of Decius' buccina. The neighs of the horses told him that Macro and Decius had completed the encirclement. All around him the auxiliaries were despatching the warriors with ruthless efficiency. Some of the women had decided to join in and he saw screaming, scratching, spitting women more like banshees than humans attacking troopers with any weapon they had to hand.

Marcus had drawn his sword but so far he had not needed to use it for his troopers were clearing the fleeing warriors and women like wheat. Then he saw that his men were not having it their own way. Outside of a large hut in the middle of the settlement a hundred or so warriors were firing arrows at his men. His men were falling to the ground even though they were armoured. For a moment Marcus was perplexed and could not rationally come up with an explanation and then he saw that a woman was directing the archers and, though he had seen her but once, he instantly knew her, it was Fainch and in that same instant he knew why his men were suffering such casualties. The arrows were poisoned. He yelled out to his decurions and troopers alike, "Poisoned arrows. Use your shields. Poisoned arrows!" He attracted Gaius' attention. "It is Fainch!"

The attack slowed dramatically as Marcus' Horse became wary of showing themselves. The mounted troopers had the advantage of being on the opposite side of the hut away from the deadly shower of murderous arrows. "Something has halted the attack on the other side Macro, you go this side and I'll go the other. Come on! Charge!"

The sudden appearance of the horses made all the difference; now the one hundred warriors had to split their arrows three ways.

"Now!" roared Marcus, "rush them!"

The arrows were now fired much more hastily and more arrows hit the air or shields than men. Marcus desperately tried to keep his eye on his main target, the witch. She disappeared behind a wall of warriors and Marcus hacked and thrust with his sword for all that he was worth. His concentration was so great that he did not see the boy with the slingshot before it was too late. Although the stone hit his helmet, which took most of the blow, it had been close enough to render the prefect unconscious. Immediately Julius, who was to the prefect's rear ordered the troopers nearest to make a barrier with their shields. After checking that he was still breathing he ordered the men, "Take him back to the forest and guard him with your lives. The rest of you let's finish this."

The enraged troopers who had had to suffer poison arrows and then the beloved prefect wounded were in no mood for prisoners. The boy with the slingshot was hacked to death by two troopers. The archers, who were defenceless once the troopers closed with them died in a flash of blades and spears. As Macro and Decius led their horsemen to purse those fleeing the other troopers led by Gaius and Julius burst into the hut. There they saw six frightened women cowering behind amphora and cauldrons. "Witches! Kill the bitches!"

Gaius was slightly behind the troopers and three of the slaves died before he could intervene. A wild-eyed trooper was stood over Ailis his sword poised to end her life when Gaius thrust his shield between them. They are slaves! Look they are slaves." The Caledonii put rings of iron around their slave's necks to enable them to be chained and to stop them escaping.

"Outside, the witch must be outside. Julius go and tell Macro and Decius to pursue her." He walked up to Ailis who was sobbing uncontrollably and put his arm around her. She threw her arms around him and wept uncontrollably. Gaius did not know what to do.

Suddenly he heard Gaelwyn shout, "Ailis!" The girl looked up and ran to Gaelwyn. Gaius wondered what was going on as they embraced and for the first time that he could remember he saw Gaelwyn cry. "It is my sister's daughter. She was stolen in a raid. She is Brigante. She is my family."

Macro and Decius raised themselves to see over the troopers who were still slaughtering warriors and the huts which blocked their view. "All we know is that she is a woman."

"Right then son. Take half the men and capture every woman you can. Tie them up and we'll worry if we have got the right one later on."

The two decurions split up and raced out of the settlement and into the open land where the few who had survived had fled. The warriors, men and boys were killed as they ran but the women and girls were all captured and tied up. It was a long process. There was a loud shout from one of Decius' troopers. He heard the man shout. "You bitch! Orders or no orders you are to going to die and then I…"

Decius grabbed the man's arm mid-blow. He could see the scratch marks from the woman's long nails and blood was pouring down his cheeks. Decius looked at the defiant woman staring with hate in her eyes. Her grey flecked hair marked her as older but her eyes were something Decius had never seen, they were the colour of spring violas! As he felt himself beginning to become aroused he put his sword to her throat and grabbed her arm. Turning it over he saw the scar running its length. "Fainch! At last, we have you. Macro, we have her! We finally have her."

Chapter 19

The clear up lasted until just after noon. Decius had taken charge once he realised that Marcus was injured. The bodies of the warriors and the dead Caledonii and Taexali were placed in the huts and they were fired. Decius was taking no chances with the witch and she was tied across a mule with two men on either side. He did not know what punishment Marcus would inflict but he would not take that pleasure away from the prefect. As they made their way up the track to the pass and the waiting horses Decius noticed Gaelwyn and Gaius comforting a female slave; intrigued but too busy to find out he determined that would be the first question he would ask back at their camp.

Marcus was conscious by the time they entered the camp. The surgeon fussed over him but the prefect was determined to return to duty immediately. "Decius, the body count?"

"We lost thirty sir mainly to the poisoned arrows."

"And the witch?"

"We have her. She won't escape this time."

"I want her in chains and guarded by four men at all times. We try her and she dies tomorrow."

Decius looked surprised. "I thought she would have died instantly sir."

"We are not barbarians Decius we are Rome and we have rules and laws. She will be given a trial but she will be found guilty. Make sure the rest of the captives can't escape. We will head back to Inchtuthil tomorrow."

"What about the rescued slaves?"

"Slaves?"

"Yes, four Novontae and a Brigante, related to Gaelwyn apparently."

"Make them comfortable. I will go and see them."

"After you have had your head looked at, had a drink and changed your uniform."

"Why change the uniform?"

"Because you look a mess now go on."

By the time the prefect was ready to greet Ailis food had been prepared. Decius had asked Porcius to arrange for the decurions to eat with the rescued slaves. Marcus was the last to arrive and all the officers stood as one when he entered. "Sit down sit down. I was injured not killed!" He glanced up at the young woman sat between Gaelwyn and Gaius. She was undoubtedly pretty which was why all the decurions had cleaned themselves and shaved. There was something about her that looked familiar; he just couldn't put his finger on what it was. "We will return you to your families as soon as possible."

Two of the Novontae burst into tears. Ailis spoke. "I think prefect that their families were all killed in the raids which took their families. The other two were so young they cannot remember their families."

"And you Ailis? What of your family."

Gaelwyn gave a gapped tooth grin and said in an over loud voice. "She has found her family."

"Ah yes, the Decurion Princeps, told me she is your cousin."

After a pause Gaelwyn said, "Not just mine but yours too prefect. She was the cousin of Macha, Lenta and Queen Cartimandua. She is your cousin too."

The silence crashed down on the table. Every eye was expectantly on the prefect, some, like Decius with amusement and some like Julius with curiosity. The prefect seemed unusually bereft of words. After taking a draught of wine from his beaker he wiped his mouth, stood up and walked over to Ailis who also stood up. Taking her in his arms he embraced her saying, "Welcome cousin." None of those present chose to notice the tears cascading down his cheeks.

It became a party and the Novontae girls soon forgot their tears. The young decurions flirted with them and the older ones happily got drunk. Marcus remained quiet, sat next to Decius. Gaius and Ailis had their heads together with Gaelwyn beaming his gap-toothed grin for all he was worth.

"Fate is a strange thing Decius. All the way to this northernmost corner of Britannia and I find the last relative of my dead wife and the murderer of Queen Cartimandua."

"Perhaps you were meant to find her. Perhaps she was meant to escape from Mona to lead you here. The pain and the deaths were the price you had to pay."

"Perhaps you are right. The Romans and Greeks believe that we are the playthings of the gods. Like small boys pulling the wings off insects to see the effect. You could be right, this could be a test and it confirms my wish now to retire. When the witch dies tomorrow my work will be complete."

"What about Calgathus?"

"That is the work of younger men like Gaius, Macro and Julius."

Just then Gaius and Ailis stood. "Sir with your permission I will escort your cousin to her tent." Marcus nodded his approval.

Decius leaned over and said quietly, "How about a small bet sir?"

"Small bet Decius?"

"Yes, I bet you that Gaius will be joining your family sooner rather than later."

"What do you mean?"

"Did you not see that he never took his eyes off her and old Gaelwyn didn't seem to mind."

Even though they had all had a heavy night's drinking every single decurion was stone cold sober by the next morning. They all knew what a portentous and momentous event was taking place. Some like Decius and Gaius had been around when the witch first spread her venom at Eboracum, others like Julius had been there at Stanwyck when it had spread but all had witnessed her on Mona as she had tried to burn their prefect to death.

"You are a witch and a priestess of Mona. You have murdered many Brigante and Romans. You have murdered my men with poisoned arrows; you have tried to kill me twice. All of these crimes are capital crimes and all of them have the death penalty. How do you plead?"

Her piercing eyes gripped Marcus in their stare. "I am a witch and I am a priestess of Mona. I freely admit all that you accuse me of and more for I was the one who tried to organise the revolt against your kingdom. I was the one who caused fires and murders at Eboracum. I was the one who helped King Calgathus to raise the northern tribes. There! Does that make your invasion any more justified? No! for I do not recognise Rome nor her power. I swear by the Mother that Roman rule will end one day and the gods of Britannia will once more rule and they are dark and they are vengeful; all those who fought for the Romans will suffer."

Many of those present gripped amulets and other sacred objects as the curse of the witch oozed from her lips.

Marcus laughed. "There was a time when your words had power witch, when you tricked and misled Venutius and Maeve even Aed the murderer of my wife. But now you have no power and I sentence you to death."

"Do you think I am afraid of death? When I die I will join my sisters in the spirit world and I will become even more powerful for I will not have the shackle that is this body. How will you sleep Roman? How will any of you sleep knowing the Fainch 's spirit is all around and will seek to do you harm?" The fear in the young men's eyes gave her satisfaction but she was irritated by the look on Marcus' face for he seemed almost at peace. "And you prefect, did you know your wife screamed for death as she was raped and soiled by thirty Brigante warriors?"

Decius tried to rise but was restrained by the prefect. "Any death at your hands would be a horrible and a terrible death and a death I have mourned these past years but do not think you can provoke me witch for you cannot. I will have my revenge. My legal, lawful and rightful revenge and when you are dead and burned and gone, then will my wife's spirit sleep easier. Then will my son Ulpius stop crying for peace. Then I too will be at peace."

Her face contorted with anger and rage. "Would that I had kept her alive to torture her. Would that you had been my prisoner for longer."

"But I wasn't and the men who are around you, my friends, my brothers risked their lives to save me. Who is here to save you?"

The word *you* boomed and echoed as a question hanging in the air and afterwards the silence seemed as loud as a heartbeat. "Crucifixion!"

The two guards holding the manacled witch led her away. To her credit she showed neither fear nor emotion. Outside the tent the cross was lying on the floor and the blacksmith ready with his nails, each one the length of a man's hand and his mighty hammer. The guards laid the witch upon the cross and held her arms. The Novontae slaves hid their faces in their hands as the first nail was driven in, the large flat head preventing the witch from ripping it out. She flinched but uttered not a sound, her eyes still boring in on the prefect as his were on hers. It was a duel of wills. As the blood started to drip the second nail was driven in. Again, she flinched and Decius noticed a tendril of blood drip slowly from her mouth. Finally, a nail, the length of a man's forearm, was pounded through her ankles. Even some of the troopers flinched when they heard the crunch of bone as it crushed her ankles. As the blacksmith stepped away the ten troopers pulled on the rope to bring the cross upright. The blood was flowing freely from ankles and hands but still she was held in place by the long nails. Her bloodless face uttered not a sound during what must have been an excruciatingly painful ordeal. Finally, as the cross became vertical and the weight of her frail body was taken on her wrists and ankles, a smile, a sigh, almost a groan came from his lips now bleeding from the places she had bitten them. Although he hated her Decius couldn't help but admire this woman who was dying so much more nobly than Gaius Cresens her conspirator. She could feel her life blood dripping from her and with the last strength she had she screamed, "Marcus Aurelius Maximunius I curse you to the end of time." Then, with a superhuman effort she pulled herself up and then threw her weight down. The result was that the nails tore through her flesh and her arteries. Deep purple blood gushed from her wounds and as Marcus stared at her eyes he saw the life leave them and Fainch the witch was dead.

King Calgathus was the first to realise that his secret stronghold was no more. Riding from the south with Lulach both ecstatic with their successes they felt themselves dragged down by the pall of smoke which still drifted across the blue skies days after the raid. As they surveyed the wreckage they could see that a mighty battle had taken place. Even as they searched for survivors, in ones and twos, those who had escaped the Romans emerged to tell the king what had happened. "They struck suddenly and we had no warning. "

"What of the Taexali sentries? Did they not try to prevent this disaster?"

"They were not as our warriors and they ran as quickly as the women."

"My son was right. Lulach find the survivors and take them with your warband to the loch. I will take my oathsworn and we will gather our warriors. We will avenge this. What of the witch? Fainch?"

"The Romans took her to their camp." The man pointed towards the pass.

When the king and his bodyguard arrived at the camp it had been dismantled but standing in what would have been the centre was the corpse of the witch hanging limply from the cross, her eyes the feeding ground for the rooks and ravens. "Your plans came to nought witch and this," the king said turning to face his warriors, "is the fate that awaits us if we fail."

His warriors roared their anger. "We will not fail!"

"We are not Taexali! We are warriors and not women!"

"Let us drive the Romans into the sea."

Tully was slowly making his way back from his successful raid on the Votadini. He had not been as successful as Lulach for the Romans had begun to reinforce their work parties from the sea but he and his men were in good spirits as they made their way along the wooded banks of the river the Romans called Bodotria. Ever the careful warrior, Tully was travelling at night to avoid being seen. His men took to the water in the estuary to half swim half paddle past the fort. During the brightest part of the day they rested in the bushes and woods which lined the banks. They weren't the best cover but they appeared to have escaped notice for they had seen few Roman patrols. Tully could see the crossing point of the Bodotria in the distance. By the time the following dawn came he would be back in his homeland and safe from the Romans.

The prefect of the First Tungrians had received his orders from the new Governor and he intended to impress him. If there were raiders in the south then they would have to cross the Bodotria five miles beyond his line of forts and camps. He had set up signal towers every five miles which signalled any movements. He wanted to impress the governor to get a better posting than this backwater of Britannia. The signal towers worked far better than he had hoped. He had been in Veluniate when he had received the signal from his outposts; a warband had been seen resting by the river eight miles away. He signalled the ships stationed off the estuary to sail along the river and provide artillery cover and he led four centuries on the road which took them to the crossing point. All three elements arrived at the crossing point at exactly the same time; it was an hour before dusk and, although Tully and his warriors were surprised they were not demoralized and a fierce battle broke out. This was not the battle the Romans liked to fight; the centuries arrived piecemeal and lacked the cohesion which normally held them in such good stead. The Tungrian prefect regretted not bringing more soldiers but had he done so he would have left the fort vulnerable and the auxiliaries were at full stretch. The warband for their part were fully rested and tore ferociously into the Tungrians diminished ranks. The ship's commanders were helpless spectators as they could not use their artillery for fear of hitting their own men and all they could do was stop the Caledonii from entering the water.

With night falling Tully led his chosen warriors in a wedge and they cut right through the centre of the auxiliary cohorts. The disjointed cohort could not resist the force of nature that was the Caledonii warriors on the rampage. Even though the warband had lost many warriors, more than the Tungrians, the Tungrians were in no position to purse and the last raiders returned home.

The Governor finally arrived at Inchtuthil. Decius Brutus met him along with the prefects who were stationed nearby. "Tell me First Spear how goes the campaign?"

"The Caledonii have been raiding our road builders and outlying camps. They are not major attacks but they have caused us more casualties than we would have liked. Prefect Maximunius has taken his ala out to try to destroy Calgathus' base, he has not returned yet."

"I have just received a report that the force of Caledonii who were raiding south of here managed to break through a Tungrian cohort. Any report of the other warband?"

"My scouts found the trail of a warband heading north from Alavna."

"And you are?"

"Prefect Sura of the First Batavian Cohort."

"Then they still have a sizeable force, in fact three depending upon whether the Prefect of Cavalry has managed to eliminate one of them. First Spear bring me a map." The map was spread across the table and the prefects gathered around it. "You have chosen good sites for you camps and forts along here but it seems to me that we need a series of forts, perhaps one here, another here and a third here." He moved his finger down to the south west, the land of the Novontae. "The raiders found little opposition here. I notice there are no forts in that area. Why is that?"

They all looked at each other. "The region was settled quickly and was peaceful. General Agricola wished to push on and conquer the rest of Britannia."

"Which his early summons back to Rome prevented. Yes, I know. General Agricola won the war but I must win the peace." The new governor stabbed his finger down forcefully on the map. "We will build forts in that area to prevent another incursion by the Caledonii."

"But Governor we are fully stretched as it is. We have less than twenty thousand men to hold a huge area of land."

"I know Prefect Sura but we must do it with the forces available." He looked at them all individually trying to gauge the mettle of these men whom he was asking to do the impossible. "I have spent all my life in Rome and I know how it works. We are the far-flung outpost in an ever-growing empire and any rebellion or revolt here does not impact in Rome. The senators and merchants only wish to milk the cow that is Britannia. We will receive no more forces and we must act quickly for I feel that we will have forces withdrawn to fight the wars in Dacia and the east."

They all looked downcast. "Will you be replacing the prefect of the Ninth from your staff sir?"

"What? Probably First Spear but not yet. Continue to improve the defences of Inchtuthil and we will use that as a rock on which the barbarians can beat themselves to death. What of this Prefect Maximunius? Do you think he will bring me a ray of hope?"

Prefect Strabo spoke up and the others all nodded affirmation at his comments. "If anyone can sir it is the prefect. He has been fighting in the province the longest of any of us from Stanwyck to Mona and up to Mons Graupius. He was with the turma who rescued Queen Cartimandua back in sixty-nine."

"He was in that ala. I have heard of him. It was the talk of Rome. Caractacus had only recently died and it even made the floor of the Senate. The Pannonians isn't that the name of the ala?"

"Yes sir they were but General Agricola renamed them Marcus' Horse as there were so few Pannonians left. They are mainly made up of warriors from Britannia now. A good ala, solid and reliable."

The 'ayes' around the table caused the Governor to look up and reflect. "It would appear that this Prefect gives me hope that we may be able to at least control this barbaric part of the province."

Less than a day away the ala was heading south with the rescued prisoners and slaves. "Well I for one will be glad to get back to Inchtuthil."

"I thought you didn't like sharing forts with the legions, Decius."

"I don't but I am hoping that Decius Brutus might have started on a bath house."

"A bath house? I think he will have had more on his mind than that. I for one hope that there is some word from the Governor. The discovery of Ailis has hardened my resolve."

"You are still going to retire then sir."

"I felt tired and weary in the last battle, if you can call it a battle and the fact that I could have died…"

"It was a lucky blow with a slingshot."

"Yes Decius and that can happen in any battle. Had the troopers not been nearby then I could have been killed."

"You worried about dying then Marcus?"

"No, you know that but this ala relies on my decisions too much. A leader needs to be in control all the time and my reactions are slower than they were. I am retiring not because I have had enough or I fear death but I fear I am no longer serving Rome by leading this ala."

Decius shook his head. Marcus was the finest officer he had ever known. He was superior to Ulpius Felix and they had both thought him the pinnacle but Marcus had taken the ala to a different level. With the encouragement of Agricola, he had made them more flexible. They could fight on foot, assault strong points and campaign independently. Part of Decius also knew that when Marcus left so would he and he was afraid. He did not know what he would do with the rest of his life.

"Look at them, Decius. Do you think they see anyone else?"

Decius turned and saw Gaius and Ailis in deep conversation. Gaelwyn rode behind them. "Have you noticed Gaelwyn though Marcus? I have known the man for, well a long time and I have never seen him smile. Since the girl was found I have not seen him stop smiling. And another thing until he started smiling I didn't know he was missing so many teeth. His mouth looks like an old cemetery!"

"Yes, it is strange how the Fates spin their webs. Gaelwyn and I only had the connection of the ala and now I find we are related through Macha and Ailis."

"I wonder why he never mentioned it."

"Perhaps he thought I would think he was trying to ingratiate himself."

"It certainly explains why he always seemed to be there covering your back and the rescue in Mona."

"The fates Decius, the fates."

Chapter 20

The signal towers recently erected along the partly built road sent the message to Inchtuthil and the Governor stood in the main gate to watch the approach of the legendary ala. He was surprised how young looking the prefect was although he noticed a certain weariness about his movements. From the line of manacled slaves his mission had been successful.

"Welcome, Prefect, I am Governor Sallustius Lucullus."

"I am Prefect Marcus Aurelius Maximunius of Marcus' Horse." Dismounting he saluted.

The Governor took him by the arm. "Come with me for we have much to discuss." He looked over his shoulder. "You have been successful."

Behind him Marcus heard Decius roaring out orders and the sound of men dismounting. "Partly sir. Not as successful as I wished but more successful than I had hoped."

The Governor paused and looked up at this prefect who had begun life as a barbarian but able to verbalize such concepts. "Enigmatic, Prefect, very enigmatic. I can see you have an interesting tale to tell. Come, we will use the Praetorium and I will send for refreshments."

When the prefect sat and took off his helmet the Governor could see the flecks of grey riddling his hair. He also noticed the recent wound on the side of his head as well as scars visible on both legs and arms. Here was a prefect who went to war.

"So successful and yet not successful. How so?"

"We found the camp of King Calgathus which we destroyed and the warriors who were guarding it but not the main force of the king."

"No for they were raiding in the south but I interrupt. I apologise. Do continue."

"We also captured many prisoners and rescued some slaves from the Brigante and Novontae people."

"Good that may be useful but again I interrupt."

Marcus smiled, "I have nearly finished sir. We also captured and executed the witch Fainch." The Governor showed no understanding. "She was the one who poisoned and killed Queen

Cartimandua. She also confessed, at the end, to advising and directing many of the revolts and rebellions against us during the past twenty years."

"Confessed? You tortured her then?"

Marcus shook his head. "Didn't need to. She was proud of it and boasted about her achievements."

"Oh don't get me wrong, Prefect, I have no aversion to torture I just wondered if you had."

"I have never needed to use it. I am a soldier sir, a warrior if you will, I prefer to face my enemies and defeat them with force of arms, not torture."

"Very noble, Prefect, but these Caledonii are cunning. We may have to resort to such methods eventually. But you are weary. When you have rested we will talk again. I have sent for the other prefects, they have been idle enough. It is time I told you all of my plans."

Gaius and Ailis had spoken for the whole journey from the north. Gaius was no longer a young man and he had long given up any romantic thoughts of wife and family. He had seen forty summers and saw his future viewing the world from the back of a horse. Ailis had woken something in him he had never known. He found her a joy to be with. He loved the sound of her voice, the tinkle of her laughter. He loved her smile and the way she flicked her long dark hair, now unfettered, out of her eyes. In fact, he found that he loved her and that came as a complete shock. He had never bothered with the girls who hung around the camps and forts and had not the first idea how to initiate a relationship. He just talked. As they had ridden along Julius and Macro had discussed their friend's behaviour with increasing amusement. I have never heard Gaius talk as much before."

"Well not about such ordinary things. He can talk for hours about weapons and tactics but talking about houses and food and…"

Ailis for her part had been in love with the warrior since the first time she had seen him. Although terrified and fearing for her life his quick reactions had saved her life and endeared him to her. But it was more than that, she found herself attracted to him as a man. She had been used by the Caledonii as a sex slave but they had not been men, they had been animals. She longed for this man to be her man. Gaelwyn had helped. A faint memory until he spoke to her in the hut she now remembered her mother's younger brother who had fussed over her when young. When she had asked Gaelwyn about Gaius she could tell from his words and tone that he respected and perhaps was even fond of the decurion and this just confirmed her feelings for him. She longed for him to say that he loved her but he appeared shy, almost like a young boy rather than a grown man.

Julius entered the decurion tent which had been erected in their new camp. Gaius was sat on his cot and they were alone. "It is good to be back eh Gaius?"

"What, er yes, good to be back."

Julius stripped off his mail and when he looked up Gaius was still sat turning his pugeo over and over. "What is it Gaius? Are you troubled?"

Gaius looked up, almost seeing the affable young patrician for the first time. "Julius, I am troubled. I feel… that is it I don't know what I feel but I think it is confusion."

"Ah," Julius smiled. "Is it Ailis?"

Startled Gaius dropped his knife which Julius picked up and returned to him. "It is but how did you know?"

Julius smiled, "I think every trooper in the ala knows Gaius."

"Knows what Julius?"

"That you long for Ailis."

"How...? But…"

"Have you told her yet?"

"Told her what?"

"That you, that you have feelings for her?"

"I couldn't do that she might laugh at me."

"She will not laugh at you believe me. Besides if you do tell her and she laughs at least you will know, but I will wager all my pay for the next two years that she will not."

Gaius looked up. Julius never ever gambled. "You are sure?"

"I may be wrong on many things but in this? I am sure."

The Governor had used the last of the luxuries brought from Rome to provide the food for the feast with the prefects. He asked for Marcus to sit by him as they ate and he questioned him about the province and Marcus' role in its conquest. When he had finished he nodded. "You are a man of Britannia as I am." He looked around and then dropped his voice. "You know that my grandfather was the last King of Britannia?"

"You are the grandson of Cunobelinus?"

"You are the first to know of him. How did you hear of him?"

"Queen Cartimandua told me of him and then her sister, my wife Macha told my son of the tales of the kings of Britannia."

"Ah yes. I am sorry for your loss so you understand my love for this land and that I intend to make it a peaceful country again."

"Yes. General Agricola came so close to succeeding. No offence sir. When he left the task was unfinished."

"I take no offence Julius is a great general and I agree with you. Some say there was jealousy. I prefer to believe that they needed his skills elsewhere. They were wrong for he should have finished his appointed task here. And now I am to do it with fewer troops."

"You have a hard task Governor."

"We have a hard task Prefect for I will be relying on you and your love for Britannia."

"Governor I would like to retire. I am no longer a young man and the conquest of the north is a task for a young man. There must be many candidates you could appoint to be Prefect. Young men with the energy, drive and ambition that an old man does not have."

The governor became agitated. "No, no. I beg of you. Just perform one task for me and I will grant you your wish. I had hoped that you would return to the land of the Novontae and build forts to protect the people."

"You have other auxiliary forces that could carry out the task."

"True they could carry out the task of building the forts but could they manage the people? Could they protect the people? No that is a task for Marcus Horse and Prefect Marcus." He paused and spoke quietly again. "I will find a replacement for you and you can train him. Will you do that for me?"

Marcus found that he like this earnest and passionate man and he remembered the chiefs of the Novontae whom he had promised peace to. Many of them lay dead, slaughtered by Calgathus' raiders. He owed it to them. "I will do as you wish sir. I will pacify the land of the Novontae."

When they had finished eating the Governor tapped the table with the hilt of his dagger. "We now come to the main purpose of this gathering although I assume you have all enjoyed the food and the wine."

"Excellent!"

"Delicious!"

"Make the most of it for I fear they will be the last luxuries for some time. We will also be losing some of our soldiers to fortify the rest of the Empire. For the moment, the Ninth will be the only legion north of Deva and Lindum." he pointed to the map, "As you can see now that the fleet has mapped out the island that the Ninth is the only legion in over half of the province, the half which has yet to be conquered."

Strabo leaned over to Decius Brutus and said sotto voce, "And you complained about not having enough action!"

"My intention is to send the Batavians and a cohort of the Ninth along the east and north valleys to establish order and finish the task so admirably started by Perfect Maximunius. It is infantry country perfectly suited to auxiliaries with legionary support. The Tungrians and the remainder of the Ninth will establish forts along this valley and pacify the tribes in this low-lying land. Prefect Maximunius will build a fort in the land of the Novontae. His task is Herculean I am afraid. I wish Marcus' Horse to patrol from coast to coast and prevent incursions by the Caledonii."

"Well that is easy, isn't it? It isn't as though he has given us a hard task has he? Just control the whole of the Novontae and Votadini, not to mention Carvetii and Brigante with less than a thousand men."

"Don't forget the fort Decius. We have to build a fort as well."

"This gets better and better." His sarcastic rant over, Decius watched the prefect's face for a clue as to his opinion. "You seem calm about the whole thing. Have you put retirement to one side then?"

"No, I am still going to retire when I have built the fort and a new prefect is appointed. Do not worry Decius it will not be you. He wants a younger man."

"Thank the Allfather for that." He swallowed a draught from his beaker. "I have been thinking about retirement. You know you made sense. I just need to find something I could do that wouldn't make me want to swallow poison. When you go, I will go."

"Excellent Decius it would be good to finish the job as we started it, together."

As they toasted each other the sentry outside said, "Visitor sir."

"Come in."

Gaius entered looking both bewildered and apprehensive. "Could I have a word sir?" Decius began to rise. "No Decius I think you might stay. It might help having my old decurion here."

"This sounds serious Gaius, take a seat."

"If you don't mind sir I'll stand."

"Well come on man get it out."

"Sir I would like permission to marry the, your cousin Ailis. I realise that marriage is frowned on below the rank of centurion but I wondered sir if you could make an exception because, well sir I want to marry her and…" he began to tail off lamely and then added as a final selling point, "Gaelwyn approves sir."

They were both desperate to laugh but Gaius suddenly looked like the young boy he had once been and always would be to Marcus. The prefect could see how earnest and serious he was.

"Well if Gaelwyn says he is happy I am certainly not going to risk the old man's wrath besides," he added seriously, "I think it is the best news I have had in a long time and it seems appropriate that we will be returning to the land of Ailis."

The rest of the evening passed in a drunken blur as the three men celebrated in true auxiliary style; drinking to their future and remembering the comrades from the past.

Epilogue

The wedding was a family affair, a Marcus' Horse family affair. The whole of the ala witnessed the simple ceremony. Gaelwyn told the decurions about the Brigante custom of bringing gifts so that the couple gained more material objects than either had ever owned. Gaelwyn, to Decius' delight, cried like a baby and kept clasping Marcus calling him 'brother'. As the gifts were given Marcus waited in his dress uniform looking resplendent. When the couple had received all their presents Marcus walked up to the couple. He leaned down and kissed Ailis on the forehead.

"Years ago, I resigned myself to a life without a family and suddenly I have a cousin, a beautiful cousin and I have in my family a man I would be proud to call son." He then embraced Gaius who himself was fighting back tears. Decius sniffed loudly and coughed. Julius and Macro smiled as they down on the sentimental old Decurion Princeps. "Finally, I have my gift." He drew out the Sword of Cartimandua and, turning the hilt towards Gaius said. "This is the Sword of Cartimandua. This is the sword of the Brigante Royal family. The Queen gave it into the keeping of her warrior Ulpius Felix; when he lay dying he entrusted it to me for my wife was of the Brigante royal family. I had thought to take the sword with me to my grave but now I can give it to you, Gaius, for now you are married to the Brigante Royal family and one day your son will have the sword which is rightfully his."

Before Gaius could refuse the hilt was pressed into his palm and the ala roared out "Marcus! Marcus!"

Outside in the forest Calgathus, Tully and Lulach lay hidden. "What is that? Is it an attack?"

"No, my son. It is the Roman's celebrating because they think they have won but they have not. You two have shown me the way we can beat these Romans not in one almighty battle where they can slaughter our men but in pin pricks. In annoying attacks. In battles where they have not had time to prepare. By attacking those outposts where there are few defenders. We will send our warbands back to the lands of the Novontae and beyond to the land of the Brigante. We will spread their soldiers so thinly that a warband of women could destroy them. Today we begin to re-take our land. Today we begin to free Caledonia."

Names and places in this novel

Fictional names and places are italicised.

Gnaeus Julius Agricola- Roman General and Governor of Britannia from 77 AD to 85 AD
Quintus Petilius Cerialis- Governor of Britannia before Agricola
Marcus Maenius Agrippa- Commander of the Classis Britannica
King Tuanthal Teachtmhar – an exiled Irish king
Sallustius Lucullus (Grandson of King Cunobelinus)- the governor who succeeded Agricola
King Cunobelinus (Shakespeare's Cymbeline) - King of Britain who fled to Rome in exile
Marcus Aurelius Maximunius- Decurion Princeps Pannonian cavalry
Decius Flavius- Decurion Pannonian cavalry
Julius Demetrius- Decurion Pannonian cavalry
Gaius Metellus Aurelius- Decurion Pannonian cavalry
Ailis- Macha's cousin
Metellus Glabrio- Decurion Pannonian cavalry
Cominius Sura- Prefect Batavian auxiliary
Metellus Gabrus- Prefect Gallic cavalry
Furius Strabo- Prefect Batavian Auxiliary
Tulius Broccus- Prefect of the Ninth Hispana
Macro- Sergeant, weapon trainer Pannonian Cavalry
Fainch- Druidic Priestess and witch
Cassius Bassus- Prefect Gallorum Auxiliary
Caolan- Novontae war chief
Centurion Aurelius- trainer for the Usipi
Gwynfor- king of the Ordovices
Gryffydd- son of Gwynfor
Agrippa- Decurion Pannonian cavalry
Inir- Ordovice warband chief
Adelmar- Usipi warrior
Pugeo – Roman soldier's dagger
Bodotria Fluvium- Forth River
Brocavum- Brougham
Caerhun- A settlement close to Conwy (this becomes the Roman fort of Canovium)
Clota Fluvium – River Clyde
Coriosopitum (Corio) - Corbridge
Danum- Doncaster
Derventio- Malton
Deva- Chester

Dunum Fluvius- River Tees
Eboracum- York
Glanibanta- Ambleside
Hen Waliau- Caernarfon
Luguvalium - Carlisle
Mamucium – Manchester
Mona- Holyhead
Morbium- Piercebridge
Taus- the river Solway
Vindonnus- Celtic god of hunting
Wyddfa- Snowdon
Decurion Princeps- senior office in an ala

Author's Note

Once again this is a work of fiction. All the Roman army elements served in Britain at roughly the time the book is set. There are Roman settlements and forts at all the named places. Julius Agricola did lead a force of mainly auxiliaries with a cohort of legionaries to defeat the Ordovices after they destroyed a cavalry squadron. When Agricola invaded Mona he did have his auxiliaries swim across the Menai Straits. I must confess how they did this with armour is a mystery and Tacitus does not enlighten us. I have come up with my own solution.

The problem we have with Agricola is that we only know of him what we do because of his son in law Tacitus, who annoyingly rarely writes sequentially and never dates events, therefore we have to speculate about many of the events. History is written by the winners; this is as true now as it was it Roman times and when the historian is your son in law one can expect a certain amount of exaggeration. Agricola was appointed to be Governor of Gallia Aquitania but it coincides with an appointment to Rome and overlaps with his time as Governor of Britannia; therefore, I have used writer's licence with the dates.

Holyhead Island is now connected to the island of Anglesey but in Roman times it was a separate entity with the southernmost part being what is now Trearrdur. This is known as Holyhead Island. The cliffs would not have been steep and the water between the two islands would have been easy to cross at low tide. The people of Mona believed in the power of the land which superseded its lack of defensive qualities.

Agricola was certainly an innovative general; the only legion he took whilst campaigning in the north was the Ninth, largely based at Carlisle. The incident with the cavalry rescuing the Ninth from an attack on their camp actually took place as did the mutiny of German Auxiliaries. The use of the fleet, the Classis Britannica, to supply the army was also an actual event and did of course result in the discovery by Agricola that Britain is an island. The site of the battle in which the Scots were finally defeated has never been accurately pinpointed and I have just used a best guess principle. Tacitus constantly talks of Agricola commanding but as auxiliaries were not legionaries it is highly likely he would have delegated command. Certainly, he had to, when advancing across so large an area, use and trust his subordinate commanders.

The campaigns against the Novontae are notable for the mixture of diplomacy and war. Siege works were found around hill forts but the lack of major archaeological evidence suggests that the people accepted Roman rule well. The naming of units after their commander was not new, Indus Horse was a famous unit from Caesar's time; as Agricola was known for his touch with the men this seemed an appropriate reward.

The attack on the Ninth occurred as written and Agricola did indeed bring an ala of cavalry to rescue them. They then went on to build the most northern fort in the Roman Empire at Inchtuthil. The curious incident of the Usipi is also recorded. Tacitus gives us one date and another Roman writer gives one with a two-year discrepancy. The facts are the same in both. The Usipi mutinied, killed their centurion stole some ships and sailed along the coast, resulting in the accidental discovery that Britain was an island. They did resort to cannibalism. One set of survivors were found in Swabia and the other in Frisia. Both sets of survivors were sold into slavery.

The Irish King did meet with Agricola as written in the novel but Tacitus talks then of Ireland being conquered. As there is no archaeological evidence for this I believe that Tacitus was referring to the Hebrides but perhaps Agricola's support for the Irish king did impact on that island.

The battle of Mons Graupius was Agricola's last in Britain. Some said he was withdrawn because he was becoming too successful. As he had not quite finished the conquest I find it more likely that Domitian needed him in the east. We do not know exactly where the battlefield was but it was fought in terrain as described and in the manner described. Tacitus says that 30000 Caledonii fought and the legionaries took no part. He ascribed 20000 casualties on the Caledonii side and only 350 amongst the auxiliaries. Tacitus was on the side of the winners and I suspect he exaggerated!

Lucullus was related to Cymbeline but when he arrived the Emperor had decided that Britain was all but conquered and he could use the troops from Britannia elsewhere. It was a mistake and Agricola's departure was the high-water mark for Rome in her conquest of Britannia.

Griff Hosker November 2013

Other books by Griff Hosker

If you enjoyed reading this book, then why not read another one by the author?

Ancient History

The Sword of Cartimandua Series
(Germania and Britannia 50 A.D. – 128 A.D.)
Ulpius Felix- Roman Warrior (prequel)
The Sword of Cartimandua
The Horse Warriors
Invasion Caledonia
Roman Retreat
Revolt of the Red Witch
Druid's Gold
Trajan's Hunters
The Last Frontier
Hero of Rome
Roman Hawk
Roman Treachery
Roman Wall
Roman Courage

The Wolf Warrior series
(Britain in the late 6th Century)
Saxon Dawn
Saxon Revenge
Saxon England
Saxon Blood
Saxon Slayer
Saxon Slaughter
Saxon Bane
Saxon Fall: Rise of the Warlord
Saxon Throne
Saxon Sword

Medieval History

The Dragon Heart Series
Viking Slave
Viking Warrior
Viking Jarl
Viking Kingdom
Viking Wolf
Viking War
Viking Sword
Viking Wrath
Viking Raid
Viking Legend
Viking Vengeance
Viking Dragon
Viking Treasure
Viking Enemy
Viking Witch
Viking Blood
Viking Weregeld
Viking Storm
Viking Warband
Viking Shadow
Viking Legacy
Viking Clan
Viking Bravery

The Norman Genesis Series
Hrolf the Viking
Horseman
The Battle for a Home
Revenge of the Franks
The Land of the Northmen
Ragnvald Hrolfsson
Brothers in Blood
Lord of Rouen
Drekar in the Seine
Duke of Normandy
The Duke and the King

Invasion Caledonia

New World Series
Blood on the Blade
Across the Seas
The Savage Wilderness
The Bear and the Wolf
Erik the Navigator

The Vengeance Trail

The Danelaw Saga
The Dragon Sword

The Reconquista Chronicles
Castilian Knight
El Campeador
The Lord of Valencia

The Aelfraed Series
(Britain and Byzantium 1050 A.D. - 1085 A.D.)
Housecarl
Outlaw
Varangian

The Anarchy Series England 1120-1180
English Knight
Knight of the Empress
Northern Knight
Baron of the North
Earl
King Henry's Champion
The King is Dead
Warlord of the North
Enemy at the Gate
The Fallen Crown
Warlord's War
Kingmaker
Henry II

Invasion Caledonia

Crusader
The Welsh Marches
Irish War
Poisonous Plots
The Princes' Revolt
Earl Marshal

Border Knight
1182-1300
Sword for Hire
Return of the Knight
Baron's War
Magna Carta
Welsh Wars
Henry III
The Bloody Border
Baron's Crusade
Sentinel of the North
War in the West
Debt of Honour (May 2021)

Sir John Hawkwood Series
France and Italy 1339- 1387
Crécy: The Age of the Archer
Man at Arms
The White Company (July 2021)

Lord Edward's Archer
Lord Edward's Archer
King in Waiting
An Archer's Crusade
Targets of Treachery (Due out August 2021)

Struggle for a Crown
1360- 1485
Blood on the Crown
To Murder A King
The Throne
King Henry IV

Invasion Caledonia

The Road to Agincourt
St Crispin's Day
The Battle for France

Tales from the Sword I

Conquistador
England and America in the 16th Century
Conquistador (Coming in 2021)

Modern History

The Napoleonic Horseman Series
Chasseur à Cheval
Napoleon's Guard
British Light Dragoon
Soldier Spy
1808: The Road to Coruña
Talavera
The Lines of Torres Vedras
Bloody Badajoz
The Road to France
Waterloo (June 2021)

The Lucky Jack American Civil War series
Rebel Raiders
Confederate Rangers
The Road to Gettysburg

The British Ace Series
1914
1915 Fokker Scourge
1916 Angels over the Somme
1917 Eagles Fall
1918 We will remember them
From Arctic Snow to Desert Sand
Wings over Persia

Invasion Caledonia

Combined Operations series
1940-1945

Commando
Raider
Behind Enemy Lines
Dieppe
Toehold in Europe
Sword Beach
Breakout
The Battle for Antwerp
King Tiger
Beyond the Rhine
Korea
Korean Winter

Tales from the Sword Book 2

Other Books

Great Granny's Ghost (Aimed at 9-14-year-old young people)

For more information on all of the books then please visit the author's website at www.griffhosker.com where there is a link to contact him or visit his Facebook page: GriffHosker at Sword Books

Made in United States
Orlando, FL
14 October 2022

23401182R00148